Hemingway, Three Angels, and Me

A Novel

~BOOK 4~

Jerome Mark Antil

ISBN: 099718020X
ISBN–13: 9780997180206 (TPB)
ISBN-13: 9780997180213 (TPB Digital)

Coming of Age - Historical Fiction
Time: Sixty-three Years Ago
Scenes: Rural America and a Southern State Capital
(Central New York Family Dairy–Farm Country)
(Little Rock, Arkansas)

Historical references offered by
Arkansas Historical Society; Forrest City, Arkansas, Historical Society; New
Woodstock Historical Society; Cincinnatus Historical Society;
NY Historical Society; and Onondaga County Historical Society.
B-25 flight and radio instructions were offered by Robert Penoyer.
WWII (1945) B-17 original bombing photos and maps were provided by
Timoth Lederman.

Para_coustics_© Sound Created _by_ LittleYork Books

Interior Illustrations: Marina Giraud
Para_coustics_ sound dubbing: Don Canterbury, PRIZM
Cover Design: Dennis Graham
Copy Editor: Jolene Paternoster
PRINTED IN AMERICA

TABLE OF CONTENTS

A NOTE FROM THE AUTHOR

All of the characters in this book are drawn from my life. Several of the stories actually occurred; including some stories of the experiences of my own relatives or the schoolmates I grew up with. The B-17 "bombing mission" photographs and maps are authentic, and the photographs were taken by a pilot, Captain Donald G. Lederman, and his crew during thirty-three strategic bombing missions over Germany, France, and Holland between January 20 and April 20 of 1945.

The Battle of the Bulge ended on January 25, 1945.

On April 30, 1945, Adolph Hitler committed suicide, and the war in Europe ended on May 9, V-E (Victory in Europe) Day.

Ole Charlie is real. I walked to his farm to get eggs every Sunday evening starting when I was nine. He was a person of fractured grammar who offered more wisdom and insight to my youth than many others who were better read and more fortunate in station. To this barefoot boy in the days of his youth, Ole Charlie was Mark Twain.

I write this series about growing up in the shadows of WWII for the entertainment of the young; however, I've received complimentary tributes to its historical value from countries around the world, from many age groups, and from veterans of WWII.

The 1940s and early 1950s were like no other time in world history. Look back through our eyes, and you will see the way life was for us—what "sacrifice," "heroism," and "conscience" meant to kids in the day as a result of that war.

You'll also learn what life was like on the vanishing family farm when family farms were the lifeblood of America.

If you weren't there, experience the times as they happened, our innocence, and our foibles in my tale.

If you were there, enjoy looking back.

—The Author, Dallas, 2016

Rosa Parks

Rosa Parks,

The example you set many years before the civil rights movement needed no march; it needed no speech.

Without a step walked or a word spoken, your selfless act of taking a white only seat on that bus very likely put your life in peril on that day in time, and your bravery continues to resonate around the world.

You are a true hero. It took courage and caring for individuals' right to basic human dignity, no matter the cost.

Your sacrifice will always be the gold standard for action.

The more fortunate who can grasp it will be encouraged to change the world and to follow your example.

—JMA

To my Pamela

CHAPTER ONE

A LOAD OFF MY MIND

By trying we can easily endure adversity. Another man's,
I mean.—Mark Twain

I'll tell it the only way I know how. Hasn't surfaced in my memory for a long time, but now it has, and I'm an old man who has never told the story that doesn't want to leave me alone until I do. As Twain said, "We can't reach old age by another man's road."

It happened in 1953, more than sixty years ago.

Most of my friends and I were born around 1941, the year of the Pearl Harbor attack, which started the Second World War for America. By the time we were five years old, seventy million people had been killed. They say more than two hundred thousand died in just a couple of days when America dropped the atomic bombs on Japan. We were in kindergarten, but we wept for the children of Japan when we saw it on newsreels at the Saturday-morning picture show or heard about it on the radio. It was awful, but the whole war was awful, and it took dropping the second of those two bombs for Japan to end the war.

It was hard to believe, after witnessing the war in Europe and the war in the Pacific, that the same inhumanity could ever hit home— or nearer to home than Hitler's Nazis or Mussolini ever got.

My story was an important story when it happened, and I kept quiet.

But maybe it's not too late. Watching the news in these times we live in today, the story seems even more relevant than ever, so I'm telling it while I'm still alive.

I'll let you draw your own conclusions about the relevance of my story.

It'll help if you believe in guardian angels.

Once upon a time, I was a twelve-year-old high school freshman. I was always the youngest, but my friends and I were normal kids: happy in our innocence, impressionable, inquisitive, and virtual sponges of curiosity. We each remembered living through a war that had had us going to bed in fear every night.

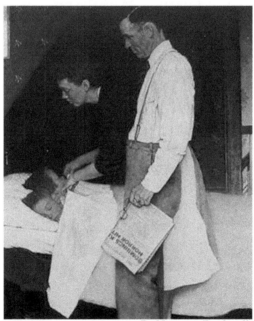

By Norman Rockwell

"If I should die before I wake,
bless me, Lord, my soul to take."

Our generation made an unspoken promise that we would never let the WWII atrocities happen again if we had anything to say or do about it.

If you know of the Crown's Pompey Hollow Book Club, you know me.

I'm Jerry.

In 1949, I was a naïve city boy in knickers from Cortland whose family had just upped and moved to farm country without telling me and had bought eighty-five acres of woods in Delphi Falls. And when I say we moved to Delphi Falls, I'm not lying. The Delphi Falls waterfall was plumb in our backyard. It was a more than seventy-foot-tall pile of rock and shale, and my, how it could thunder and roar a dreadful fit both day and night, and without a minute of pause.

To this nine-year-old, I couldn't possibly imagine water being able to make such a confounded racket. There were times my imagination would get the better of me, like the time I thought the thundering noise would about give me a heart attack, and no one would be able to hear my cries for help and I wouldn't be found for days, maybe weeks and lost in the woods and raised by bears.

As time wore on, I got more settled to its presence, but my imagination kept the fright alive whenever my bedroom window would rattle in the wind.

Then there's the other thing.

My dad thought it would be an adventure, so he encouraged Farmer Parker, across the way, to invite me to go for a ride on his horse-drawn manure spreader just to see how it all worked—farming, the cycle of cleaning out the barn, and of fertilizing the hayfield.

This city boy walked over to his barn nervously in the pitch of darkness one Saturday while Farmer Parker was in his barn finishing his morning milking chores. He had already loaded the manure-spreader wagon and hitched up the horses, Sarge and

Sallie, and he pointed to where I was to sit, which was on the right side of the bench in front. We were up on the highest hilltop in the middle of the hayfield spreading the manure when something important came up. It was all still piled pretty high in the wagon, billowing steam and operating at full crank, but a gust of wind had ripped my secret treasure map of the Delphi Falls cemetery out of my hands while I was sitting on the wagon bench next to Farmer Parker, asking him a question about the map when the map sailed into the air, my mind raced, as it sometimes did in those days. For a split second, I figured the map was important enough to me at the time, so I jumped off to go back around and fetch it.

I should have listened to Farmer Parker when he said, "I wouldn't be doing that, son."

But I didn't.

Needless to say, stepping behind that manure spreader, I learned a valuable lesson—I surely did.

I never did it twice.

Now, I didn't actually start the Pompey Hollow Book Club back those sixty-five or so years ago. Some would rumor I had, but it wouldn't be so. A more truthful legend was I might have inspired it.

Our club was started after the war. It was started on an Easter Sunday, to be precise. But on the Thursday afternoon before that Easter, after hearing we had already planned a Sunday meeting at the cemetery, my mom said, "Easter Sunday is a holy day of obligation, young man. You're going to confession. Get in the car."

It was six of us who started the club. We were nine and ten years old the year we saved the rabbits from slaughter and caught the store burglars in Groton.

That was three years before this story I'm about to tell, but you'll need to know the characters.

It was Barber who dreamed up the club name. On Easter Sunday, it was. He pulled himself up and stood on the cemetery stone, pointed through a gape in a tall pine up to a cloud, and declared that "ain't a mom in the county would stop us from going to a club meeting, even on a school night, if we were called the 'Pompey Hollow Book Club.'"

That being said, Mary Crane stood up, pushed out her lower lip, puffed a curl from over her eye, and suggested that such a lie about the club's nature might work better if we considered stopping saying "ain't."

A girl that perceptive just had to be our president—that was the consensus. Wasn't a doubt in anybody's mind, with the possible exception of Bases, but he had to get to the stone quarry for a Sunday game to fetch baseballs from the creek and had no time to filibuster a sentiment. We took his walking down the cemetery's path as his relinquishing the floor. That was good, as it meant no one needed to bring up certain arguments in Mary's favor—no one needed to say that she could throw farther than Bases could, that she could hit a home run farther out of the park than he could, or that she was probably the only person in the entire group who knew what "coeducational" meant.

The rest of us spat and made it so.

In that one act, we made Mary Crane America's first female president, at least to the best of our limited understanding of politics.

Now meet Holbrook—you'll like him.

My best friend from my first day of school, back in 1949. He was about blind without thick glasses but proud with neatly combed hair and a plastic comb sticking out of his back pocket. We met walking to the cafeteria, and he didn't laugh once at my dad's necktie my mom made me wear like a city boy in the heart of dairy-farm and bib-overall country. He even talked with me just like I was a normal kid. I learned that he had sixteen siblings, mostly girls, that he had no home telephone, and that his dad had bought their house for seven hundred dollars and was paying it off by working as a brakeman for the railroad out of Syracuse. Holbrook's sweat-stained lunch sack had more creases in it than a polka-band accordion, so I suspected he was poor as a church mouse with all that family. That's why I nudged my lunch quarter into his ribs and made him give me his sack lunch, which was a ketchup sandwich for appearances' sake made by his momma, a woman with seventeen young'uns to feed.

I suspected square meals at the Holbrook household were pretty much a crapshoot or lottery event.

From that day on, through every year we were together at that school, Holbrook got my quarter for a hot lunch, and I got his sack lunch in an even trade.

Early on, I did it because it was the right thing to do, and best friends always knew what to do.

Later, I kept doing it so he could use his Tully Bakery after-school part-time-job money to pay down on the hot water heater he'd given his momma for Christmas when he was eleven. Boiling clothes-washing water on a cookstove to do laundry for seventeen people was getting the best of her day. When I asked him what he'd given her for Christmas that year, he said, "Some rest."

Any best friend would have kept giving him the quarters.

Then there's Barber. That boy worked his daddy's farm from the day he could walk. He's still on the land today. He's not all that much taller now than in this story, but he liked to talk so much that we nominated him to be the club's meeting caller. That was a proud moment for him, and he's never taken it lightly or looked back. In the day, the lad was known to be able to carry on mean-ingful conversations with an empty milk bucket.

You already heard about Bases—I mentioned him before. He did nothing without a baseball mitt on his hand, eating included. He chased after foul balls from the creek for a dime apiece at the Sunday games in the stone quarry. A quiet boy, Bases had limited interest in anything that didn't involve wearing sneakers or base-ball cleats, but he could always be relied on for help.

And there's Randy.

Randy was a good friend to all of us and still is, at least to all of us still around to this very day. Back in 1953, his dad, smiling, happy, Mr. Vaas, drove the big old 1942 Dodge diesel milk-can-hauler truck from small farms to dairies before sunup, and then he'd go drive a school bus. At times Mr. Vaas could be seen hauling a load of kids to the Saturday-morning picture show up in Cazenovia when he had to go to the feed store for a load; or he could be seen taking us to club meetings at the Delphi Falls cemetery in between his milk-can stops at farms.

We'd called Bobby Penoyer "Mayor" ever since he'd walked into the second-grade classroom with thick and wild black hair. He'd been looking on a mission and had been on a scout for a desk without jackknife hearts or initials carved on it. Rumor was that his ancestors had come to this country as Pilgrims. We all reckoned he'd grow up and get elected mayor or something important like that, as he had determination in his face most of the time, so "Mayor" stuck.

And wouldn't you know we were right? Mayor grew up to become a mayor.

Others would join the club from time to time during our adventures. Getting into the club wasn't more troublesome than just showing up at meetings.

Now, not all of our adventures were easy, and there were times when we'd call a special SOS meeting, hoping the older guys would show up and help us catch crooks and criminals.

We had our reasons.

Marty Bays was one of them; he was closer to our ages than some of them but still older than we were and in a grade or two ahead. Red hair and freckles, he was exceptional at math and science and the best at figuring things out—he was a good strategist. That talent and the fact he did most everything on horseback or with his daddy's pickup made him a perfect fit. He had an early farm-driving permit for hauling milk to the dairy before school started. Marty could show up where we needed him and give us a lift to boot.

The other older guys who helped us during an SOS included my brother Dick, who was sixteen in 1953, and his friends, Conway, Duba, and Dwyer. Most had cars or a truck by the time they were sixteen, but they knew how to drive long before, when we started out in '49. They only hung around if we needed them for something dangerous or if Dick and Duba weren't otherwise preoccupied with drag racing from Hastings store in Delphi Falls down the Oran Delphi Road and up Cherry Valley. Dick, Duba, Jimmy, Minneapolis Moline Conway, and Jimmy Dwyer weren't afraid of snakes or sheriffs, they said, and they knew just enough about both sides of the law to help us broaden our scope. They dared to do things to help us—things we couldn't work up the nerve to do or to try to get away with. It was a gift they had.

If I can paint a proper picture of my brother Dick at the time, you'll understand the rest—Duba, Conway, and Dwyer. Best I can describe Dick is by saying that in Jerry's first book, he showed up in chapter one with a black eye he'd just gotten—from a girl.

That pretty much puts them all in a nutshell.

Me in Little Rock 1953

As for me, I was twelve, the youngest of my friends, average height. I hadn't started my growth spurt yet. Black hair, a brush cut, (quarter inch all the way around). Hazel eyes and a chipped front tooth from trying to catch a sandlot football and missing.

You're going to meet my dad. Adults called him "Big Mike"; kids referred to him as "Big Mike" and politely called him "Mister," to his face. He towered over us at six foot six, and his dress hat added a few more inches. Always in a nice tie and suspenders. Dad had a bakery in Homer and one in Carthage, and he drove throughout central and upstate New York, visiting grocers most days. On Saturdays he would take me into Homer, where I would go to the post office and get the bakery mail and deliver it to his office right after I'd savored an ice cream sundae and a hot chocolate at Leonard's Coffee Shop.

Mom is "Missus" in all my books. My brother Mike is "Gourmet Mike." You'll learn why soon enough.

That's about it—other than my young love for Olivia Dandridge and my painting my bike canary yellow with my dad's shutter paint after I sat in the movie house and watched her three times in *She Wore a Yellow Ribbon* with John Wayne.

Oh, and there's Ole Charlie.

I called him "Mr. Pitts" when I first started walking the mile up to his place every week to get the eggs for my mom. He later told me to call him Charlie, and when he died he left me his kerosene lantern, some wicks, and a box of kitchen matches. Those days, I always said my bedtime prayers, and his lantern sitting on my windowsill would catch my eye, and I'd throw in a prayer for Ole Charlie.

I was convinced Ole Charlie was my and my friend's guardian angel.

I still am.

We lived in a rural area we dubbed the "Crown." It was a humble, hardworking, Currier-and-Ives patch of pastures, towns, villages, and fifty-four small family farms nestled in the rolling hills, where everybody got along and most knew your family name. The Crown stretched from Cazenovia down to Delphi Falls, back up to Pompey Center, down to Fabius, back up to Pompey, down to Apulia Station, up to Lafayette, and straight down to Tully. From there it crossed over to Gooseville Corners and back again up to Cazenovia.

This year was a happier time than all the wartime '40s—1953 was a coming-of-age time for us, and that November was the best of it. It was the time of year for the auto show, and we'd all hitch rides to the armory up in Syracuse just so we could stare at and drool over the next year's new car models raised up high on revolving-platform stages under spotlights. We saw the Buick, the Oldsmobile, the Studebaker, and the Cadillac—all of them. My favorite that year was the Mercury.

We celebrated new car models and the show. It was almost as if the Ringling Brothers Circus were coming to town with a big magic clock that would sound, reminding us school holidays and the Thanksgiving and Christmas parties and dances were on their way and our kitchen calendars.

It was truly an autumn of golden sunsets; full-wafer moons; brisk, cold air; deep, brilliant reds and yellows; and chimney smoke.

All was quiet in the Crown—or so it would seem.

Big Mike

CHAPTER TWO

THE ARKANSAS TRAVELER CIRCA THANKSGIVING 1953

Just the way Dad and the doc told me it happened.

My dad, Big Mike, wasn't "in his cups" the Saturday he walked over to Doc Webb's, but he was about to work on it having something weighty on his mind. He watched Doc's jeep crawl out of his barn, flagged him down, and Dad leaned back on it. He stretched his long right arm and set a full bourbon bottle on the hood while his left hand loosened his tie and unbuttoned his collar button. As a courtesy, Doc turned the engine off, figuring his run to Hastings for cabbage and pipe tobacco could wait. He knew my mom, "Missus," and Dick and I, "the boys," had driven to Little Rock to help Aunt Mary during Thanksgiving week, as she was fixing to have a baby.

The doc understood that it was pretty much common knowledge that a family man left setting at the supper table alone too many nights in the quiet of dairy-farm country was prey to certain apparitions and depressions in the head. My dad, for one, didn't favor being alone all that much since his one-year stretch away from us in the tuberculosis sanatorium, but on that day in particular, it seemed he had something other than loneliness gnawing on his mettle.

Around then the general-store owner from Fabius, Mike Shea, drove up and pulled over, looking for a friendly afternoon card game of pitch. But he joined in the conversation instead by politely poking an ear out his car window to tune in on the topic.

Gentleman that he was, Dad restarted the story of his being asked to join the country club in Cortland and how, when he mentioned the fanciful invite to some friends at the bakery, he learned that the country club didn't take Italians, Jews, or Negroes. Hearing the news from his friends, a Jew, an Italian, and a Negro, near made him cringe—or "bristle" might be a better word—so he left the bakery, rationalized that buying a fifth of Kentucky bourbon might solve his burn, drove home, parked, and walked over to Doc's place to blow off some steam, uncorking the bottle and his contempt along the way. And here we are.

"Oh, Big Mike," said Doc. "The sneaky and persnickety ways at that high-*falutin*' club full of pantywaists have been pretty much a public embarrassment for some time. No secret there. It shouldn't come as any surprise to you now."

"I guess I did know it deep down—just didn't want to believe it," said Dad. "I gave them the benefit of the doubt."

Mike Shea stepped out of his car and rested his elbows on top of its opened driver door.

"Big Mike, I've known you for some time—what's it been, since the thirties? There's something in your craw, but it's not a country club that isn't worth spit in the bigger scheme of things. They've been hiding their sins behind a dress code for years. Want to tell us what's really on your mind? You're among friends."

What Doc and Mike Shea didn't know was that after being put off by the country club's bigotry, Dad got home only to get a postcard from me.

"It's just that I was thinking about my boy, is all."

"Which boy is that, Big Mike?" asked Doc.

"Jerry."

Dad pulled my postcard from his back pocket.

"This here is a postcard from him postmarked Little Rock, Arkansas, 1953. It's addressed to Big Mike, Delphi Falls, NY:"

> Dad, when my letter comes can you give it to Mary Crane? I marked it PHBC—secret! PS: I don't like Arkansas. Jerry.

"Now I get it," said Mike Shea. "It's the 'I don't like Arkansas' line that's bothering you. You saw it—prejudice—firsthand down in Cortland today, and you saw the way some things have been there for years. You're afraid the boy will be seeing the real Jim Crow where he is down South. You're listening to the same news we've been hearing about Negro kids in Little Rock not being allowed in public schools, and now Ike is trying to force integration. You know what it's like down there today, and it bothers you that Jerry might be in the middle of it all. Am I close to the button?"

Dad nodded his head, remembering a time of his early travels.

"I went all through the South on my way to Texas one time back in the twenties. I'll never forget it. People would seem to look right through the Negroes down there like they didn't even exist. I know he's seeing it all for the first time."

"The boy's resilient," said Doc. "Just have a sit-down with him when he gets home. He's a smart kid. It's not the way things are most places."

Dad leaned in.

"Gents, I saw a drug store down there with a small square hole in its brick alley wall. If a Negro wanted to pick up a prescription, he had to stick his arm through the hole and wait for someone to take his money and put the medicine in his hand. Negroes weren't allowed in the store."

"Jerry's a strong lad," said Mike Shea. "He'll see the wrong."

"Just have a talk with him," said Doc.

Dad slid my postcard back into his pocket and reached for the bottle, pulled its cork, and lifted it.

"So tell me this. Why didn't I drive over to the country club, speak up, and give them all a piece of my mind, like a man?" he growled. "I just bought a bottle of bourbon and drove home."

He took a swig of bourbon.

"It's 'cuz all those country-club members and their businesses buy a lot of bread, pies, and cakes, maybe?" said Mike Shea.

Dad pursed his lips and nodded, not wanting to admit it but knowing that Mike Shea was right—that everybody protects their own interests. He set the bottle back down and looked off into the distance. Mike Shea had hit a nerve. Nobody spoke for a spell. My dad just stared off at a hill behind Doc's. He spoke up.

"There's not a doubt in my mind, gentlemen. More than two hundred years of slavery has shredded America's moral conscience, and it's been torn like an Achilles tendon."

Hearing such eloquence, Mike Shea felt obligated to close his car door, and he motioned for Dad to hand him the bottle for a belt. After tipping it back, he lowered the bottle, looked over at Doc, flexed his neck, and gritted a whiskey-wrenched swallow.

"You may be driving me back to the store, Doc. You'd better not drink so you're able - just smoke your pipe."

He took another snort, shivered his head, and handed the bottle back to Dad.

Doc interrupted the thought and explained the bright side.

"Abolition did finally come, gentlemen—took a while, but it came. Bully for Lincoln, and bully for abolition! We got it right!"

"You don't get what the man's trying to say, Doc," said Mike Shea.

"What am I missing?" asked Doc.

"It came all right, but it came without absolution. Abolition without absolution was like putting a bandage on two hundred years of slave ownership. That right, Big Mike?"

Dad nodded his head in agreement.

Doc pushed his hat brim up with his thumb and scratched his head.

"I'm a simple dentist. Do either of you care to explain that one?"

Mike Shea did the honor.

"Why, the abolition vote alone was like hanging mistletoe over the doorway to freedom, Doc. As if freedom was just a light switch you could turn on and off."

Dad thought that was poetic, took a snort, sucked in some air through his teeth with a wince, and handed the bottle back over to Mike Shea.

He stared at the ground for balance and, as if he were thinking back on his travels as a young man hiking around America, mumbled, "Some of us with consciences embraced it, but the recalcitrant only considered abolition like mistletoe—poisonous if swallowed."

"Recalcitrant?" asked Mike Shea. "Mighty big city word for out here, but it works. Is mistletoe poisonous?" he added.

"It could kill you," said Dad. "I learned that walking through the South—Alabama, Georgia, and Mississippi—when I was eighteen, seeing the country."

"I don't get it," said Doc. "Wasn't abolition—freeing the slaves—what we all wanted?"

That one there drew silence before Mike Shea broke the spell. He raised his fist gently to his chest, lowered his chin, puffed his cheeks, and muffled a belch.

"We never said we were sorry, Doc."

"What!"

"I like that," said Dad. "We never said we were sorry."

"We freed the slaves without giving them education, Doc. They were unable to read and write—they weren't allowed to learn when they were slaves. We just opened the floodgates and let them loose to feed and fend for themselves like they were free-range chickens," Mike Shea added.

"We didn't educate the freed slaves. Is that what you're going on about?" asked Doc.

"Worse, Doc—we didn't educate anybody," said Mike Shea.

Dad set the bottle down on the hood of the jeep and said, "I read where General George Patton ordered all the German civilians in a town to march five miles up a steep hill, escorted by armed American soldiers, to see the bodies at the Buchenwald Camp, where Nazis had killed and burned Jews. It took two days for the Weimar residents to file through the camp. Twenty-five thousand Jews were gassed and burned at the rate of a hundred a day."

"He wanted them to see what they had turned their backs on throughout the war," said Mike Shea.

"So we never said we were sorry," said Doc. "Hmm."

He took a puff on his pipe and stared off at a tree.

"I met a priest from Alabama," said Dad. "I think it was 1927—I was at Penn Station in New York City. He told me some Southern states created vagrancy laws after abolition. If the Negroes there couldn't prove they had a job, they were court ordered into two years of servitude."

"They kept slavery going for fifty or more years," said Mike Shea.

Dad took another belt and handed the bottle to Mike Shea.

My, but it was a powerful set of intellects standing around Doc Webb's jeep all right, as I remember Dad telling me the story. Not many knew the three that way, as their usual masks were most always those of friendly pillars of the community, men with ready smiles, mild manners, and gentle politeness their long-since-passed mothers would have been proud of.

At about that time, the two Mikes weren't sure if the moment was being spurred on by a few snorts of aged Kentucky bourbon or talk of a country club Dad had no intention of joining. They'd lost track, as neither was keeping score.

"It's now eighty-eight years and counting," said Doc as he figured the number on both hands. "And we've still never said we're sorry."

Well, apparently Doc had figured the score. Abolition had happened in 1865, and that there was 1953.

"So how do we say we're sorry for something like that?" asked Doc.

"Doc, we spent more than two hundred years setting bad examples and teaching children the wrong way by those examples. Now we're trying to force integration, like it or not. Spending eighty-eight years teaching them—all the children—what's right in all classrooms would have been saying we're sorry," said Mike Shea. "Integration would have already happened if we'd done that."

"How?" asked Doc.

"The kids would have integrated on their own without any help from any National Guard if we'd taught them right," said Mike Shea.

"This sort of thing can only be taught," said Dad.

"Look where not doing it has gotten us. Now the Italians and Jews and God knows who else are in the same fix in America, being singled out by some bullies who get away with it," said Mike Shea.

"Is it too late?" asked Doc.

"It's never too late," said Mike Shea. "But we have to start believing that teaching it in the classroom is as important as teaching math or science if we're going to change things."

"Environment has nothing to do with what a person can learn and achieve," said Dad. "Abe Lincoln reading by candlelight in a log cabin proved that."

"The problem won't be fixed with lip service," said Mike Shea. "It'll only get worse until we do take responsibility for it in the classroom."

Dad was thinking about my postcard and me, his twelve-year-old boy in Little Rock who was likely seeing Jim-Crow bigotry firsthand for the first time. And then it wasn't too long before the loneliness and disappointment melted together and sobered Dad enough to cork the bottle and walk alone back on up the hill on this side of Farmer Parker's land to get home and lie down.

Doc and Mike Shea walked across the road to the house to play a few hands of pitch.

Big Mike

My dad was a remarkable man. Autodidactic, the man could finish a *New York Times* crossword puzzle while driving between country-road signs. He was a lad of thirteen and nearly fully grown when his father fell from the barn roof. He quit school and walked from Minnesota to North Dakota, working all the wheat fields and covering his hands with callouses from the leather reins he held as he drove teams of four and sometimes six horses pulling great, thundering thrashers. All the while, he sent money home to his mother.

Big Mike at thirteen in 1915 in North Dakota

He would tell me stories of how, at day's end, he'd climb and sit on top of a Black Hills mountain ridge and sing out loud.

"Oh, give me a home where the buffalo roam, and the deer and the antelope play," he'd sing, just to hear his echoes as he watched the stars.

Sitting on the mountain one night, looking up at a million stars, he made a promise to himself that he would go see the country and set foot in all forty-eight states by the time he was twenty.

When he was seventeen and driving a horse-drawn bread wagon, he met a young man his age and height, the Charles Lindbergh fellow, another adventurer. Legend is that they both stood in front of a grocery store and shared their pledges to explore the country, and they kept their promises by going off separately to see more of America than either of them needed to in order to get a proper hang of it. With his goal kept, Dad went home, built a bakery in Homer, and became "Big Mike," and Charles Lindbergh kept his pledge too. He went west to build an airplane—the *Spirit of St. Louis*—that he wound up flying to Paris, and he became the famous, "Lucky Lindy."

Standing in the kitchen and waiting on the coffee percolator, Dad tapped my postcard on his palm like he was playing the snare drum in a dirge at a Frenchman's wake.

I was away from the state for the first time in my life; I was twelve, and Dad had been thirteen when he'd done it, and maybe he was thinking the postcard warranted a telephone call to protect me from what I might be seeing in Little Rock. And maybe then he remembered there were no ready telephones back when he saw the states, and maybe it was best I do my own exploring, see the good and the bad for myself, and make my own conclusions.

He poured the bourbon into the sink drain, dropped the empty in the trash, picked up his coffee mug, and stepped into the bedroom. He paused at the doorway, turned, and then sat on the edge of the bed in the dark, and he thought some more before picking up the receiver.

"Operator."

"Myrtie, I need the Cranes on the wire. Can you find them up Watervale way, maybe Berry Road?"

"Did Missus and the boys get to Arkansas?"

"It was a long drive, but they made it in time to help out."

"Has the baby come?"

"Not yet—maybe tomorrow."

"Here you go."

"Hello?"

"Betty, this is Mike."

"Did Missus and the boys make it safely to Little Rock?"

"They did. A postcard came with a message for the club—Jerry wants me to get it to Mary."

"Mary's up the road with Aunt Lucy, helping her get her house ready for a social. She's having friends in Sunday."

"Aunt Lucy? Is she your sister?"

Mrs. Crane chuckled.

"No relation. She goes by Aunt Lucy. She does live-in work for a family in Syracuse. She bought the Ryan place three houses up and lives there weekends when she's not working. She asks Mary and a friend for help washing dishes, setting the table, and serving at her party—that sort of thing. It's extra money for them, but I don't think they'll take it."

"A letter is coming from Jerry. Secret, he says."

"Secret Pompey Hollow Book Club messages, eh?" Mrs. Crane mused. "Here they go again."

"I don't know what's in it," said Dad. "Knowing Jerry, if the boy took the time to write it, it's important to him."

"Well, of course."

"Tell Mary I'll make spaghetti for whatever night his letter gets delivered. The club might as well meet here, where there's light to read by, instead of at their usual spot over at the cemetery with kerosene lanterns. Besides, it's getting colder."

"I'll be sure to tell her."

"I could use the company. It cheers me up, seeing their zeal—watching them grow up."

"You're not going to be with family for Thanksgiving?"

"They'll be in Little Rock all week. Thanksgiving is the busiest time for the bakery, what with bread stuffing for turkeys, pies, and all. It always has been."

"You're welcome to come here."

"Thank you, Betty, but young Mike and his girlfriend will be home from Le Moyne. He's cooking our bird."

"Is that who Jerry calls 'Gourmet Mike'?"

"One and the same. I'm sure he'll come up with some new twist on a traditional Thanksgiving meal."

"Jerry's becoming a regular Huckleberry Finn, traveling all that way. It must be quite an adventure for him."

"Mark Twain lived in Elmira, Betty, fifty or so miles from here all the time he was writing *Huckleberry Finn*."

"You don't say."

"And pretty well set in the comforts of a home his wife had, I understand. I think Jerry's seeing some things for the first time, firsthand, in Arkansas."

"Did Missus have business there?"

"The boys' uncle Don and aunt Mary live there. They have a baby due before Thanksgiving, hopefully tomorrow. They needed a hand with their little one still in diapers."

"They'll have their hands full."

"She's gone full term. She'll be in the hospital four or five days, and Uncle Don has to work."

"I'll let Mary know. They love your spaghetti. I'm sure they'll look forward to it."

The telephone call ended, edging Delphi Falls a little closer to the 1953 holiday season.

My dad, lanky "Big Mike" at 13 in 1915, singing, "Oh, give me a home, where the buffalo roam, and the deer and the antelope play." He sang just to hear the echoes.

CHAPTER THREE

A CALL TO ORDER!

*Can't grow up with the kids and not have heard the
stories a million times.*

On Saturday morning, the Crane's telephone rang.

"Hello?"

"Mrs. Crane, this is Dale."

"Hold on, hon."

Through the earpiece Barber could hear the clap of a screen door, followed by some stomping. Stomping on the entry mat was a ritual usually used when wet, cut grass or damp autumn leaves stuck to shoes.

"Hello," said Mary.

"Didja go to the square dance?"

"No, un-uh. Why?"

"No reason."

"You called to ask me that?"

"No."

"Why'd you ask?"

"Never mind."

"Must be a reason. Boys don't bring up a dance after a dance is over for no reason."

"My mom—"

"It's a girl, isn't it?"

Mary sang a whine: "Barber likes a girllll…Barber likes a girllll… and he wants to know who she danced with or if she smooched, right?"

No answer.

"Who is she? Tell me. I promise I won't tell."

Mary was getting nowhere fast.

Barber had hoped for a bit more decorum from the club president.

"Mom told me you called," said Barber. "You want me to set up a meeting or something?"

"Sort of, but not yet," said Mary.

"Huh?"

"Oh, well go ahead and call everybody. Might as well tell 'em to be ready. Big Mike is making us spaghetti either tonight or tomorrow, depending on when the letter from Jerry comes. I'm waiting for him to tell me."

"Jerry sent it from Arkansas?"

"Yes."

"Roger dodger," said Barber. "What's it about—did anybody say?"

"We're getting a letter from Jerry is all I know."

The two hung up, and it wasn't ten minutes before Mary telephoned Barber.

"Go ahead—set it up for tonight. Meet at Farmer Parker's at five."

"We're going to eat at Farmer Parker's?"

"No, but let's go say hello to Farmer Parker first. We'll see if he's doing okay with his strained back, then we'll walk over to Big Mike's for supper."

Since 1949, my friends and I have grown up and blossomed out spiritually, mentally, and physically—every which way you could imagine. We were about as tall as our folks, and some of us had changing voices and hair growing in new places. We were then in our teens, but the rules for club procedure we'd set and spat on when we were nine and ten still stood true. It was because of this unconditional respect for one another that the club worked. Together we caught crooks and thieves and pickpockets and set good examples.

We ran Farmer Parker's farm, helping out when he wrenched his back and was laid up a couple of weeks before this particular story started. We even buried his dog.

We liked Farmer and Mrs. Parker all get out, but we knew Charlie Pitts was our kindred spirit. Everybody remembered walking with me at one time or another when I used to walk up to his place to get eggs. We'd meet and play in his barn. It wasn't much to look at in the daylight, but it came to life when we'd play in it. At night, with the three lanterns lit, the golden-straw loft, the one horse stable and one cow pen, and the corn manger in the center, it glowed like a hand-painted Christmas card. When Charlie died, they burned his house and barn to the ground for fear his cancer would spread. We had our meetings over his grave at the Delphi Falls cemetery after that.

Holbrook was an hour early for the meeting. His dad dropped him off on Cardiner Road so early that he decided to climb the back hill behind our alfalfa field up to his and my camp on top of the left cliff overlooking the waterfall. He needed to kill some time and to decide if he wanted to camp out after the meeting. A lot of his decision would depend on the snap in the air and on if there was any canned food left in my knapsack, which he thought was down in my room.

The rest began trailing toward Farmer Parker's at about four thirty.

Blocking the setting sun while pulling over Farmer Parker's side-road hill, Mr. Vaas slowed first and then ground a gear down as he turned his '42 Dodge milk-can hauler into the cinder drive-way, taking a wide cut on a piece of the lawn. His truck was like a live lion, rocking there in idle, its diesel engine like its purr, rat-tling Farmer Parker's toolshed and making the tools inside clank on the walls while Randy, the Mayor, and Mary piled out of the truck's cab.

Mr. Barber's new four-door gray Packard was the last to pull in. Its big whitewall tires rolled majestically onto the drive, crunch-ing the cinder, which resulted in a sound like corn popping, while Bases and Barber climbed out. Barber took his dad's keys and stepped around back. He opened the trunk and lifted out three packages wrapped in butcher paper and tied with string. After slamming the trunk down, he handed the keys back to Mr. Barber.

"If you're not late, Bub, I'll pick you up," said Mr. Barber. "If you're late, call to see if I'm up or hitch a ride or walk."

Family farmers were at their best after a good night's sleep, con-sidering their days started at four in the morning. The car backed out and was the last to drive away.

They gathered around in the milk barn and said hello and other politenesses to Farmer Parker while he stripped a cow. They satisfied themselves that things were fine with the old man, as he was back at his chores. Up at the house, Mrs. Parker was roll-ing dough for some holiday pies and had a bowl filled with what looked like the mix for a Christmas fruitcake. Mary mentioned how lovely her prize roses were at that late season, and she gave Mary a taste of a jam.

"The secret is my cutting them back before snowfall," she said. "Just after Thanksgiving I'll be trimming the bushes a tad...just a tad. Their branches enjoy an early spring rain and the sun."

After paying their respects, they moved single file out down the worn walking path on the north side of the house and left of the wood plank, next to the strawberry patch. They stepped down off the lawn, crossed the road, and headed up the long dirt drive to our house.

"Farmer Parker must be lonely milking in the barn without Buddy," said Mary.

"Why?" asked Holbrook. "Buddy was too old to go to the barn and watch him milk for more than a year. Why would he be lonely?"

"Buddy was always on the porch and would say hello to him when he went down to the barn and hello again when he came back up," said Mary. "Now he's dead and buried up on the pasture hill, and Farmer Parker with no dog to greet him."

"He told us that he couldn't ever replace Buddy," said Holbrook.

"You want to get him another dog, don't you?" said Barber. "I can smell it."

"Let's find him one before Christmas," said Mary. "We can give it to him early."

The view looking down from the cliff top at our house and the waterfall

CHAPTER FOUR

SPAGHETTI SAUCE AND SECRET THOUGHTS

Dad met them at the screen door and stepped from the house as he took his apron off and handed it to Mary.

"Come in, come in, and make yourselves at home. Go on in and start your meeting—go as late as you'd like. I forgot the sausage, so I'm going to pop over to Hastings for some. I won't disturb you. We'll eat in about an hour or so."

Dad handed Mary the envelope from me as he stepped off the porch. He took the apron he had given her, gave it to Holbrook to hold, walked to his car, and drove away.

Stepping into the empty house, Holbrook beamed when he smelled the aroma of oregano, cooking green peppers, and a garlic-tomato sauce wafting about, simmering with warm hints of the Italian sausage on its way. "Big Mike's" Italian sausage was Holbrook's favorite food.

Gathering in the dining room, they each selected a chair around the table. They left the head chair empty out of respect for Dad, Big Mike.

"Anybody got anything before I read Jerry's letter?" asked Mary.

"Mom sent these packages for Aunt Lucy," said Barber. "They're for her charity for Christmas."

"I didn't know you had an aunt Lucy," said Randy.

"She lives up from Mary," said Barber. "Mary, tell her they're from Gertrude. She'll know."

Mary set the packages on the floor by her chair.

"I think she's only home on Saturday and Sunday," added Barber.

"I know," said Mary. "I work for her sometime."

"Jerry and I put up her backyard clothesline," said Holbrook.

"Who is she?" asked Mayor.

"Just a friend," said Mary. "She works in Syracuse."

"She collects Christmas presents to give to charity. Whatever people donate, she wraps and sends out," said Barber.

"She's not my aunt," said Mary.

Mary looked around the table.

"Anything else?"

"Go ahead and read Jerry's letter," said Mayor.

"Read it," said Holbrook.

"Read the letter," said Randy.

Mary carefully started a rip on the envelope with her fingernail, neatly opened its top, and lifted out what appeared to be four folded pages. She unfolded them like they were a man's handkerchief.

Anxious eyes were glued to her hands and the papers in them. She puffed a curl away from her eye.

"Well, here goes."

She paused and thumbed through the pages.

"What are you waiting for?" said Holbrook.

"I don't see 'dear,'" said Mary. "I'm looking for the beginning. I can't find 'dear' anywhere."

"Start on the top page and read it. We'll figure it out," said Barber.

Mary shrugged and started reading the letter.

It's hot here but probably snowing up where you guys are in Delphi Falls, I bet. People talk with an accent. My mom calls it a "drawl." She says everything's so hot that people have to talk slower. It's like how they talk faster in Boston because it's so cold there, she said. Something like that. They don't have enough beds with all their kids, so I have to sleep in the empty apartment on the second floor. The apartment owner said it was okay for me to sleep up there on an army cot. It's scary alone in the dark. It's not like I can build a campfire. I know how to change a diaper now, and I've been trying to get Uncle Don to tell me stories about when he flew his B-17 from England over to Germany in the war, but he works a lot. His guys flew missions and bombed Hitler, Aunt Mary told me. She showed me the picture album of him in uniform and a picture he took out his window on a bombing mission. She told me his plane was *Lady Helene* and showed me pictures of his bomber crew.

Mary paused and looked up as my dad walked into the house, making his way to the kitchen carrying a grocery bag from Hastings. Holbrook held up his arm with the apron in his hand, and Dad grabbed it as he walked by.

"Don't stop, young lady. I'll be in the kitchen. Pay no mind to me."

"Where was I?"

"His plane was *Lady Helene*," said Randy.

Mary continued to read the letter.

But that's not what I want to tell you guys. Dick and I took a bus downtown. We got off at the zoo, and that was fun, but then he showed me how Negro people in Arkansas aren't allowed to do everything white people can do. They call Negro people "colored" here, but it isn't polite, my mom says.

"They do in Syracuse, too," mumbled Bases.

"Shut up!" said Holbrook. "Read, Mary!"

"My dad told me," said Bases.

Mary continued.

> Down here they have drinking fountains like we have at school, but they're outdoors here because it's so hot, but they always have two. Know why? One has a sign on it that says For Whites Only, and one has a sign that says For Coloreds Only. We even wanted to go to a movie and sit in the balcony, but they wouldn't let us. Know why? The ticket lady told us the balcony was for coloreds only. She actually said that out loud where everybody around could hear her.

"He'd better be careful," said Mayor. "I think they have laws down there that are different than the laws up here—laws from Civil War days."

"Maybe they put the drinking-fountain signs up for slaves a long time ago and forgot to take them down after the Civil War," said Bases.

"Give me a break!" Mary said impatiently.

"I know they have KKK all over the place—at least that's what I heard," said Barber. "They're nothing to be messed with."

"He'd better tell Dick not to be mouthing off at anybody down there," said Holbrook.

Mary found her spot on the page and read on.

> Will somebody send me the master code sheet we made up for Eisenhower's grandson, just in case I need to write a secret message? Ask my dad where to mail it, or look on this envelope. Make sure my name is on the envelope. That's all for now, but it is scary here. Jerry

PS: Tell Holbrook I took my knapsack in case he's looking for it to go camping, but tell him to ask my dad for some food to take up. He can use my pillowcase. Tell him the Spam is in the cabinet over the icebox.

Mary looked up.

"He wants the master code. Where is it? Does Duba still have it?" she asked. "He had it last."

"I wonder why he wants it," said Mayor.

"I'll ask Duba for it," said Randy.

"Maybe there's something he's afraid to tell us without a code," said Barber.

"I think Duba gave the code master to Marty in case he needed it when we caught the pickpocket," said Mayor. "I'll ask Marty."

Dad came in the dining room, wiping his hands with a kitchen towel, and interrupted the meeting.

"I put the spaghetti on to boil," he said. "I have a few minutes before serving it and couldn't help overhearing what you're talking about. Mind if I sit in a spell?"

My dad knew he was always welcome but asked as a courtesy.

"Is it like that down there?" asked Holbrook.

"In Arkansas?" asked Dad.

"Yes," said Holbrook.

"It's like that, in different ways, in many places," said Dad.

"Not in Syracuse," said Bases.

Dad sat down and looked Bases in the eye.

"Son, there's a football player who Syracuse University wouldn't give a football scholarship to this year because of his skin color. One of the best young high school athletes in America. His name is Jim Brown. You'll be reading a lot about him, I'm sure. They didn't want him because of his race."

"For real?" asked Holbrook.

"For real," said Dad. "He's sponsored by a white family he lived near in Manhasset where he played high school lacrosse —the Molloys down on Long island—that's influential with Syracuse University somehow, but they only managed to raise the money for his tuition and expenses. They put him on the team, but it's my understanding that Jim Brown doesn't have a football scholarship, just because of his skin color."

Dad didn't want to bring up his experience with the country club in Cortland.

"I know what Jerry is saying is right," said Barber. "The man across from Chubb's bought a television at the state fair, and he told my dad that somebody on television was showing news or something about how they won't let Negro kids go to school in Little Rock, Arkansas, with the other kids because of their color."

"You mean Jackie and Alda wouldn't be able to go to school in Arkansas?" asked Mary. "I hardly believe that."

"He'd better be careful down there," said Mayor.

"Put the letter away for now, and grab a plate," said Dad. "I'll serve the food, and we'll talk about this while we eat."

Wasn't long before they were back in their seats with plates of spaghetti piled high. Dad set two platters in the center of the table, one with sausage links and one stacked with Italian bread. He took a seat down at the end of the table.

"I have an idea your meeting wasn't over," he said. "So we'll call this a supper break. And while we're eating, let me get some words in for you to think about. There's more spaghetti and sauce in the kitchen if anyone wants more. Help yourself."

Dad twirled his fork in the spaghetti on his plate and looked around at the faces. He'd known the same bright eyes and sincere smiles from the time we were pups. The kids who didn't have a mean bone in their bodies—the kids who weren't kindly when someone got taken advantage of—were growing up.

He set his fork down.

"When I was a young boy, back in about 1910," Dad said, "I remember asking my mother why the Indian kids I knew in Minnesota lived on reservations. She told me she didn't have an answer—it was the same way it was when she and my dad came to America from Saint-Jean-Port-Joli, Quebec."

"Are you from Canada?" asked Holbrook.

"My parents came to Canada from Normandy."

"In France? You mean like the D-day Normandy?" asked Holbrook.

"Yes," said Dad.

Everyone put their forks down and leaned in to listen to one of the Big Mike stories they knew almost always came with his spaghetti-and-sausage suppers.

"I was born on a farm in Minnesota the youngest of seven brothers. I was so proud to be American and even prouder when my dad would sit tall and tell people his little Mike was the seventh son of a seventh son. He died from complications after falling off the barn roof when I was about your ages now. Losing my dad was like you and your friends losing people in the war. I was thirteen and quit school to help my mom, and I made a decision that I was going to fulfill my dream to see all forty-eight states, learn about America for myself, and learn why Indians live on reservations."

Big Mike's boyhood home in 1902

"For real?" asked Holbrook.

"Well, that was more like what they'd maybe call a 'metaphor' of my dream or an 'allegory,' son, or maybe a 'figure of speech'— not sure which. I just wanted to see what kind of people made up this country and how they lived."

"I know about metaphors," said Mary.

"That's before cars were invented, right?" asked Barber.

"I started in the Dakotas, working harvests in the wheat fields and sending money back home. I drove teams of four and sometimes six horses pulling thrashers all the way down the wheat-belt states and then back up through other harvesting states. Doing that and later on while working in the bread business. At eighteen I worked driving a horse-drawn bread wagon in Minnesota, and then I was promoted up to traveling around helping bakeries with their marketing and sales. I finally reached my goal of traveling to every one of the forty-eight states. Some states more than once."

"How old were you when you finally did it—you know, saw them all?" asked Holbrook.

"Just about twenty-one, at about the same time I fell in love."

"With Missus?" Mary asked, smiling.

Dad flicked his eyebrows like Groucho Marx and nodded a smiling yes.

"The point I'm trying to make is that I've seen a lot of things in these states we all call America. I've seen things I'm proud of, and I've seen things I'm not so proud of. I've met a lot of people."

"What was your favorite thing to do?" asked Randy.

"Besides reading a book?"

"Yes, sir, your favorite thing you did."

"I jumped across the Mississippi River," Dad said, laughing.

"For real?" Mayor asked. "Are you making that up?"

"In the far northern part of Minnesota, the Mississippi River starts as a spring or two. It's about four feet wide at one point, and I sure enough jumped over it. Had a picture of it but lost it somewhere."

"Holy cow," said Randy.

"When I was thirteen or fourteen, I would sit on a mountain edge in the Black Hills every night and sing 'Home on the Range' at the top of my lungs and listen to my echo."

"You did all that at thirteen?" asked Randy.

"First time I did it, I was. I worked wheat fields each season for a few years. I was a lanky one back then, too," said Dad.

"What else?" asked Holbrook.

"While I was cooking tonight, I heard Mary read what Jerry wrote, and I've seen all what he's seeing now in many places—and worse."

"Worse?" asked Mary.

"We have a nice life here. Everybody in the Crown gets along. We're sheltered from a lot of the bigotry that exists around the country. I just want you to be prepared for it as you grow up and move on. Maybe someday you can figure out how you can make a difference."

"What have you seen that's worse?" asked Holbrook.

"I've never seen one, but there've been lynchings. People hung or burned alive by mean and ignorant bigots because of their skin color. Human beings treated like barnyard animals, disrespected and degraded or even murdered."

Dad looked over and saw tears glistening in Mary's and Randy's eyes. The others sat in stunned silence with purse-lipped disbelief. Up to then they'd all pretty much related that sort of thing to Hitler and the Nazis. This all brought it home.

Judging by a tear rolling down her cheek, Mary was the closest to somebody of color.

"Aunt Lucy is...you know—" Her voice cracked.

She was thinking of lynchings and of being burned alive.

"Colored?" mumbled Bases.

Mary looked down at the table with her eyes closed and nodded a slow, sad yes.

"There are two things I'd like to say," said Dad. "You're bright young people. I'd appreciate if you gave them both some thought."

"We promise," said Holbrook.

Dad raised himself up from the chair and stood every inch of his full six-foot-six height. After untying the apron from around his waist, he dropped it onto the chair's seat.

"Barber, what am I?" he asked.

"Huh?" Barber said, completely startled.

"Look at me—tell me what I am, son."

"Aren't you Big Mike?" asked Barber.

Dad wasn't satisfied with that answer. He looked about.

"What am I?" he said again.

"Anybody!" he said. "What am I?'"

"You're a baker," said Randy.

Dad raised his arm and swirled his fist in the air near the ceiling.

"Yessss!"

"So what is Mr. Barber?" he continued.

"A farmer?" asked Mayor.

"How about Mr. Holbrook—what is he?"

"He's a brakeman on the railroad," said Holbrook.

"Now tell me, Mary—you tell me. What is Aunt Lucy?"

"She's a live-in housekeeper. Oh, I get it," said Mary.

"And the Gaines family down the road and left up the hill—what are they? Anybody?"

Murmurs worked themselves about the table.

"Farmers," said Holbrook.

"They're farmers," said Randy.

"Gaines farm—they're farmers," said Barber.

Mary rose up from her chair, walked around the table, and gave Dad a hug. She whispered "thank you" into his chest.

Mayor spoke up.

"You said there were two things. What's the other thing?"

"Number two is that people are people—the bakers, the brakemen, the farmers, and the housekeepers. The word 'color' has nothing to do with it. Talk with people—hear them out—about their lives and about who they are. Give them a chance. You can't do that without becoming friends. Don't make assumptions about who people are or talk behind their backs. If you have questions about people's different cultures or different backgrounds, break bread with them. We're all one brotherhood, and life is too short. The issues aren't about color; they're about not understanding other cultures. Sit down at their tables and listen and learn. Not your table—theirs. Don't ever feel so threatened that you allow anyone to be caged into categories like colored or into places like the reservations where the American Indians lived."

"What does 'culture' mean, anyway?" asked Holbrook.

"Let me explain it in a simple way," said Dad.

"Okay."

"I'm a Roman Catholic. Some of you are Baptists, Methodists, or other religions. Any of you ever think it's funny the way we Catholics are always standing and kneeling in Mass?"

"It is funny, and it would wear a body out just going to church," said Mayor.

"When we get into or out of our pew, we genuflect, or touch one of our knees to the floor. Want to know why?"

"Tell us," said Holbrook. "Why?"

"We believe that the church is God's house. We believe He is at the altar. Out of respect for His presence, we always genuflect when we enter or leave His home."

"That's so nice," said Mary.

"How about you, Mayor?" said Dad.

"I really understand it now, and it makes sense."

"So now you know a bit of the Catholic Mass culture. Does it help you appreciate our ways better?"

"It does."

"Isn't that better than just going on making assumptions without knowing?"

"Yes. It's not so funny after you explain it."

"So you're saying we need to learn the culture of things or people instead of laughing at what we don't know," said Holbrook.

My dad smiled.

"I'm in the church choir with Jackie and Alda," said Mary.

"The Gaines girls?" asked Dad.

"Yes."

"Have you ever shared their table?"

"No."

"Have any of you thought of inviting them to join the Pompey Hollow Book Club?" asked Dad.

"No, sir."

"And they live a stone's throw from here. Is that because of the color of their skin?"

"Never! No way," Mary said. "None of us even think like that—never. They're in different grades in school is all."

"Seventh grade, I think," said Randy. "Alda is a good softball pitcher."

"Come to think of it, Gaineses' place is the only farm in all of Delphi Falls that's actually on Pompey Hollow Road—well, at a corner of it anyway," said Barber.

"So, Mary, let me ask you something," said Dad. "If Mr. Gaines and Mrs. Gaines are farmers, what are Jackie and Alda?"

Mary didn't hesitate.

"Jackie's a great choir soprano, and Alda's the best softball pitcher," said Mary.

Dad beamed.

"Atta girl!"

Mary beamed a happy, understanding grin.

"Grab your plates, and take them to the kitchen. Just stack them, and come back and finish your meeting," he said. "I'll cut the cake and see you get home if you need rides."

They all "got" it—Dad's message.

When they ate the cake, it was a happy time. Mary called the meeting to order again.

"That's all I have," she said through a mouthful of cake. "Write Jerry's address down if you're going to write him in Little Rock. Randy, if you get that secret-code master, be sure to tell Barber in case he has to set up another meeting."

"I'll know tomorrow," Randy said to Barber.

"Meeting adjourned," said Mary.

Each thanked my dad for the food and the talk. They stepped out of the house and off the stoop a little taller then, knowing how they could make a difference in the world.

The gathering officially broke up when the shiny, long Packard drove in to pick Barber and Bases up. They would've walked home, except Mr. Barber had some night chores that had kept him up. He rolled a window down, stuck an arm out, and pointed to Mary.

"How're your folks, young lady?"

"They're fine."

"Thanks for taking the packages to Aunt Lucy."

"No problem. I'm going there tomorrow after church anyway."

"She's good people. Gertrude met her at a bake sale. We try to help any way we can," said Mr. Barber.

Mr. Barber offered Mayor a lift up to Penoyer Road, but the lad opted to ride back with Randy's pap when he came so he could pass some time jawing with his friends. Holbrook felt the air to see how cold it might be getting. He said he'd either go with Randy's pap too or camp out again. He didn't quite have his mind made up yet.

The Packard rolled down the dirt driveway.

"I'll never understand that whole thing," said Mary.

"What whole thing, Mary?" asked Dad, speaking through the screen door.

"The Civil War thing. I thought it ended all that. I don't get it."

No one spoke.

When there are no answers for a question, silence speaks the loudest.

My dad was a good man teaching some good kids.

"I wonder how Jerry's doing," said Mary.

"I bet it's warmer in Arkansas than it is here," said Holbrook.

With my pillowcase and provisions over his shoulder, he stepped off the porch, walked down the drive, crossed the bridge, and cut through the alfalfa field, climbing the hill to camp out.

CHAPTER FIVE

NECESSITY IS ANOTHER INVENTION

Early the very next day, the Sunday before Thanksgiving, in Little Rock, Aunt Mary gave birth, and both were in the hospital doing fine. Twelve hundred miles away, up in Delphi Falls, on the same morning, there was a Pompey Hollow Book Club meeting called for noon at the cemetery.

Church-day meetings were a tangle for Mary, as she typically had Sunday papers to deliver, early choir practice, and holy services to sing. Most all the club members went to some kind of church somewhere. On that particular Sunday, at two o'clock, Mary also had a job helping with the dishes and picking up after a social for her friend Aunt Lucy.

Because Barber had called the meeting without asking her, which was atypical, Mary felt a sense of urgency and thought that something might be in the air down in Arkansas. She made a special point of being there. Her dad dropped her off.

Now here is a spot in my story where it'll do you good to forget what you might have heard and to try to understand the way times really were back then in many parts of America. They are the times we remember. The civil rights movement story is not quite in the order you've been told it is. This story happened in a time my dad called the "puberty-of-the-freed-slave" American experience. This day in time, the early 1950s shouldn't be confused with the civil rights movement of the 1960s. This story happened long before the civil rights movements of Medgar Evers or of Martin Luther King Jr. and his "I Have a Dream" speech.

To me, Rosa Parks was and is the original American heroine.

That brave lady in America proved it by demanding basic human dignity for all in the '50s.

Now, Medgar Evers and Martin Luther King Jr. inspired people and did brave things encouraging change, and yes, they were ultimately assassinated. Not to make light of it, but they didn't do those things thinking they were going to be murdered.

The very second Rosa Parks decided to sit in that white-only bus seat in Montgomery, Alabama, just to make her point and refused to move, she had to have known in her mind that she'd sat down at the risk of being lynched within the hour and possibly hung in a tree or burned just for doing it. It could have been worse: the culprits might have gotten away with lynching her in that day in time. As it turned out, she was reported by the bus driver, arrested, and jailed.

Not a doubt in my mind, the bravest person in America is a woman, Rosa Parks, who showed us what right was and what human decency was, all the time knowing what could happen to her. The lady never uttered a word of speech, but what Rosa Parks did was heard clear around the world. Oh, was it ever!

The '50s in America were frightening, racially speaking.

They were the Jim Crow–law times when people were called "colored." There were actual racist laws on the books, and they were very real in many Southern states.

For example, there was the Jim Crow law in Missouri, which read, "Separate free schools shall be established for the education of children of African descent; and it shall be unlawful for any colored child to attend a white school, or any white child to attend a colored school.

Or the Jim Crow law in North Carolina, which stated, "Books shall not be interchangeable between the white and colored schools, but shall continue to be used by the race first using them."

And then there was the Jim Crow law in Georgia: "It shall be unlawful for any amateur white baseball team to play baseball on any vacant lot or baseball diamond within two blocks of a playground devoted to the Negro race, and it shall be unlawful for any amateur colored baseball team to play baseball in any vacant lot or baseball diamond within two blocks of any playground devoted to the white race."

Can you just imagine?

And even though slavery was abolished in 1865, many Southern states kept it alive by legalizing "servitude" laws for vagrancy. Any person of color who couldn't verify an employer automatically received a sentence of two years of "servitude."

For years, these American injustices of race were masked and drowned out by brass bands marching on the Fourth of July – in villages and on the main streets with pomp and circumstance, flag-wavers prancing about celebrating a disingenuous, selective freedom. The Civil War had stopped nearly one hundred years before, but we teens in the Crown were only just becoming aware of racism. We'd been too busy with the aftermath of a depression and a war to give it the attention it deserved.

If my story can show you how it was in America when we grew up, maybe you can figure how little we've done as a people to make it right and help fix it, once and for all. I don't care how old you are or how young you are. You can do something to solve it. You can make a difference. You can make it happen.

Things brewing in 1953, and they were about to boil over, thanks to President Eisenhower, and I was a twelve-year-old lad finding myself in the heart of it down in Little Rock.

There was a vermin sort of human being hell-bent on killing the minds and spirits of a whole race. Worse, those worms felt superior because America was enabling them to do it. Most Americans knew it wasn't right, but a whole nation turned a blind eye.

According to the club, especially after reading my letter about it and knowing I was in Little Rock where the headlines were being generated, the fools being mean and the fools letting them get away with it were all pretty much the same.

Mary looked at her watch.

To get things started, she picked up a pinecone and opened the meeting by pitching it and bouncing it off Mayor's shoulder. He was the one who'd had Barber wake everybody up on a sleep-in Sunday with an early telephone ring.

Mayor stood up and turned to the group with a look in his eye.

"Marty is supposed to be here," he stuttered.

He stretched his neck, looking down the cemetery's cinder drive.

"I sure hope he gets here."

(You'd know Marty if you'd read any of the Pompey Hollow Book Club books. Red hair and freckles, he's smart as a whip and a year or so older than most who were sitting around Ole Charlie's gravestone that day.)

"Did anybody find the code master Duba had?" asked Mary.

Mayor chose an effective technique—interruption—to stall for more time.

"I was thinking," said Mayor. "Since he's way down in Arkansas, Jerry's traveled more than any one of us. Can you just imagine? I wonder how many miles that is."

Bases lifted his baseball glove as his point of disorder.

"I went to Binghamton once."

"That's in this state, Bases," said Randy. "Binghamton is in New York State."

"Well, I went," said Bases.

His point was unclear, even to him.

"Duly noted," said Mary, looking down at her watch and shaking her head.

If Mayor had been relying on Marty to carry the meeting, it wasn't looking good for him.

"What's in Arkansas, anyway?" asked Holbrook.

"I only know it's on the Mississippi River," said Mayor. "It's across from Tennessee."

Boys in the '50s carried *Huckleberry Finn* like it was a reference guide for the way summers should be. Just the sound of the words 'Mississippi River' and 'Arkansas' and 'Tennessee' flowing from Mayor's lips raised him a notch among his male friends. His talking of the mighty Mississippi almost as though he knew it would have conjured up daydreams of travel and mystery and rafts and adventure to any young boy in 1953. I could just imagine them sitting there imagining me as Huck on a raft trip down to New Orleans and on to South America.

"How do you know so much about it?" asked Holbrook.

"Arkansas?" asked Mayor.

"Yes," said Holbrook.

"I didn't have a map, so I did the next best thing. I picked up the telephone and asked Myrtie, the operator, what she knew. She could only guess, but she told me a lot," said Mayor.

Horses' hooves could be heard trotting a steady canter as Marty came up the cinder drive on his palomino, Sandy.

"Whoa."

Leather creaked as he dismounted the horse, holding a satchel by its strap in one hand and his reins in the other. He dropped the reins to the ground, walked toward the group with his hat in his hand, and performed the cowboy affectation of wiping his brow with his shirt sleeve, even though it was too cold outside to work up a sweat. He reached into the satchel and pulled out two wooden cylindrical wheels with small knobs on each end. They were covered with letters and numbers.

"Does anybody know what these are?" he asked, holding them up with pride.

He was counting on no one knowing.

"Minneapolis Moline Conway and I figured them out with Mr. Ossant's help in woodshop. We made them after seeing a picture and a drawing. Here's a hint: somebody real famous invented it."

"Pass one around so we can look at it," said Mary.

"Where'd you get the picture of it?" asked Randy.

"A teacher took it at the Smithsonian Museum on her senior trip to Washington, DC, last year and gave it to Mr. Ossant."

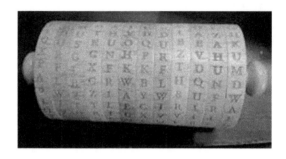

"Rolling pins for elves," grinned Holbrook.

"These are exact replicas of the wheel cipher. Thomas Jefferson himself invented it in 1790," said Marty. "That Jefferson was a pretty smart character, ya know."

"Trust Marty to know smart," said Mayor.

"And characters," said Mary.

"A wheel what?" asked Holbrook.

"It's a wheel cipher," said Marty.

"What's it for?" asked Mary.

"Jefferson had to go to France, ya see, as an ambassador or something big wheel. He invented it so he could pass coded messages over to Benjamin Franklin and John Adams without the French guys reading their secrets and knowing what they were up to. Franklin and Adams went with him to France. It was right after the French helped us win the Revolutionary War, so there were spies all about. Nobody trusted anybody."

"Did he put it together himself—like, did he cut the wood wheels? What kind of tools would he have had to have?" asked Bases.

"Jefferson?"

"Yeah. Did he put it together?"

"Oh, I imagine he probably had one of his slaves make it," said Marty. "He dreamed it up, and—well, an important guy like that would naturally delegate the work and have a slave put it together."

"How's it work?" asked Holbrook.

"Pretty simple. Look-see here: It has twelve small, separate wooden wheels attached to it. Try turning them. Each wheel has all the letters of the alphabet jumbled up, and none of the wheels are the same. If you turn the wheels, you can spell a message across any one of the lines. After that all you have to do is turn the cipher around and write down a whole other line of letters, any one of them. Send that other whole row of letters in your message. That's the code. Whoever gets it adds any line to the same code letters you sent, and then they turn the wheel around until they can read the sentence you coded."

"And nobody else can decipher the code?" asked Mary.

"Not unless they have one of these, they can't," said Marty.

"And both of these wheel gadgets have the same letters on them?"

"Yup, all the same."

"How long did they take you guys to make in shop?" asked Randy. "I only made bookends."

"It took Conway and me a week to make four of them," said Marty. "The wheels are the easy part—you just need a jigsaw and a wood drill. Adding the alphabet was the challenge. We screwed up two trying to get it right. We first tried to carve them one letter at a time, but that was going to take forever. Since I know about newspapers, I found an old set of thrown-out printer's-type letters from a shut-down newspaper in Tully. We just made sure we had the whole alphabet and shook the letters up in a shoe box. Then we hammered the letter's impressions into a wooden disk on each cipher wheel four at a time, one for each cipher wheel. We shook the letters up before we started every new disk so no disk was the same."

"We should get it to Jerry," said Mayor.

"Already sent him one right after Randy asked Duba for the secret-code master. Duba couldn't find it and called Conway, thinking he had it. Conway called me and suggested we send the wheel cipher, so I called Randy, who gave me the address to send it to. I sent it airmail, special delivery. Jerry should have it any day now. The club owes me a dollar forty, and we owe my dad two bucks and ten cents. I had to borrow some for postage."

"Sounds complicated to use," said Mary.

"It won't be if Jerry gets in trouble," said Marty. "He'll figure it out quick if he needs it."

"Marty's right," said Mayor. "Who knows what messes Jerry's going to meet up with traveling through all those states? Don't suppose anyone has read *Huckleberry Finn* or about all the trouble he gets himself into. Don't suppose."

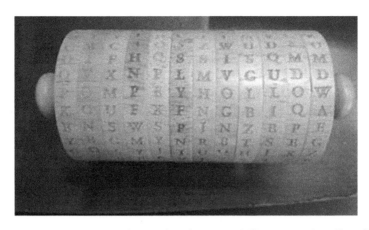

Mayor sets the cypher wheel to read "Pompey Hollow."
The code is BNSWSPJNZBPE.

"Who would Huck have sent messages to on the river, anyway?" asked Randy. "Jim couldn't read or write."

"Wait a minute," said Mary. "That can't be right."

"What can't be right?" asked Marty. "It's a fact. Slave Jim couldn't read or write."

"Not that," said Mary. "Jefferson wrote and signed the Declaration of Independence in 1776. How could he have had a slave in 1790?"

"My grandpa moved our whole family from Missouri, which is where Tom and Huck were from in the first place," said Marty. "The stories he could tell. It's another world out there in some parts, that's for dang sure. Slavery didn't end until 1865, Mary. I wouldn't be telling Mrs. Cox in American History class that you didn't know that."

"Can I have one to take?" asked Mary. "I want to put 'send me a postcard' in code on a postcard to Jerry. I collect postcards."

Marty passed a cipher wheel to Mary.

Mary's mind wandered as she examined the clever wooden mystery machine, turning its wheels about and aligning up letters. She seemed unsettled and in a daze, like she was wrestling with a matter of some unfinished business.

That was when a chilled breeze through the pine tree startled her. She leaned down and picked up the three packages Barber had given her to deliver to Aunt Lucy and then stood up straight, holding them with a hug.

"Has Jackie or Alda ever talked to any of you guys about being in the club?" asked Mary.

"What do you think?" said Barber.

"I'm just asking."

"No, you aren't," said Marty. "You're wondering if there's a reason we didn't ask them into our club."

"I promise, I wasn't asking that," said Mary.

"Surprised you'd ask it," said Marty.

"Nobody has ever been turned away from this club," said Barber.

"Shut up," said Mary.

"Nobody," said Holbrook.

"I didn't mean it the way it sounded," said Mary.

"This craziness in Arkansas is making us all edgy," said Marty. "Don't worry about it."

"You're in the church choir with them," said Mayor. "Why don't you ask them?"

"Mary, if they say yes, see if they have a telephone, and get me the number," said Barber.

"I think I'll walk over and ask them," said Mary. "Somebody call my dad, and tell him to pick me up at the Gaineses' place."

"I'll call him when I get home," said Randy.

"What's the best way?" asked Mary. "Climbing Farmer Parker's hill here down and around that way or walking into town and over that side road?"

"Into Delphi Falls and over," said Barber. "I'll walk with you as far as Delphi Falls Road."

The Gaineses' place, just up the hill from Maxwell's

CHAPTER SIX

MARY SHARES A TABLE

The Gaines farmhouse was on Delphi Falls Road at the Pompey Hollow Road corner hill. Walking up to it for the first time, it looked a lot bigger to Mary than she'd suspected it was. She told me she reckoned that because it was set back under all the big trees on such a sharp turn down the steep hill to Maxwell's corner, passersby mightn't have time to look.

The side door was open a crack. She could hear talking inside, so she rapped her knuckle on the glass pane. Hearing no response, she edged the door open enough to see three people sitting around a tree shade–darkened kitchen table and a brightly lit light bulb on a cord hanging down. Mrs. Gaines, with a skillet of vittles in hand, was restocking a platter on the table. Jackie was reading aloud from a magazine she had rolled to a single page, while most were busy passing food, eating, and listening.

"Crop fertilizers have become more reliable and predictable, according to Cornell Extension reports. Check with your farm-supply dealer for literature. They will most likely have all the information about their safe use. This winter promises to be productive for farms planting early. Good timing on your seeding and proper fertilization are important, along with the weather, of course."

'Bout that time Mary decided it might be best to announce herself before somebody turned and saw her dark shadow walking in unannounced and she caused a heart palpitation.

"Hellooo," cooed Mary.

"Mary! Hi!" squealed Jackie, turning in her seat and standing to greet her school chum.

"Sorry for popping in like this, everybody."

"Not at all, child. Come take a chair and join us," said Mr. Gaines. "Why, you're that Mary girl Alda speaks of. We so enjoyed all your beautiful voices in this morning's services, didn't we, Mae?"

"They are truly blessed. Such a joy, a rainbow of lovely voices," said Mrs. Gaines. "Welcome to our home, young lady."

Alda waved her hand at Mary and offered her a pretty smile from across the table.

"Thank you, Mrs. Gaines," said Mary as she pulled out a chair and sat down.

The lady of the house stood erect with the heavy skillet in hand.

"Now, Mary, there's no Mrs. Gaines in this house. No Mr. Gaines neither. I'm Mae, and my husband there is Allen. And we're neither 'Ma' nor 'Pa,' so get that one out of your head too if you're thinking of it, and we're definitely not any 'honey this' or 'honey that.'"

She pinch-pouted her lips and squinted with friendly, laughing eyes at the way she was overexaggerating the whole name thing.

"Mae and Allen is who we are. You already know the girls."

Mae said her piece and turned toward the cookstove for another load.

"Mae and Allen? Well all rightee. With your permission, I can do that," said Mary.

"Would you like some puffball, young lady?" asked Allen.

"Puffball?" asked Mary.

"Haven't you ever had puffball, Mary?" asked Jackie.

"Aren't those the big white balls we kick in the woods, and they puff with dark-brown powder? Do you eat them?"

Mae slid a couple of sliced-and-sautéed pieces of puffball onto one side of Mary's plate and some scrambled egg on the other side.

"You have to peel the outside off first and clean the center good before you cook them," said Jackie. "Momma uses bacon fat."

"Did you go out and find these in the woods, Jackie?" asked Mary.

"Jackie!" exclaimed Alda. "Why, that girl is afraid of bugs. I have to go find the puffballs; Jackie sticks around here berry picking, maybe chasing up peapods, and calling the cows in. She does the safe stuff."

"That's not true—I like butterflies," said Jackie. "They're insects."

"I chase peapods," said Mary. "Do you have good bumps around here?"

Some country kids in the early '40s and '50s did the household chore of keeping a lookout for bumps in the road. When the big harvest trucks loaded with peapods headed out from farms for the Apulia Station peapod vinery and hit the bumps, peapods would bounce off the back of the truck. Peapods were on most tables on the nights harvest trucks drove by.

"I have two good bumps," said Jackie. "One's on the curve here, and one's below on Pompey Hollow Road."

"One bump for me," said Mary. "On Berry Road, but it's a doozy. Lots of peapods fall off."

"Give your puffball a try, Mary. If you don't like them, somebody will," said Allen.

"I didn't mean to interrupt you, walking in like I did, Jackie. What were you reading?"

"Mornings I read the Cornell Extension farm reports to Daddy," said Jackie. "He's a good farmer and likes to stay on top of the latest news. I read about innovative ways to farm and animal diseases—farm news like that."

"Were you finished, or did I—"

"I was done."

Mary surmised from that that Allen could neither read nor write, but in that day, it was no source of embarrassment. Throughout the depression and the drought, Allen and millions of others in America lived through nomadic times looking for work just to survive a time when some weren't fortunate enough to have an education.

She savored a bite of the puffball.

"This is really good. It tastes kind of like breakfast sausage."

Mae smiled.

"Plenty more."

"Well now," said Allen. "Maybe you'll show them a little more respect when you come upon one in the woods."

He crackled a smile, pleased that Mary was enjoying the experience of their warm table.

"Plenty more."

"You're always welcome here, Mary, and I mean no disrespect, but was there a particular reason you dropped by today? You never have before," Mae said.

"Oh, I have some time before I have to go to work, and I thought I'd come by and see if Jackie and Alda would like to join our club."

"What club is that, child?" asked Mae.

"Momma," said Alda. "It's the Pompey Hollow Book Club. Just about everybody who's anybody knows about that club."

"Girl, just where'd you learn that sass? Not here in this house, you surely didn't."

"Sorry, Momma."

"Well, you'll have to pardon me, young lady. I must not be everybody or anybody. Your momma must have been in a library reading a good book when all the news about the—what did you say the name of the club was again?"

"The Pompey Hollow Book Club, Momma."

"Our books are in libraries, and I take great care to get them back on time. I haven't heard of this particular club."

"It's more of a club where we try to do good," said Mary. "It's not so much about books. We just call it that."

"How can we join, Mary? We're not in your grade," said Jackie. "We're only in seventh."

"Our club doesn't care how old anybody is," said Mary. "We started it when we were nine."

"I want to join," said Alda. "Can I, Momma?"

"If it doesn't interrupt your chores—and don't forget we're canning today. Did you girls pick up the cellar like you were told?"

"Yes, Momma."

"I help my mom make jams," said Mary. "It's fun."

"Daddy's a good cook," said Jackie.

"Big Mike's a good cook too. He made us spaghetti last night."

Mary looked over at Mr. Gaines.

"What do you like to cook?"

He set his coffee cup down.

"Worked the Pullman from Chicago to New Orleans and back up for nigh on twenty-two years. Never missed a day. Cooked the meals, every breakfast, lunch, and dinner long before I bought this here farm."

"What's a 'Pullman'?"

"Oh, a Pullman—it's about the fanciest train cars for passengers there is. It has sleeping berths with rich velvets, expensive pillows, and running water. There're lounge cars with full bars stocked with the best liquor money can buy, and there's a dining car as good as the finest New York City restaurants.

"Oh my," said Mary.

"I worked the kitchen in the dining car. I slept between meals on a bunk board in the crew area of the baggage car. I met some nice folks, don't ya know. 'Spect I made some friends along the way. I met some most interesting folks, I surely did."

Allen picked up his coffee cup and gazed off into the memories.

"Daddy gets lots of Christmas cards from all over," said Jackie.

"That's your daddy's business, now isn't it, young lady? Mary doesn't want to hear such bragging."

"Well it's true, Momma," said Alda. "We hang them on the Christmas tree after Daddy looks at them."

"Daddy also makes the best corned-beef hash in the entire world," said Jackie. "With the grinder he clamps to the table."

She pointed at the clamp indentations on the edge of the wooden kitchen table.

"I'm partial to pickled tongue," said Mae.

"Tongue takes a whole month, done right," said Allen. "We have a patch of dill in the garden."

"Where's your job today, Mary?" asked Jackie.

"Aunt Lucy's place. She lives up by me. She's having people over. I wash dishes and pick up the house when she has a social. These packages are for her from Mrs. Barber."

"Dishwashing is good for the soul," said Allen.

He chuckled.

"It's because of Aunt Lucy that I'm singing in the choir, Jackie," said Mary.

"Huh?" said Jackie.

"I wanted to learn gospel and wanted to learn how to sing it well, and Aunt Lucy told me the best way was to try joining your church because you and Alda were in the choir. She was right."

Jackie beamed.

Mae smiled a kindness over Mary's way.

"Are the bags linen for the party, Mary?" asked Mrs. Gaines.

"Oh, no, ma'am. Aunt Lucy collects clothing and blankets from the folks she does live-in work for in Syracuse and sends them to the poor all around during Christmas. She wraps them up nice and sends them to the needy. Barber gave these packages to me to give to her. They're from Mrs. Barber."

"Bless her," said Mae.

Mrs. Gaines balanced the family's social culture with positive influences, albeit gently, as she knew the racial attitudes outside of the Crown. She filled their world with the busyness of friendly drop-ins, runs to the library, and church gatherings. A Native American herself, she would take her girls on hikes around the DeRuyter Lake shores to look for arrowheads. Mary saw in her eyes and could sense that the Gaines and Aunt Lucy shared a culture.

"Mary, Aunt Lucy is welcome here. Would you tell her where our farm is?"

"Yes, ma'am. I surely will."

"Bring her by anytime. That would be nice. We'd like to meet her," said Mae.

"Yes, ma'am."

Mary had finished her second breakfast of the day and was about to get up when Jackie held a basket of bread rolls up to her.

"Daddy brings these rolls home from a customer in Syracuse—he gets a whole bagful when he goes in on Saturdays to sell the eggs and chickens."

"Want to see our room?" asked Alda.

"Sure," said Mary, grabbing a roll.

"Mary," said Alda. "How will I know when you're going to have a meeting?"

"Barber will call and tell you. Don't worry—if you're out doing chores, he'll keep calling. He's our meeting caller. I need you to write down your telephone number. If you want to come, meet us at the Delphi Falls cemetery at whatever time he says."

Allen winced at the thought of the cemetery.

"Well, it'll be quiet—that's for sure," he said, smiling.

Alda and Jackie, happy Mary dropped in

Mary heard the car beeping for her out front in the drive, hurried her good-byes, and walked out, gnawing on her roll. She had a pleasant feeling about the visit—and about sharing a table, as Big Mike had encouraged her to.

Mr. Crane dropped her off at the home of Aunt Lucy, who listened to her every word about the Gaines family, eating puffballs, and their house and barn. She couldn't wait to meet them.

"You can take me there after Thanksgiving, dear," she said. "After Thanksgiving would be nice. Thanksgiving is always the busiest time for a housekeeper."

CHAPTER SEVEN

AN ARKANSAS MIDNIGHT

I needed to determine what that noise I was hearing in the dark, vacant, second-floor apartment I had to sleep in alone was.

It was very late on Tuesday night in Little Rock when the whisper first came in the pitch-dark room.

"Jerry?"

Silence.

"Jerry, can you hear me?"

I moaned a bit, pulling the blanket over my head, and turned on my cot with a squeaky bounce to face the wall.

"Jerry, I don't got all night. It's already almost too late, so you need to get up a spell."

Under the blanket, my head flinched at the voice; I darted up, tightening the knotting up blanket's blinding bridle. I wasn't used to Arkansas sounds in the night yet, and in the empty apartment, the echoes of voices seemed to be exaggerated. This noise sounded like a voice. I thought maybe it was a dream.

"Jerry, this is Ole Charlie. You got a minute?"

Why, I'm here to tell you that I did sure enough hear that, and at the sound of that voice, I jumped up, flipped that blanket

down from off of my head, and felt my eyes grow bigger than
Holbrook's peepers were the time that dead body came to life up
near the Berwyn bathtub. There I was in the middle of the night
in Little Rock, Arkansas, alone in a dark, vacant apartment, and
I was staring straight into a glowing kerosene lantern with dead
Charlie Pitt's head floating just above it and looking me straight
in the eye.

"Jerry, it's me," said the spirit. "Charlie."

I bolted out of that cot, I tell you, and I charged through the
ghostly vapor of that lantern and the floating head like Barber's
ringed-nose bull chasing a red flag. Then I grabbed onto the wall
and felt my way along it in the dark to a door so I could find the
bathroom sink. I paused and looked back long enough to see if the
lantern and Charlie were still there. The lantern was, and it was
glowing like a halo.

Once in the bathroom, I closed and locked the door, switched
the light on, and filled the sink bowl with cold water—the coldest
water available in Little Rock.

That's about when I began mumbling to myself.

"What a nightmare," I said. "Holy Cobako! What a danged
nightmare."

I splashed two handfuls of water into my face and then two
more splashes.

"I wonder why Charlie would be in my nightmare," I muttered.
"Before he died I used to walk the spooky mile to his house in the
dark every week to get the eggs. I never have nightmares about Ole
Charlie."

I cupped water from the bowl and that time splashed it over my
hair. I reached for a towel, put it on my head, and stood up to towel
off. When I opened my eyes, there he was again, just as clear as the
Wizard of Oz. Ole Charlie was in the bathroom mirror.

"Yikes!" I yelped, muffling my voice with the towel so I wouldn't
wake anybody in Uncle Don and Aunt Mary's downstairs apartment.

"Jerry, if you calm down, we can talk better. You know me, my friend. I'm Charlie, and I'm not going to hurt you. I just want to talk."

"Bu...bu...bu...but—"

"And keep your voice down, son."

"Charlie died. How can you be Charlie?"

"Well, this is me, my friend. I am Charlie."

"If you're Charlie, tell me something only Charlie would know."

"I learned you how to free-range chickens, Jerry, and I gave you a lantern, five wicks, a box of kitchen stick matches, and my hunting knife for Christmas the year I died."

"You are Charlie!"

"It's nice to see you, my friend. Now let's go to your room to talk."

"Why can I only see your face, Charlie?"

"We do it in stages, son. If you'd woken up and seen my whole body, you could have had that heart attack you were always going on about, and that would have been just one more thing."

"So what are you? Are you a ghost, Charlie?"

"I'm your guardian angel, Jerry. You and your club friends— I'm your guardian angel."

"I knew it!"

"I know you did, son. Thank you for your prayers."

"I knew it all along."

I didn't dare turn my back on him yet, so I backed into the other room. I sat on the edge of the cot while Ole Charlie became life sized in his bib overalls and straw hat. He squatted down cross-legged on the floor by the glowing, golden lantern as though it were a campfire.

"How did you die, Charlie? Nobody ever told me why you died. Tell me everything."

"I'm a guardian angel. It was the cancer. I died a considerable time before you put a stamp on the postcard and dropped it in that Arkansas mailbox."

"You know about my postcard?"

"I'm your guardian angel, Jerry. I know pretty much everything."

"Dang, it's like you're a ghost, Charlie. Ghosts are dead people, like zombies."

"Can't be a guardian angel less you're dead, son—that's a rule."

That loosened me up a bit.

"It was in 1950 that I passed. You and your pap were up in Carthage. I fell to the ground openin' the wooden gate out behind the chicken coop, and I died. They rested me in the Delphi Falls cemetery."

"We went to your funeral, Charlie. Mary Crane tried to sing a gospel but kept crying. How'd you become our guardian angel?"

"You know I wasn't an educated man, Jerry. I was just a simple hoe-tillin' garden farmer on a half-acre bog—couldn't read no more than a measurin' stick when I died. Never had electricity and didn't listen to the radio, so conversatin' didn't come all that natural to me. You saw I built a two-room house with a wood cookstove on the west wall, a necessary out back against the hill, and barn with a corn manger that you kids said glowed at night like a hand-painted Christmas card. You remember my horse, Nellie; my cow, Bessie; and some chickens?"

"I remember, Charlie."

"Well, heaven put me in charge of keepin' an eye on you. Even now while you're mostly teens, people in the Crown pretty much know that the Pompey Hollow Book Club is more about catchin' criminals and wrongdoers than about readin' books. They know you're a well-meaning devilish sort who don't mind bendin' some rules and overlookin' some laws that might inconvenience a pursuit of doin' what's right."

"Does God think we're bad, Charlie? Is that what He thinks?"

"God thinks that you were all born before the war and that kids in the 1940s grew up fast. You had to—you learned what honor, valor, and sacrifice were in the truest sense by livin' those ideas every day and night. Millions of people around the world were being killed in your young lifetimes."

"It was scary, Charlie."

"There wasn't a one of you or your friends who didn't lose someone in the war, so heaven looks the other way on occasion."

"I remember being in kindergarten before we moved to Delphi Falls, Charlie. Sister Mary Francis would take us to the funeral parlor next to Saint Mary's school every day before we walked home. We'd pray for the dead bodies lying there. Some were old people, and some were dead soldiers in uniforms. We'd pray every night at bedtime that the war would end."

"You're a prayerful lad. It's a good thing."

"So when did you become our guardian angel?"

"First off, I knew I was dead when an angel—Angel Arnold— appeared while I was lyin' there on the ground by my back gate. He said they'd made me guardian angel to the Pompey Hollow Book Club the minute I dropped. Well, it still bein' pretty new to me—bein' dead and all—I tried my best to tell this Angel Arnold fellow they had the wrong man for an important job like that, me not bein' a smart man. But that's when he told me, 'Charlie, good is mostly what we're looking for in a guardian angel. Smart will come on a need-to-know basis and will come naturally when you need it. Come follow me.' Jerry, it works out that Angel Arnold was my guardian angel for most of my breathin' time on Earth—nobody tells you these things when you're alive. He knew my pap—he fought in the Spanish-American War with him under Teddy Roosevelt. They even buried him in Cuba."

"Wait a minute!" I said. "Wait a minute! If that's so, why are you telling me you're my guardian angel tonight, here in Little Rock? Am I going to die or something, Charlie?"

"You're not going to die, son—least not yet."

"So why did you come?"

"Oh, there's a reason, son. It started earlier this particular evenin' when Ole Charlie here was settin' on my favorite tall pine branch up in the Delphi Falls cemetery admirin' a glowin' November full moon."

"You can zip around like that, Charlie? That's a thousand miles—more."

"I can, son."

"Are the leaves changing colors back home, Charlie?"

"Oh my, but how they sparkle and glisten in the autumn frost."

"I'm homesick."

"Well, there I was, up tall on my branch. I was in a moment of thought about the Christmas ahead when I looked up and saw the moon flicker."

"Huh?"

"Yes, sir, the moon flickered. It surely did. It even flickered a full on and off two times."

"Is that like some kind of voodoo thing or a miracle or something, Charlie?"

"A flickerin' moon can be seen only by guardian angels, and it can mean only one thing, son. Those angels who can see it are called to a special meet up. Heaven calls them 'angel congresses.'"

"Holy Moses."

"This meetin' will be at the strikin' of midnight tonight."

"Tonight!"

"It's always the night of the flicker of a full moon, Jerry. Two nights if it's a three-quarters moon. An angel congress means somethin's up. It's our way of gettin' new assignments and gettin' questions answered."

"Where do you have to go for it?"

"I usually favor meetin's on top of your pap's barn-garage roof."

"Angels meet on top of our barn-garage? For real?"

Big Mike's barn-garage under a perfect angel-congress moon

"Your barn-garage at the falls shows the glow of the moon the best."

"Holy Cobako!"

"Nobody can ever see us, but we're up there on occasion."

"Where do you have to go tonight, Charlie? You know, for that congress thing?"

"Something told me it's best we have the angel congress here with you in Arkansas."

"What!"

"Premonition, son—a good ole premonition. You're in my flock, see. Ole Charlie had a premonition that you might could help yourself through these attitudes and laws you're seeing down here for the first time by helping me with an assignment."

"You promise I'm not going to die, Charlie?"

"I can't promise that, son."

"You know what I mean—tonight or here in Arkansas."

"You'll have a nice long life, Jerry, if you don't go giving yourself that heart attack you keep spoutin' of."

"Charlie, if my mom heard us talking and came up here right now, would she see or hear you?"

"Only you can see me. Only you can hear me."

"What do you need from me, Charlie?"

"Not certain yet, son, but knowin' that there's an angel congress tonight and that it's going to be here in this room was settlin' somehow. You and I have one more day before Thanksgiving if we need to do something special while you're here in Little Rock. The day after Thanksgiving, you'll be heading back to Delphi Falls."

"I can't wait to get back home. Were you nervous coming all this way, Charlie? It's pretty far."

"Well, like I was sayin' before I came here tonight, I was perched on my limb, gazin' up at the moon over Delphi Falls and thinkin' of the holidays I remember and the smells of firewood smoke dustin' over the hills. I imagined the roastin' turkeys bein' carried in from barns for pluckin' and from stores for roastin', bringin' families together. I imagined the flaky crusts of apple and pumpkin and mincemeat pies ready to dress up a table along with tart cranberry jams and gravy-covered turkey slices. Giblets and bread stuffin' and candied yams with marshmallows all soon on their way again to open a season of kindness startin' with Thanksgivin', the officially beginnin' of the countdown to Christmas."

"I'm sorry you had to die, Charlie."

"I miss my ole barn and the glow it give off when the golden lanterns were lit."

"It did, Charlie. It would have been a perfect Christmas card. I can still remember the whetstone-wheel bench with its flat wooden pedal."

I sat there looking at the lantern.

"So when is this thing—the meeting? What did you call it?"

"Angel congress. It'll be here, in this room, in about four minutes."

"Huh? Will I be scared?"

"No need to be scared. Just sit and listen. We'll talk again after it's over and they've gone."

"Who are they?"

"I'm not sure, son. Other than my guardian angel, Arnold, I don't know who or how many will be here."

"Are they ghosts, too?"

"We like the word 'spirits,' Jerry. We like 'angels' even better."

"I have to pee."

"Go do your business. We still have a little time."

CHAPTER EIGHT

BLUE MOON OF NOVEMBER

"Who's the young man, Charlie?" asked Angel Arnold.

"He's one of my flock."

"Is there a reason he's here?

"I had a premonition," said Charlie.

"Angel congresses are for angels, Charlie, not for the living. Care to explain your premonition?"

"Well, Arnold, I conjured it this way: At first, when the moon flickered, I couldn't understand why I was being called to a congress at all, with everythin' bein' so peaceful up in the Crown. 'Sbeen pretty quiet, with nothin' really happening since the pickpocket got caught. Settin' there on my limb, Ole Charlie here gave it some more thinkin'. I said to myself that one of my own flock—that young fella settin' over there on the cot—was down here in Little Rock all alone. Well, he's not alone exactly, but he's away from the Crown and his friends. I knew he was experiencin' sights of things the Lord wouldn't find favor with—things the boy had never seen before—down here for the first time. "

"And?" asked Angel Arnold.

"Well, he's a prayerful lad, Arnold. So that's when I said to myself that maybe some angel down this neck of the woods maybe heard the boy's bedtime prayers about what he's been seeing here, and maybe that same angel passed an idea on to you. That's when I thought maybe you really wanted me to conjure it just so I'd think it was my idea to be down here in Little Rock, where the boy is. Thought maybe you had somethin' brewin' down here that the lad might help on—you know, somethin' an angel can't do but somethin' that's important for the Lord. Not that you'd take advantage of a boy's adventuresome nature."

Angel Arnold smiled at Charlie.

"Or of mine," added Ole Charlie.

"You're pap would be proud of you, Charlie. You're a good shepherd."

"Thank ye kindly, Arnold. I did think it good."

When Angel Arnold turned toward me, it gave me the chills. I was still under the illusion that Ole Charlie's being there was a dream, a figment of my imagination.

"Son," he said, looking me straight in the eye. "What's your name?

I couldn't believe another angel was actually talking to me, but I went along with it.

"Jerry," I mumbled.

"Saint Jerome," said Arnold. "Impressive. Jerome is quite a namesake indeed, Jerry. He translated the Bible, you know. You have a middle name, son?"

"Mark."

"Saint Mark? Another revered."

"It's after Mark Twain, sir."

"No need to be 'siring' me, young man. I was volunteer cavalry."

"Charlie, the lad's perfect," he said.

"Jerry's a good lad all right," said Charlie. "He has a good heart. A brave pup too. Why, did you know it's his pap who owns the barn-garage we meet on up in Delphi Falls?"

"Is that a fact?" said Arnold. "I like meeting on that barn-garage roof. It's the best in the world, Charlie. I can sit and watch the reflection the moon gives off the big white rock stuck up high on the cliff across the creek."

Arnold turned back to me.

"You ever watch the reflection of the moon off that white rock, young man?"

"I see it from the top of the cliff a lot," I said. "Sometimes my friends and I sit on it under a full moon. The rock is pure white - reflects the moon real good."

"Just imagine that, Charlie," said Arnold. "This boy's perfect."

As I sat on the cot, my mouth dropped in awe. Sure enough, I had just talked with an angel I'd never seen before—and now the two of them were standing there like I was some important VIP or something.

Angel Arnold started reminiscing and telling stories of when he served with Ole Charlie's father under Teddy Roosevelt in Cuba back at the turn of the twentieth century.

Teddy Roosevelt and his cavalry Rough Riders in 1898

"Rough riders, we were for sure," he said.

Angel Arnold told me of how he'd become a guardian angel sudden-like after a raid up a hill somewhere in Cuba. He said he thought it was a cannonball "what took" him, but he never asked.

In the middle of one of his stories, something happened; it was like a flashbulb went off, lighting up the whole room for two or three seconds. I bolted back when the room went to dark again except for the lantern light. Rubbing my eyes, I saw another angel appear in the flash. He was a darker, younger angel and was standing there with Ole Charlie and Angel Arnold. First he looked over at me for a few seconds almost like he knew me, and then he looked at Ole Charlie.

"Angel Charlie, I want you to meet Angel William," said Angel Arnold.

William seemed way too young to be a guardian angel. My guess was that he looked like a teenager.

"Thank you for seeing me, Charlie."

"No choice in these matters, son. Happy to make your acquaintance."

"Charlie, William here is guardian angel to a flock here in Arkansas, mainly in Little Rock, some in southern Little Rock, and a few up in North Little Rock. He needs your ear a spell."

"Why mine?"

"Remember a few weeks back when we brought you Angel Sir Arthur Conan Doyle to help you with that English pickpocket fellow?"

"Oh, he helped me, Arnold, he surely did. He'll be comin' back when the lad gets out of jail."

"Well, now Angel William here needs some help and guidance in kind of the same way—but from you this time, Charlie. It's for some in his flock down here in Arkansas."

Just sitting there observing with my best Hardy-boy investigative techniques, I watched Ole Charlie's eyes and could see the old-man angel was beginning to think. He was thinking about my being in Little Rock, about my letter to Mary, and about what it was like for the Negroes down there. He was thinking about how nobody in the Crown ever acted a mean way to anyone up home, regardless of their skin color.

Something was trying its best to fit together, was on Ole Charlie's mind. It was all too coincidental, our being there together. He still needed answers.

That's when he looked up at the young angel.

"Angel William, might'n I ask something of you?" said Charlie.

"Anything," said William.

"Son, are we here because you've been listenin' to the bedtime prayers of that young man settin' over there on the cot, and you've been hearin' the miseries he's been seein' and feelin' down here in Little Rock?"

"I won't lie."

"You can't lie, son. It's an angel rule."

"I did overhear his prayers, Angel Charlie. And I did ask Angel Arnold to see what he could do to maybe get you to help my people down here like Angel Arthur Conan Doyle helped you."

"Beggin' pardon, Arnold," said Ole Charlie, "but Angel Sir Doyle is truly an expert on a number of things. I'm not much of an expert on anythin' more than chickens. I've never been out of the Pompey Hollow except for the First World War and now."

"Charlie, we think we have an idea. First, though, William needs your and the young man's ears—that's all he's asking. We think you may be able to help. We may be able to use Jerry's help, too."

"Well, we can give him that. You have our ears, son."

When Angel Arnold said "Jerry's help," I began to shake, sitting there on the cot. I grabbed a fistful of blanket for balance.

That's when Ole Charlie turned and looked over at me and said, "You may want to listen up, son."

William gathered his thoughts.

"Charlie, there's a man staying in the Capital Hotel just east of here. He came into town, went to a church, prayed some, and left and checked into the hotel. He's been checked in for two weeks now and has never been seen out of his room. He stands by the dresser in his underwear, typing on a typewriter. He didn't check in under his real name."

"How do you know?" said Ole Charlie.

"Well, we can see him through his hotel room's window, and we know he checked in under the name 'Manolin Santiago.' His real name is Ernest Hemingway," said Angel William.

My heart sank. I sure knew about Ernest Hemingway. Mom said she was getting me his new book for Christmas.

"Why would a man up and change his name like that?" asked Ole Charlie.

"There's secret word going around that President Eisenhower is considering sending army troops down here into Little Rock. Those troops would guard the Negro children who want to go to public school but are being stopped by the governor's office," said Angel William.

"Are you meaning to tell me that children need troops to walk them to school here?"

"If they're of color, Charlie."

"I can't imagine that."

"Charlie, the governor has even threatened to close all the public schools if the president insists on integration."

"Why, the nerve!"

"Now this Hemingway fellow is a famous writer all over the world, and I think he doesn't want folks knowing he's in town. It could cause suspicion. This man has a nose for smelling around for stories during times of conflict—even during wars. We know he's Ernest Hemingway," said William.

"Can't say I know the man," said Ole Charlie.

"Like I said, Charlie, he's a writer," said William.

"I can't read."

Angel Arnold interrupted.

"Charlie, this Hemingway fellow wrote something that William found. He read it, and it's important to his story."

"Why's it important?"

"I'll tell you in a minute."

"How did you get ahold of it?"

"We found it on a bench in a church some years back."

"Please give a listen, Charlie. It'll all come together in time."

"I said you have my ear, son, and I meant it. Jerry's too."

With that, Angel Arnold excused himself, stepped over by me, gave me a wink so I wouldn't be scared, and sat on the floor at the other end of the cot.

"I've heard this already," whispered Angel Arnold. "Don't want to be a distraction, so I'm going to set here a spell while William talks about Mr. Hemingway's paper."

"Yes, sir," I said.

"Oh, ain't no need for 'sir,' son. I was calvary—did I say that already?"

Ole Charlie got on the floor next to the lantern, cross-folded his legs, and sat up proper out of respect.

Young Angel William backed up next to the wall, stood up proud and unfolded some papers. "PH" was scrawled in big letters in black crayon on the front page. He held it up for Ole Charlie to see.

CHAPTER NINE

A PAGE-TURNER PLOT

"Charlie, this Hemingway fellow wrote several books," said William. "Some about wars and Paris and some about bullfights, but one in particular is about a young Cuban boy named Manolin and an old fisherman named Santiago."

"Where did I hear those names, son—Manolin and the other?" said Charlie.

"Those are the names he checked into the hotel with."

"Oh, that's right. Now why would a man do that if he weren't hiding somethin'?"

"His new book is called *The Old Man and the Sea*, and it's going all over the world now for all the people who are reading it. People will listen to him, this Hemingway man."

Ole Charlie sat up so proud. He seemed satisfied that they'd come to him and thought he could help.

The young angel stood, catching a thought, tears welling from his eyes. Ole Charlie pointed to the crayoned "PH" on the paper he was holding up and asked if he knew what it meant.

"It stands for 'Papa Hemingway,' Charlie. He was proud when he became a papa. That's why this is all so special."

The young angel stood there. He folded the paper and looked at the floor.

"What was that in your hand, William? What are those papers?"

"It's a story this Hemingway wrote about a lady having a baby back in 1937. It's about how her son had to run find the doctor late at night and how the baby girl was a blessed baby, so special. The baby's name was Anna Kristina. That's the story on these papers, Charlie. This is every word Mr. Hemingway wrote about it."

Ole Charlie sat and waited.

Angel William clasped his hands.

"And we think this Ernest Hemingway fellow is in Little Rock to write about the school children who aren't being let into public schools."

There was a worried look coming over William's eyes, which were filled with tears. I could tell Ole Charlie was suspicious, as the angel was acting as though he wasn't the one who needed help.

"I'm thinkin' you know this baby girl," said Charlie. "The one in the story you're talkin' about."

"I do."

"How do you know her, son?"

"Anna Kristina was my sister."

"So you're the young boy who ran to fetch the doc, aren't you?"

"Yes."

"Where was your pap when this was happenin'?"

"Pa went to Louisiana for bait-shrimp work before Momma had the baby, but he never came back. He never saw the child."

"What is your momma's name, son?"

"Daisy Pearl, but I called her 'Momma.'"

"And Daisy Pearl—your momma, son—where is she?"

"We lost momma when Anna Kristina was four."

"Not a well woman, was she?"

"Charlie, I was a mess-cook helper in the navy in 1941. I lied about my age and joined up—thought I could see the world in the navy. I was killed in the Pearl Harbor attack."

"How old were you, son?"

"Almost seventeen."

"Oh my."

"My dying is what put Momma down, Charlie. Her dying made Anna Kristina's life a struggle. She having to survive best she could. She was orphaned and went into foster homes."

"Orphaned at four? Was there any family to help her?"

"I have a brother, Aaron."

"Where was Aaron, son?"

"Brother Aaron couldn't deal with either of the losses. He upped and ran away and joined the army air corps right after Momma died. It was all too much for him. He didn't wait for the draft. They taught him a lot—all about planes and how to fly bombers—so that was good."

"Liked to fly, did he?"

"He was a good pilot but never had a chance overseas. Most of the coloreds in the air corps were kept on the ground working on planes. Oh, the Negro boys from Maxwell and Tuskegee, maybe, but they didn't see action less they were Red Tails in fighter planes."

"Charlie," said Angel Arnold. "William here is Anna Kristina's guardian angel."

"Good choice. Seems like a nice lad."

Angel William went on.

"Aaron lives in North Little Rock. He doesn't talk much. Ever since the war, he's not been himself. They broke him, I think, giving him that training with airplanes and all but never sending him over for action. That made him feel lesser than the man our momma always told him he was. She would tell us to stand straight and tall and would say that we could do anything and be anybody if we kept looking up. That's why Aaron joined the air corps after she and I died. He wanted to show her he was a man."

"Taking care of his sister would have done that, son."

I looked over at Angel Arnold; he looked back and winked at me. We both could tell Ole Charlie knew something was brewing.

"One of them is in trouble, right?" asked Ole Charlie.

"Yes."

"Anna Kristina in trouble, is she?" asked Charlie.

"She's pregnant. She's sixteen and pregnant."

"The girl can count on Ole Charlie here for prayers."

"She was raped, Charlie," said Angel Arnold.

Ole Charlie slumped down in misery with that thought. He started, and stood up.

"I'm not an educated man, Arnold and William, but there's somethin' you're both not tellin' Ole Charlie here, and I'd much appreciate your gettin' on with it. A little girl's all alone—maybe in harm's way. The girl must hold favor with somebody, or else this Hemingway fellow wouldn't be writing about her."

William spoke up.

"Charlie, the baby's father is white."

Not knowing that that mattered, Charlie asked, "Did the lad hurt her, son?"

"He forced himself on her, but he didn't physically hurt her. He's twenty-two, and she's sixteen, so that's rape."

"Does the young man care about the girl? Does she have any feelin's for him? Did anyone find out?"

Angel Arnold stood up from the cot and walked over to Charlie.

"The lad's been steering her heart with wrong intentions for some time the way some do, but he's not our problem right now, Charlie."

"Tell me everythin'."

"It's his pap," said Angel Arnold.

"What about his pap?"

"His pap works for the governor at the state capital building. If that man ever finds out…well…I mean that he's been known to burn crosses, and he has a short tolerance for Negroes and says so right out in the open in public. He's not letting their children go to public schools. Why, if this man-demon ever finds out that an innocent colored girl like Anna Kristina is having his grandbaby, that baby won't stand a chance of seeing the light of day."

"How far would he go?"

Angel Arnold gave Ole Charlie a deadly stare.

"He'd go that far, Charlie."

"Is she far along?"

"Eight months."

Ole Charlie circled around the room, muttering to himself.

"That little girl's here in Arkansas. Until tonight, I didn't even know where Arkansas was. But I do know we're up here in Jerry's room flappin' our gums. By the way, what's this Ernest Hemingway fella got to do with it anyway, and why's he here again?"

"All we know is he's hereabouts, Charlie. He lives in Cuba part time, and we first saw him writing about the First World War in 1917 while he was in the Red Cross hospital for wounds. We know he likes bullfights and that he jumps in the middle of good fights and writes about them when he's not throwing a fist at the devil. Like I told you, Hemingway heard that President Eisenhower might be sending troops to the schools. He must smell a story."

"Does he know about any of this, Arnold—the rape and her carryin' and all?"

"No," said William.

"How do you know he's not like the others down here, a bigot?" asked Ole Charlie.

"Hemingway is a citizen of the world, Charlie," said William. "His fight for anyone's freedom knows no racial boundaries. Only the ignorant think otherwise."

"Charlie, we think Hemingway's story about William's momma might stir his gut again," said Angel Arnold. "Stir it enough to make him want to help."

"You mean for him to read it?" said Charlie. "Well if the man wrote it, he's already read it—that only makes sense to me."

"Yes. But he wrote the story sixteen years ago. He well could have forgotten it. If he reads it again and hears the story of the fix she's in now, he might want to help."

At about that time, my Pompey Hollow Book Club experiences got the better of me, and I interrupted the three angels who were standing there talking about the situation.

"Charlie, can I say something?" I asked.

All three stopped talking and turned toward me.

"Go ahead, son," said Arnold.

"If Ernest Hemingway wrote a story that will remind him about this girl, and if he read it again, and then after he reads it, somebody told him about the trouble she's in now, he sure might help. I agree. He likes kids, and that's why he calls himself Papa Hemingway. Mom told me that…and that's why he just might see me."

"So is it true that that's where the 'PH' comes from?" said Charlie.

"Yes," said William. "Papa Hemingway."

"What's your idea, son?" said Arnold.

"Well I know he wrote the book *The Old Man and the Sea* about an old man and a young boy. He respects kids. Give me that paper he wrote, and I'll go take it to him tomorrow and get him to read it somehow, and then I'll tell him about the girl and the trouble. I'll see what he says."

"A brave lad," said Arnold. "You'd do that, son?"

"Just tell me where the hotel is. I'll do it."

"Now I know why we're here," said Ole Charlie.

"An unborn baby, Charlie, isn't in a flock at all until its birth," said Arnold. "A baby in the womb is in God's kingdom. Angel rules change in order to care for them—the unborn babies. That's why we've chosen Jerry and why the lad can see us now. We knew it would be in his nature to help, but he alone had to make the decision on his own. Otherwise this all would have been just a dream for him."

I'll never forget that moment.

"How will you manage to get out of the house alone, son?" asked Ole Charlie. "None of us will be able to go with you."

"I'll think of something to tell my mom. Maybe like I'm taking a bus or going to the zoo or something. I'll get off the bus at the zoo so it won't be a lie and walk to the Capital Hotel, where Ernest Hemingway is. Maybe I'll just walk the whole way."

William had a smile on his face, as though his prayer had been answered. All we needed was a plan for what I would say after I got to the hotel.

Just as Ole Charlie was about to talk, there came a knock on my bedroom door.

All of a sudden, out of the blue, there came a loud whisper that about made me wet myself.

"Jerry?" the voice said. "Is there someone in there with you?"

CHAPTER TEN

GRACE UNDER PRESSURE

I barely slept a wink that night.

When I opened the door, my mom was there. She'd come upstairs because she'd heard noises. I convinced her I'd been sleepwalking, having a dream, and talking out loud in my sleep. She was okay with all that, poured me a glass of water and put me back to bed, although I do remember her asking me why I had left the bathroom sink running.

"Oh, that," I told her. "It was the weirdest dream."

She believed me and let it be.

That morning, the Wednesday before Thanksgiving, I folded the "PH" papers Angel William had given me, stuffed them into my jean's back pocket, and went down the hall stairs to Aunt Mary's first-floor apartment for breakfast. I paused outside the door, my hand on the doorknob. I remember standing there, thinking my life had changed the night before. I would never be the same. I wasn't sure of the rules for meeting angels and talking about it, but until I was sure of them, I knew I had to keep it all a secret. I also knew, more than anything else, that folks were depending on me. I took a deep breath, exhaled, and opened the door.

"Drink your juice," said Mom. "Dick and Jerry, see to it that Aunt Mary's kids, Tommy, Timmy, and Teddy drink their juice."

"When is Aunt Mary coming home?" I asked.

"Tomorrow, dear," said Mom. "She had the baby Sunday; they'll hold her for five days to make sure everything's normal. She'll be home for Thanksgiving tomorrow."

"When are we going back to Delphi Falls?"

"On Friday, Son. Eat your oatmeal. We leave early Friday morning."

I knew I had no time to spare.

"Dick, where are the maps you and Mom used to drive here?"

"They're in the glove compartment," said Dick. "Why?"

"Is there, like, a city map of Little Rock in there too?"

"No, but Uncle Don has a city map on his desk in the living room. What's up?"

"I need you to show me something on it after breakfast."

"What do you want to know?"

"A place."

"What place?"

"Can't you just show me something without a lot of questions?"

"Why're you being snappy?"

Mom remembered my "nightmare" from the night before.

"Dick, show Jerry the map, and answer his questions, please. Be a good brother."

I appreciated my mom's sticking up for me.

Then she went and ruined it all.

"What do you need to know about a Little Rock map, Jerry?" she asked.

"I'm just going for a walk is all. I'm going for a walk, and I don't want to get lost. I don't know what the big deal is."

"Dick, show Jerry the map and help him," said Mom.

After breakfast, Dick and I went to the secretary desk and unfolded the Little Rock city map. I pulled my sleeve up and looked at what I had written on my forearm with my ballpoint pen. I told him where I wanted to walk to and from. He pointed to a spot and said, "Here's where we are."

"I'm looking for West Markham and Main," I said.

"What's at West Markham and Main?" Dick asked.

I poked Dick in the ribs, giving him that "just shut up and help me, and I'll tell you later" look.

Dick obliged me. He handed me a blank envelope from the desk.

"Write this down," he said.

I pulled the hassock over to the chair Dick was sitting on and sat on it, using my knee as a writing surface.

"You walk on Battery for three blocks to Wright Ave."

"Which way?"

"What do you mean?"

"Do I go left on Battery or right?"

"You go out the door and go left."

"Okay."

"Left on Battery for three blocks until you come to Wright Avenue."

"Got it."

"You go right and walk for—hang on. One, two, three, four, five, six—you go for seven blocks to South Chester Street.

"South Chester Street."

"You walk thirteen blocks up to West Third Street."

"Which way?"

Dick pointed to the map.

"Look here—go this way."

"Okay."

"You walk eight or ten blocks, and you'll be here."

Dick pointed to the spot on the map.

"Thanks," I said.

I folded the envelope and stuck it in my pocket. Dick followed me out onto the porch.

"What's up?" said Dick.

"I just want to go for a walk is all. I have two rolls of one twenty-seven film left, and I want to take some pictures."

"Yeah, right."

Dick wasn't buying it. He knew something was fishy, but he knew me, and he knew I was stubborn. I would tell him when the time was right.

Every step of the way was intimidating. I found myself muttering questions to Ole Charlie, hoping he'd maybe appear and walk with me. I watched city buses drive by and smelled their diesel fumes. I saw Negro ladies in starched maid's uniforms getting off buses at corners and walking to driveways and up to the side or back doors of houses. I could hear a radio through an opened window of a brick house. Some lady was singing inside.

The hotel was big with beautiful red awnings. It seemed to fill the city block like Hotel Syracuse, the hotel I had worked in that summer, did. A granite sign on its corner said that Ulysses S. Grant had stayed there. As I stepped into the lobby, a doorman in a long velvet coat and what looked to me to be a top hat started.

"May I help you, sir?"

"No, thanks. I'm meeting somebody."

"Very good, sir."

Inside a man was on a tall ladder decorating a pine tree for Christmas. The ceiling of the lobby was a colorful stained-glass design that let in light from the roof many floors up. I walked slowly through the lobby, looking for elevators. Seeing one, I walked over to it and stepped in.

"Floor, please?"

I pulled my shirt sleeve up and looked at the ballpoint markings on my forearm.

"Three, please."

"Very good, sir."

I walked off the elevator and looked at the sign telling me that room 305 was to the right. I was about to have a heart attack—I felt it could happen at any moment. I went to the door, stood there, and gulped.

Knock, knock, knock.

No answer.

Knock, knock, knock.

"Go away!" someone inside said.

Knock, knock, knock.

The door swung open. There he was, standing tall and breathing through his mouth in baggy pants and a sweater. His hair and white beard were dripping wet like he had just splashed his face and head to wake himself up.

"Who are you, and what do you want?"

"I have a delivery for you."

"There are no deliveries for me. I'm not here. Go away."

He started to push the door closed. I stuck my foot down, blocking it.

"I know who you are, sir. I'm supposed to make the delivery in person."

Hemingway paused, stood straight and tall, and cocked his head with a smirk.

"Just who am I, son?"

"You're Mr. Santiago," I said.

Hemingway harrumphed and started to push on the door again to close it.

"Some other time, young man," he growled.

"Wait. I know who you really are."

I looked up and down the empty hallway.

"Your name is Ernest Hemingway. I promise I have something important for you, Mr. Hemingway. Please let me in."

He pulled the door open.

"You're a deceptive young pissant, son. Come in and say your piece, and tell me who the bastard was who told you I was here before I throw you out a window."

By then I was trembling from my head to my feet. It wasn't that I was afraid of the man. I remember I was afraid I would say the wrong thing to this man who the entire world knew.

"Mr. Hemingway, I have some papers here. It's important that you read them out loud while I'm here, and then I'll go if you want me to. I'll keep the secret that you're here. I promise."

"You're a writer, son. You want me to read something you've written so you can tell your friends Hemingway read your work. I get it."

He turned and grabbed a bottle of scotch from his bedside table.

"You wrote it, Mr. Hemingway."

Hemingway looked around at me with the bottle's cork in his teeth. He spit it out.

"What the hell?"

"You wrote it, sir—really."

I pulled the papers from my back pocket and unfolded them.

"Let me see."

"Only if you first promise to read it out loud."

"You're trying my patience, kid. You like to fight?"

"You have to promise."

"You've read it, son. Just give it here, and I'll know if it's mine."

"I haven't read it, but it's yours, Mr. Hemingway. I know it is."

"If it's mine, where did you get it?"

"I can't tell you that."

"Can't? Or won't?"

"If I told you the truth, you wouldn't believe me, Mr. Hemingway. You like the truth. It would be the truth, but you wouldn't believe me."

Hemingway tipped and finished a jigger of scotch.

"You've been reading too much O. Henry, kid."

"Promise!"

"You run a hard bargain, son. Give me the papers."

"Thank you, sir."

When I handed him the papers, he looked at me with a wrinkled brow.

"You ever thought of bullfighting, son?"

My mind raced to an image of Barber's grumpy, old ringed-nose bull.

"No, sir."

Hemingway told me to sit on one of the twin beds. He sat on the other, opened the paper, and scanned a page or two.

"Well I'll be damned," he said.

"Are you going to read it, Mr. Hemingway?"

He looked at another page.

"Well I'll be goddamned," he said.

Hemingway reads Hemingway.

CHAPTER ELEVEN

HEMINGWAY READS HEMINGWAY

Hemingway looked up at me with an inquisitive look. For the first time, I felt he knew there was more to me than sheets of paper. He placed all the sheets on the bed next to him and picked up one page at a time.

"Keep your mouth shut, kid. Listen."

I remember nodding yes.

Hemingway cleared his throat with two hacking cigar coughs and began reading:

Daisy Pearl was named after a slave her mother admired. She was in her late forties the night her water broke and she cramped over, slumping against a wall by the cast-iron Franklin cookstove.

It might have been heat that took her into early labor, but some thought she was too old. Her shoulder felt the burn of the wall as bursitis pain ripped through her worse than the cramps, causing a wail that could be heard in the still-night Arkansas air clear past the tracks, and those were two shanties away.

William heard his mother scream and took off running barefoot through lightning bugs for the doc's place in the vicinity of the Sears. Doctor Jefferson didn't live near the tracks, but this was 1937, and she was the only colored doctor there was, and she kept a lantern lit signaling "Welcome" for this sort of medical inconvenience. Day or night made her no nevermind she would remind folks.

The head came out and touched the kitchen table more than three months early and in candlelight. The little mite was shy of four pounds—Doctor Jefferson surmised that by cradling the baby up in the palms of her hands, which reflected the glisten of the walking lantern over next to her open bag on the ledge of the sink. Baby wasn't bigger than the doc's two hands end to end.

"She's not breathing, and I can't find a pulse," said the doc.

With Daisy Pearl lying back, her head leaning off the chipped porcelain tabletop, Doctor Jefferson tried what she knew but pronounced the baby dead.

The doc cut the cord to Daisy Pearl's favor, wrapping the balance around the baby, while an emptiness shared about the night, riding on shadows like waves with no names roll to shore the way they do. A little one didn't stand a prayer birthing this early in term, and she was meant to come and leave alone, dead. Daisy Pearl leaned up on her elbows, paused, and pursed her lips, staring off into a lonely dark, avoiding looking down at her baby. She thought of her own momma being born in a cotton field and of her grandmother having to keep picking the cotton until sundown, stopping only to nurse.

This happened fast for Daisy Pearl.

She stepped from the tabletop, turned in the dark, and rolled the lifeless body and the cord in a section of the blood-spotted morning newspaper she had been lying on. She lifted the lid of the firewood bin and put the package on some kindling at the left end of it but paused, and she asked William to hold the lid up for her. She disappeared into the next room and returned muttering gentle little-girl words in prayer for her lifeless doll, and she carefully folded a hand-stitched baby blanket, lifted it to her face, and smelled it and kissed it a final good-bye. And resting it on top of her dead baby, she slowly lowered the lid.

"Pastor Wright will say proper blessings and handle the matter of my baby girl with the Lord tomorrow," she whispered in the dark, trying to convince herself she'd be fine. "First light, William, see to it you pass the word to him."

"Yes, Momma," William told her.

"And be sure to tell Pastor Wright my baby's name. Let him know it's Anna Kristina."

"Yes, Momma."

"Anna Kristina is your baby sister's name," Daisy Pearl said. "Don't you ever forget that name, William."

"God bless you, Daisy Pearl," said the doctor as she closed her bag with a snap and lifted the walking lantern.

"Sister, you get some rest. You're momma enough as it is already with two fine grown boys. This wasn't to be is all. Promise me you'll get some rest."

Doctor Jefferson pushed on the screen door and left for home, and she didn't ask for any money, and she didn't let the screen door slam.

It was three the next morning when William's brother, Aaron, came home from working at the railroad depot. The train yard foreman fetched him the day before to help stack boxes and shipping crates for a dollar, if he didn't mind earning slave wages. He put the two fifty-cent pieces on the table for his momma. He felt around the table and picked up the candle, lit it, reached over, and lifted the lid off the stockpot filled with bouillon simmering a gristly soup bone. He set the lid back down and leaned over to open the ice-box, looking for food like any boy would do after a hard night of sweat and toil.

Other than the shadows of three eggs and bacon lard, the shelves were as barren as the night and just the same as he'd found them before he'd gone off to work. He closed it shut and settled for a can of salmon from the cupboard. He pitched it into his mouth with the fork he'd gotten from off the sink. About the time he dropped the empty can in a trash bucket, he felt air from a window crack, and decided to stoke the cookstove for his momma's stockpot before going to bed.

He stepped over and lifted the lid of the woodbin. He noticed the baby blanket she had been stitching on for some time now. He reached back for the candle and pulled the blanket out. His eye caught the rolled-up newspaper on the stack of wood, and he picked it up in his big right hand. He turned the package about to feel what might be in it, and the bloody water seeped out and dripped red over his hand and shirt sleeve. He bolted back in fear, quickly dropping it and the lit candle to the floor.

That baby started crying from inside that package on the floor—that's what my notes say. Oh my, how she did cry, they say, and she was alive and saved.

Anna Kristina was reborn on the morning after she first came into the world.

"It's a miracle," Doctor Jefferson said.

"Praise Jesus," Daisy Pearl rejoiced.

The woman gently lifted her left breast, pressing the nipple near to the baby's face, while her outstretched little finger tenderly touched the newborn's gums and lips to stimulate her suckling instinct.

"This baby has two birth dates," said Doctor Jefferson.

"Praise the Lord," said Daisy Pearl.

"The cord I left on her and the warmth of the newspaper inside that woodbin must have acted like an incubator, and the shock of the fall to the floor must have jarred her little lungs awake."

Hemingway stopped reading and looked over the last page like it was a fond old memory—like it was an old friend he remembered sweating over and had probably misplaced in a tavern under a whisky glass somewhere.

I was wiping away tears with my hand. The tears were not about the story but about the trouble I knew the same girl was in. I felt like I knew her personally then.

"Can I say something, Mr. Hemingway?"

He looked up at me. Somehow I had a feeling that he was looking at me differently. Like it was important to his life that I was there.

"Did you write that, Mr. Hemingway?"

"You know I did. It's true, and it's alive."

He looked at me with a wince in his eye.

"What is your name?"

"Jerry."

He extended his hand.

"I'm Ernest, Jerry. Call me Ernest, or call me Papa."

"Thank you, Ernest."

"Talk to me, Jerry. Speak with honest sentences."

"I'm thinking you must have known this baby girl—the one in the story," I said.

"I knew the doctor."

"Oh? The one in the story?"

"Don't waste breath on stupid questions, Jerry."

"How do you know her?"

"I met her at a Red Cross relief station before the war. She was giving tetanus shots to civilians. She told me the story. Now I remember. First black woman I could have really loved. I wrote it to give it to her as a thank-you for putting up with my bullshit at a bar. Leaving the bottle of bourbon for it and taking off was her idea, not mine. I never saw her again."

"Well the lady you wrote about, the Daisy Pearl lady, died after her son was killed at Pearl Harbor," I said.

"Aaron was killed?" said Hemingway.

"William," I said. "Her youngest son. He was sixteen. He lied about his age and joined the navy."

Hemingway paused. He was experienced with war and dying all over the world. Every casualty meant something to him.

"He died bravely. He died for his country. We owe him," he said. "Why are you here, Jerry?"

"Anna Kristina."

"Anna Kristina in trouble, is she?"

"She's pregnant by a white guy. She's sixteen and pregnant by a white guy, Mr. Hemingway."

Hemingway gazed at me for more.

"She was raped."

He stood and yelled, "What!"

He grabbed a pillow, swung it around, and threw it against the bedside lamp, tearing the lampshade and knocking it over.

"What kind of bastard would do—"

"They said he forced himself on her, but he didn't hurt her. He's twenty-two, and she's sixteen. That's rape, right?"

"How old are you, Jerry?

"Twelve."

"You're an old twelve, my friend."

"My friends and I grew up in the war, Mr. Hemingway. We were old at six."

Hemingway plopped down on the edge of a bed with his shoulders slumped.

"Say what they may. I do believe in God, and I pray. I've never judged a man by his color or his creed – take issue with anyone who does. That's why I'm here, dammit. I don't know how this journey of yours started, but it was heaven sent."

"You can say that again," I said facetiously.

"Tell me everything you know. Tell me why you came."

That's when—and I remember it like it was yesterday—Ernest Hemingway sat there and listened to me, a kid from Delphi Falls, and my story about a girl in trouble and a white boy's father.

"His father works for the governor of Arkansas. If he ever finds out...well...I mean, they say he burns crosses and hates Negroes and says so right in public. He won't even let their children go to the public schools. Anna Kristina's baby may not stand a chance if he ever finds out it's his son's baby."

"I've seen his slime before."

"So you don't know where the girl is, Mr. Hemingway?"

"It's been fifteen years, Jerry. That's a long time when there's been a world war and a lifetime thrown in."

"Oh."

"Is that why you came? To see if I could help?"

"Yes."

"Get me names; get me the kid's old man's name. Let's catch that SOB. Get me something more to go on, Jerry."

"So here's the deal, Mr. Hemingway."

"Ernest or Papa, dammit!"

"So here's the deal. I'll try to get some information today and tomorrow, but I have to leave on Friday. If I find stuff after that, I won't know how to mail it to you if nobody knows you're here."

"Where are you going?"

"My mom, my brother, and I have to be going home. We live in Delphi Falls, all the way up in New York State."

"If you live way up in bum-stump, New York, how in the hell did you wind up in this mess here in Little Rock?"

"You live in Cuba, and you're here."

"I'm Ernest Hemingway, Jerry. I live nowhere and everywhere."

"Stop fooling around. Tell me how I get messages to you."

"Ernest Hemingway, this hotel. I'll tell the desk."

"Okay, good."

"Can you come back later or tomorrow?"

"Why?"

"I'll address postcards for you to use until then. You write messages. And mail them."

"How long will you be staying here?" I asked.

"I'll be here until I leave, Jerry. After that I'll go to Cuba to drink or to Africa to kill, but they'll forward my mail."

"Thank you, Papa. You won't regret any of this. I promise."

"So how are you involved with all of this, Jerry?"

"I'll tell you everything if we get to save this girl. I promise. Right now, I can't."

"Be a writer, young man. You're observant, and you have a soul."

Ernest Hemingway shook my hand, stepped into the hall, and watched me walk down it and around the corner to the elevator. It was like I was important.

Uncle Don, ready to fly a B-17 to England to start his missions in 1944

CHAPTER TWELVE

THANKSGIVING IN ARKANSAS

On Thanksgiving morning Mom told me not to go far; she said she might need me to do something. There wasn't a soul outside like there had been on the weekdays I'd been in town. Most of the kids must have been sleeping in because it was a holiday or in kitchens smelling pies and sausage and bread stuffing. I knew I'd have to figure out a way to get back to the hotel to get Hemingway's postcards before we left.

Battery Street in front of Aunt Mary's apartment duplex had a one-block strip near Twenty-First that had a boulevard of lawn down its middle wide enough to play touch football on. I was plopped in the center of it, sitting alone. My mind couldn't stop bouncing like a Ping-Pong ball between thoughts of friends back in Delphi Falls and thoughts of meeting Charlie, Arnold, and William. And I wondered if I'd hallucinated the whole angel thing, if I was getting touched in the head, and if I'd ever see them again. Then there was Ernest Hemingway. I knew he was real, but I knew nobody, including my English teacher, Miss Doxtator, would ever believe I'd met him.

I looked around to see if anyone was watching me and gave it a try.

"Charlie, are you here with me?"

I waited.

"Charlie?"

I gave him about a minute.

"Charlie, will I ever see you again? Angel Arnold? William, are you here?"

I was all alone.

With so much to think about and nobody to talk to on Thanksgiving, I thought about the Arkansas heat. All the adventure and the three angels aside, I kept complaining that it just wasn't normal to be so warm on Thanksgiving when it was probably snowing in Delphi Falls. I was also disappointed that I hadn't been able to have a sit-down with my hero, Uncle Don, for the talk he'd promised about the war and about flying B-17 bombers. Between his job and having to visit Aunt Mary and the baby in the hospital, he came home late to sleep and got up early to shave and leave for work, which meant he barely had any time.

I went back inside, but Mom ordered me to get out of the kitchen if I was going to mope around feeling sorry for myself and keep sticking my finger in the butter sauce for the fruitcake. She had a turkey to baste and rolls to bake, and all the while she had to keep from burning the green-bean-and-onion-crisp casserole.

"Go outside and play," Mom said. "Just don't go wandering off."

"Play with who?" I said, pleading my case.

"With 'whom,' dear. Go out and play with whom."

My head sank.

Mom rethought her command, understanding it was a holiday, after all. She had Dick busy doing something he got a lot of training for when he was in trouble—washing dishes and scrubbing pots and pans.

She waved the turkey baster like Sousa's baton, pointed toward the door, and suggested I go wait outside for Uncle Don to come home with Aunt Mary and the new baby.

"They'll be here any time now. Go outside and watch for them!"

Uncle Don was my hero. I didn't have a problem with that proposition.

"When they get here, be a gentleman and carry Aunt Mary's bag," said Mom.

Sure enough, up drove the green Oldsmobile, a sleek '49 four-door car. Uncle Don jumped out with a grin, skipped around to the other side, and opened the door for Aunt Mary, who was holding their fresh, new baby son swaddled tightly and warmly in a blanket. I opened the rear door, grabbed her bag, and followed behind them while Uncle Don offered her his arm for the walk up the sidewalk and into the house. When Aunt Mary got inside and saw that one of the busier jobs of a homemaker's year, preparing the Thanksgiving supper, was well in hand, she figured the swelling in her ankles would go down if she could put her feet up a spell. I fetched two pillows from a bed to support her back. Mom held the new baby until Aunt Mary was in a comfortable position, and she rested back on the pillows and raised her feet on the arm of the sofa with a sigh.

Her other three were awakened by all the commotion and gathered around their new baby brother.

Uncle Don stood guard over the turkey. He took his holiday carving seriously. He took his carving set from its box, raised the deer-horn handle knife in one hand and the sharpening steel in the other, and sharpened the knife's blade with a few traditional holiday-bell-ringing slither-swipes up and down.

"Come and get it, people," said Mom. "Jerry, your seat is down next to your uncle Don's."

Aunt Mary rolled onto her side, got her balance, stood up from the sofa, and cribbed the sleeping new baby.

"Mom, what's this on my chair?" I asked.

"It's a package and some mail. I thought they'd be a nice Thanksgiving surprise for you. I forgot about them this morning, or I would have given them to you."

"Did they come today?"

"Yesterday."

"These could be important."

"Stop being so dramatic, dear. Put your napkin on your lap."

"Tommy and Timmy?" said Aunt Mary. "Take a seat next to a grown-up."

"Dick, why don't you put Teddy in the high chair and bring it up next to me. I'll watch him," said Mom. "You sit between little Tommy and Timmy so you can help them. Give Aunt Mary some rest."

I ripped open the package from Marty and held the cipher wheel in my hand, turning it about, staring at it, and wondering about it. I handed it to Uncle Don while I looked at the postcard and the two letters. The postcard from Mary Crane was in code, and one of the letters was from Mayor, and one was from my dad.

Dick got the high chairs arranged and the small kids organized, and he was the last to pull up a chair and sit down.

Uncle Don set the cipher wheel on the table in front of my plate and picked up his carving knife again.

"It looks like it's for codes," he said.

"It is?" I beamed.

The first things that came to my mind were Ernest Hemingway and secret messages.

Uncle Don finished carving the turkey.

"Missus, will you kindly do us the honors?" asked Uncle Don.

"Lord, we thank you for this precious new baby and for all his nice young brothers who can watch over him. Thank you for this food and for our loving get-together, and please watch over Big Mike back home while we're away, and give us safe passage tomorrow as we start our journey home. Amen."

"Thanks, everybody, for coming. You were such a great help for us," said Aunt Mary. "And I know you boys missed Thanksgiving parties and dances to come here to help. Thank you."

"Want me to read Dad's letter in case it's about Thanksgiving?" I asked.

"Of course, dear. But quickly, before the food gets cold—and elbows off the table."

"I'll serve the turkey and potatoes," said Don. "Pass the plates this way."

I tore the envelope open and pulled a sheet out. "Jerry, me boy!"

I looked up at Uncle Don.

"Dad always calls me that."

Have fun in Little Rock, and take lots of pictures of your adventures. Invite your uncle Don and aunt Mary to bring the kids to Delphi Falls for Christmas and New Year. Santa will come here. See you all when you get home Sunday, Son. Love, Dad.

I looked over at Uncle Don. "Will you come?"

He was busy serving turkey and potatoes.

"I'd love to see the falls again," said Aunt Mary, "Don, you'll have vacation time by then, and the babies travel well."

"We'll let you know next week, Missus, if that's okay," said Uncle Don.

Mom smiled her approval.

"Grown-ups, go ahead and pick up a serving dish or a bowl, take some for yourself and some for the little one beside you, and pass it on," said Mom.

"Small portions on the little ones' plates, please," said Aunt Mary. "There is always more. And try to watch over them so they don't spill their drinks."

Aunt Mary's saying those words about watching over the little ones made me think of Ole Charlie, and just as I thought of him, I could see his head looking at me from on top of the buffet table. He was holding a finger over his lips as if he were telling me not to give it away that he was there. He appeared at about the time I was lifting a warm gravy boat. It gave me cold chills down my spine. I guessed I was either having a premonition like he'd had or was about to have a heart attack—and only time would tell which it was.

"Uncle Don," I said. "Did you shoot down a lot of planes in the war?"

"Give it a rest," said Dick. "Uncle Don doesn't want to talk about the war."

"I flew a bomber, Jerry. You know that. From our base, we all flew the B-17 bombers."

"But the picture-show newsreels called the B-17 a 'flying fortress' because it had so many guns. You must have shot down some Nazis."

"Oh, well that's true. Our mission was to drop bombs on targets we were ordered to bomb and to get back to base without being shot down. As we moved out and back, if we were attacked by German fighter planes, our boys in the gun turrets would try to protect us on all sides. They did their fair share of shooting down enemy planes. Our fighter planes shot down more, though—sometimes it was our Red Tail guys, and sometimes it was the British fighter planes that helped protect us."

"Did you bomb Germany on D-day?"

"I was in flight-school training here in the States when D-day was going on. After training, I flew my airship overseas right to where I was stationed in England. My crew started our missions after Christmas while the Battle of the Bulge was still going strong, and we flew missions right up until two weeks before the war ended in Europe."

"Did you drop bombs on Hitler?"

"Good Lord, Jerry," said Mom. "This is Thanksgiving."

"Don can't tell you about his missions, Jerry. They were all top secret," said Aunt Mary.

"Never?" I asked.

"I can't tell for ten years, Mary. It's ten years only on top-secret equipment and codes. That'll be in April of 1955. But our missions weren't secret—bombing missions went out daily all through the war, and I'll answer whatever general questions I can, young fella."

"Were you scared?"

"I'd say we were nervous, not scared. The war tested our nerves, what with the German V-2 rockets bombing London and our bases every day. We were nervous on the missions we flew, knowing there were sometimes three thousand planes in the air at the same time and that we could bump into one another and crash. Life in the air corps was pretty much all about being aware so you didn't miss a small detail, staying in formation, and looking out for close planes while watching for enemy fighter planes. That kept us alert. We'd sometimes look out ahead and up high—"

"Twelve-o'clock high?" I asked.

Uncle Don smiled.

"Twelve-o'clock high, and at first they'd all look like a dozen or so sewing pins scattered about in the distance. Within seconds they'd become life-sized fighters diving at us and shooting their fifty cals. We were scared in the flak, though, from the ground cannons. Sometimes they would blow three- or four-inch holes in the walls of our plane."

"What is 'flak,' Uncle Don?" asked Dick.

"'Flak' was the kind of vest we wore—a flak jacket—to protect us from the ground cannons that we called the 'ack-ack guns.'"

"'Ack ack'?" I asked.

"They were antiaircraft guns, or 'ack ack' to us."

Uncle Don put his fork down and raised his hands like he was holding a machine gun.

Flak-cannon rockets exploding around
my bomber wing in 1945

"It's what they sounded like—*ack-ack-ack-ack-ack.*"

My mouth dropped as I listened to his every word.

"The enemy would shoot a lot of shells into the air all around our planes, and they'd explode with shrapnel, sometimes hitting us. They could knock out engines, set fuel tanks on fire, and even kill gunners or crew members. On night flights they'd explode like balls of fire. In daylight runs they'd explode like puffs of white powder, but they were just as dangerous—just as deadly—day or night."

Mesmerized, I let my fork fall out of my hand and onto my plate with a clang.

"Jerry, eat," said Mom. "Let Uncle Don have some peace and enjoy his meal."

"Did you see planes get shot down?"

Lead bomber (second from top) after being hit on Mission nineteen, "Bomb Berlin" March 18, 1945

Uncle Don paused. He looked with a stare at the cranberry dish.

"Yes," he said, almost to himself.

I didn't say a word. I could see his angst.

"Our group's lead bomber was shot down on my nineteenth mission," said Uncle Don. "My plane became the lead bomber after that."

"That's enough, Jerry," said Mom.

And then I almost blew Ole Charlie's cover with my big mouth. I looked over at Ole Charlie's head on the buffet table just as if he were sitting and eating with us.

"Charlie," I said. "If Hitler and Mussolini were so bad, why did God let them shoot down our planes?"

"Charlie?" asked Mom.

"Who's Charlie?" asked Dick.

Gulp!

"I meant 'Mom.' Did I say 'Charlie'? Crazy me. I meant to say 'Mom.' So Mom, why did God let them do those things?"

I thought I was going to wet my pants.

"As soon as we get back, you're seeing Dr. Brudney, young man."

"Huh? Cheece - a guy can't even get his mail when it comes and now I can't ask questions," I whispered.

"First the nightmares, and now you're talking to yourself. You need a looking at by a doctor," she said.

"It's puberty," said Dick. "I got pimples, and Jerry went nuts."

Thinking of my question, Uncle Don pursed his lips, raised his eyebrows up, and looked down the table at Mom over his glasses. He let her field that particular unanswered question about God and Mussolini and Hitler.

It remained unanswered.

After we had our Thanksgiving celebration, it was like a starting gun went off in my brain; all of a sudden, I realized I didn't have much time. We were leaving for Delphi Falls the next day.

As I should have suspected, Ole Charlie was planning a busy afternoon for Uncle Don and me somehow—I just didn't know how. But after seeing him on the buffet table, I knew enough to watch for his signs and to just trust Ole Charlie and go with the flow.

CHAPTER THIRTEEN

JUST DESSERTS

"Don and Jerry, why don't you take the children into the living room and keep them busy while Aunt Mary and I clear the table and cut the pies," said Mom.

Uncle Don picked up the cipher wheel in one hand and his cup of coffee in the other, stood, and went to his easy chair to study the wheel. He turned it about and twisted the wheels; he examined the lettering and the numbers. He studied it, looking for clues as to how it had been put together.

"Come help in the kitchen, Dick," said Mom.

"Why me and not Jerry?" whined Dick.

"Kitchen, mister," said Mom. "Jerry has been waiting all week to talk with his Uncle Don. We're leaving tomorrow. Let them be."

Dick passed a sneer to me.

I was on the living room floor, looking at the picture of the New York State Fair's Ferris wheel on Mary Crane's postcard and opening my letter from Mayor. The kids were sitting around the crib, staring at the new baby.

"Did you use a lot of codes when you were on your B-17 missions?"

"We did. A fair amount of them, anyway. Code words, code names—they'd change them sometimes in case the enemy had broken them. Let me figure this cipher wheel out. Give me a minute with it."

"I can't read this postcard from Mary Crane. It's in some kind of code."

"Hand it here. This thing might break the code," said Don.

The postcard in hand, Don stood up from the easy chair and walked over to a tall secretary desk against the living room wall. He sat down, taking a pen in his hand. He started turning the wheels on the disk to match Mary's code letters until he saw they formed complete words on another line.

Mary Crane's original message was simple: "Send a postcard. I collect them. Mary."

But unbeknownst to me at the time, as Uncle Don turned and sat down with the postcard, Ole Charlie did some manipulating and added another coded line or two to Mary's message in her handwriting. They were lines only Uncle Don would see, and they disappeared the second he set the postcard down when he was finished with it. I later learned Ole Charlie did that knowing it was in Uncle Don's nature to help, so he included the message to see if he would.

While Uncle Don tried to decipher the code on the postcard, I opened my letter from Mayor and read it out loud.

Dear Jerry,

Conway and Marty built the cipher wheel in woodshop. Somebody took a Kodak picture of it at the Smithsonian during the senior trip last year. Arrange the letters to read a sentence on one of its lines. Turn the cipher thing around, and write down the letters on any other line as your code. It's easy. When the other end sets a line on their cipher wheel to your code line, they'll turn the thing around, and your message will come up on another line. It'll be the only line with words, so they can't make a mistake. Be careful down there. Tell Dick to watch his mouth. I didn't say that—somebody else did—but it's a good idea. Be careful! Mayor.

I scratched my head.

"Uncle Don, did you understand any of that?"

"Jerry, come over here a sec," said Uncle Don.

I jumped up.

"I figured out the code. It took more than one of the cipher wheel lines," said Uncle Don.

"Read it," I said.

Uncle Don turned and read from his notes.

"Send a postcard. I collect them. Mary."

"PS: Go to Mission Methodist for Aunt Lucy. Ask them what they need for their poor so she can send it down.'"

"I know Aunt Lucy," I said. "Holbrook and I put up her clothesline post."

"Let's go," said Uncle Don.

"What's Mission Methodist?" I asked.

Uncle Don picked up the telephone directory and looked it up. He stood up quickly and grabbed his hat.

"Get in the car."

"Now?"

"Mary?" Uncle Don yelled. "Jerry and I will be right back. Something important has come up."

"Who'll watch the kids, Don?" asked Aunt Mary.

"Get Dick to watch them."

Uncle Don waved the coded postcard in Aunt Mary's direction like it was an important semaphore and then set it down on the secretary desk.

"I have a feeling this is important," said Uncle Don. "They're leaving tomorrow, so Jerry and I have to do this today. I'll explain it all later."

Since the postcard's message was written in code, Uncle Don felt he was compelled to act on it right away.

He couldn't explain why. I knew why, and Ole Charlie knew why. It was in his nature to help.

It was in Uncle Don's nature to do heroic acts.

I imagined our ride like a ride in a B-17, with Uncle Don pilot-
ing and resting one arm on the steering wheel and one on his
knee. We drove through Little Rock like there was no time to
spare, careful to watch for street signs, stop signs, and clues for the
next turn. Unbeknownst to us when we started out, our journey
took us into the poorer section of southern Little Rock, down by
the tracks near where little Anna Kristina had been born in 1937.

As our green Oldsmobile slowed and pulled to a stop, the
Mission Methodist Church stood there tall and proud, in need of
paint but a beehive of activity.

Uncle Don turned the engine off.

"Come with me," he said."

We stepped from the car, walked to the steps of the church,
and paused there, looking around. People standing about – all
ages, ladies on the steps in pretty holiday hats and choir singers in
starched robes. Don sauntered over and tipped his hat to two women
standing and talking. They stopped and waited for him to speak, as
he was interrupting their precious Thanksgiving go to meeting day.

"May I ask you ladies who's in charge here?"

"We're a church, sir. Ain't nobody in charge."

"God's in charge," said a voice.

Uncle Don chose to lighten the load for those ladies with an
explanation. He had a sense there was something intimidating
about a tall white man in a tie from some uptown vicinity poking
his nose around their church, which was their safe zone.

"Ladies, a lady in a church group up north has asked that we
kindly inquire as to whom Northern ladies like her might send
Christmas packages for your poor-box missions and other offer-
ings. It's like an outreach program they have, I suppose. Who
might I talk to about that—would you know?"

The ladies looked at each other and then back at Uncle Don,
sizing him up. He had the look of a man with integrity, it seemed
to them, and his shoes were polished, and his fingernails were
clean. Their guess was that he wasn't meaning no harm.

"Sarah Wilkins might help you," said one of the ladies.

She pointed her white-gloved hand.

"Up there by the front door."

"Much obliged, ladies," said Uncle Don.

"She's the lady in the black dress and the black hat," said the other lady.

"Thank you," I said.

Uncle Don tipped his hat and made his way up the steps, and, again tipping his hat but that time holding it over his heart, he introduced himself and me to Sarah and explained why we both had come.

Not only did the lady gleefully write down her name and the church address and the sorts of items they were in need of, but she also—and I could tell it was with some of Ole Charlie's manipulation—paused a moment and looked up at the sky as though she had just remembered something to ask Uncle Don. It was a question she had no idea Ole Charlie was suggesting she ask.

"Do you know a man in North Little Rock who flew bombers in the war?"

Uncle Don was startled.

"How did you know I was a bomber pilot, ma'am?"

"Lawdy me, I didn't," she gasped. "Why, I don't even know what made me say that."

She looked down at her purse and then up at Uncle Don.

"Were you a bomber pilot, sure enough?"

"Yes, I was. But no, ma'am, I don't know any pilots here or in North Little Rock. I know one pilot vet, Hal Hoffman, over in Carlisle, east toward Memphis, but he runs a crop-dusting service."

"He isn't doing well at all," said Sarah.

"Who isn't?" asked Uncle Don.

"The man in North Little Rock I was speaking of—the man who flew the bombers."

"What do you mean, he's not doing well?"

"It was the war. It did something to him."

"The war did something to a lot of people, ma'am."

"Not like that."

"Do you know his address?"

"His name is Aaron. I'll write his address down for you. I knew his momma. She was my best friend since we shared rain-barrel washtubs. She passed in forty-two—passed with a heart attack, she did, but I think it was a broken heart."

That's when I turned a full three-sixty turn, looking for Ole Charlie. I knew he was there, but I didn't know where.

"Holy Cobako," I mumbled to myself.

"God bless her soul," said a voice.

"Praise Jesus," said another.

"While you're up there, mister, see if Aaron knows where his baby sister, Anna Kristina, is. Test the waters, though. The man hasn't seen her since she was five. I haven't had the heart to tell her he's alive or where he is, with his condition the way it is, so delicate and all. I'll write her name down in case you forget."

"What seems to be his problem?" asked Uncle Don.

A lady standing next to Sarah Wilkins offered us some information.

"He come here one Sunday back in forty-seven—never came back, ever," she said. "It was his brother's and momma's deaths what started it. It was the war what finally did him in."

"That's right, he came for his momma's funeral in forty-two," said a voice. "Again in forty-seven and then never again."

"God bless that man," said Sarah.

"A troubled soul," said the lady next to Sarah.

"He might not answer the door," she said. "You just keep pounding till he does. He may be troubled, but he's a gentle enough soul. He don't bite."

"Can I tell him where his sister is? Do you know?" asked Uncle Don. "That might cheer him up."

"If'n he comes here, God will have his sister waiting for him. He surely will. I promise you that. You can tell him that too. She needs the man at this time. But he has to want to come to her."

I just knew Ole Charlie had done some manipulating business. It was a clever idea. He knew that Uncle Don was a good man and that maybe a bomber-pilot-to-bomber-pilot talk would open the door and be all it took to get rolling in the right direction to help that unborn baby.

Uncle Don pulled a map from his glove compartment and handed it to me so I could give him directions up to North Little Rock. Soon enough we found our way, the street we were looking for, and the address number and pulled up in front. Folks were out and about on porches of neighboring houses. Some were in rockers visiting; some were sitting a spell on stoops; and some were standing, smoking pipes and cigarettes, and catching up on family gatherings and grandchildren.

"Jerry, hang on to this sheet of paper—it's the list of what the mission church needs. You'll have to figure out how to get it to the right people in Delphi Falls. It has the mission's address written on it."

I knew right off that Old Charlie had manipulated the list.

"It says 'Aunt Lucy,'" I said. "I can give it to Mary to give to her."

Uncle Don stepped out of the car and tried to remember what names were on the list he'd read, but a young boy scootering by on the sidewalk balancing on an orange crate with roller-skate wheels nailed to a board distracted him.

I just knew Ole Charlie had arranged for Aunt Lucy's name to appear on the note and for the boy on the scooter to distract Uncle Don.

I shrugged my shoulders, folded the paper, and stuffed it into my pocket.

Uncle Don knocked on the door.

No answer.

He waited a full count of twenty seconds and knocked again.

The door opened.

A man about Uncle Don's age was standing there, not saying a word. He seemed particularly annoyed with the intrusion into his privacy, particularly by a white man.

Uncle Don felt the uneasiness, but as sure as his B-17 crewmen wouldn't go home after their twenty-five missions because they'd volunteered to stay on until Hitler was stopped, he wasn't about to give up and walk away from a man he felt a brethren with as a bomber pilot—a man who obviously had something burning his gut.

"I was with the Eighth," said Uncle Don. "B-17s—heavy bombers. *Lady Helene* was our ship all the way in forty-four and forty-five. You?"

Aaron looked Uncle Don up and down.

"Who are you? What do you want?"

"We flew thirty-three missions," said Uncle Don. "The last was—"

"I was assigned to the Four Hundred Seventy-Seventh Medium Bombardment Group to fly B-25s. Mitchells."

"Pilot?"

"Yes, I flew the B-25. Never shipped out, though," said Aaron.

He turned his head and looked at the doorjamb and repeated himself.

"They never shipped me out."

"Where were you boys stationed?"

"Selfridge Field."

"B-25?"

"B-25."

"A sweet ship and a light bomber, the B-25. Important ship. How'd she handle?"

Aaron started to smile but held it back.

"Wore her like a glove," said Aaron.

"The name's Don," said Uncle Don, extending his hand.

Aaron paused, looked down at the outstretched hand, and then looked up into his eyes.

"Aaron," said Aaron, shaking it.

"Can we come in, Aaron?"

"What'd ya want?"

"Can we come in?"

"Come on in."

Aaron leaned back, holding the door for Uncle Don and me to walk through.

"I don't have anything to offer you," said Aaron.

"This isn't a social visit. This is my nephew, Jerry. We came to ask you something."

"Ain't no harm in asking."

Without looking like a snoop, Don peered around the living room at pictures of Aaron in his uniform and of another young sailor in uniform. There were vintage studio sepias that appeared to be portraits of Aaron's mother, a kindly lady wearing a pearl necklace. He looked Aaron in the eye. In it he saw a shadow of the man in uniform in the picture on the wall behind him.

"Aaron, I want to start off by apologizing to you."

"Why? I don't even know you."

"I've been waiting a long time and for the right place to say this, so don't stop me now."

"You don't know me."

"There's no excuse for the way some people were treated in the Second World War."

Aaron caught Uncle Don's eyes, which were looking at his military picture on the mantle, and added a snide comment.

"You mean us Negroes?"

"Well—"

"Ain't you heard, man? We're 'colored people' now," Aaron said sarcastically.

"No excuse at all," said Don. "There were a lot of great talents like you, willing, trained, and able to fly bombers with the best of us and to help the fight, who never got shipped overseas for action.

There were the thousands of Japanese Americans who were locked up in internment camps. I want to apologize for all that."

"It wasn't you that did it," said Aaron.

"Let me try to make sense out of it."

"Ain't but only one sense to it," said Aaron.

Don held his ground.

"America was attacked and bombed by the Japanese, who killed more than three thousand boys and gals on a sleepy, early Sunday morning. We were scared."

Aaron lowered his head.

"Pearl Harbor. I lost my brother, William, in that one. He was about to turn seventeen."

Uncle Don bolted back, biting his lip, and looked over at the picture of the lad in the sailor's uniform. He looked back into Aaron's eyes.

"There was war all over the Pacific, with Jap suicide bombers diving into ships, killing crews and sinking entire fleets. Most didn't know the Japs dropped more than a thousand balloon bombs all over the western United States."

"Is that a fact?" asked Aaron.

"Roosevelt kept it top secret so it wouldn't cause a national panic."

"Well, I'll be."

"And on the Atlantic side, Hitler was taking over all of Europe, killing millions. Millions of civilians, Jews, and Russians—it never stopped. Hitler's U-boat submarines alone sank about a thousand ships a year in the Atlantic. We sank German subs right off our own East Coast."

"We could have helped," said Aaron.

"Not a doubt in my mind ever—there never was a doubt in my mind," said Uncle Don. "There'll be a day soon when there won't be a doubt in anybody's mind. The Red Tail boys helped a lot."

"That's right, that's right. Now there you go. The Red Tails. So why'd they send those Red Tails over and not us B-25 boys?" asked Aaron. "They were colored too. Tell me that one."

"Those were different times," said Uncle Don.

"Not all that much different today," said Aaron.

"When it was all over, Aaron, I asked Jimmy Doolittle why you guys weren't shipped out. I met the man after the war in Washington somewhere. He was giving a speech at a VFW luncheon."

Aaron sat up.

"You knew Jimmy Doolittle? He used B-25s on his raid over Tokyo."

"I got to shake his hand. Know what he told me?"

"What?"

"He said that this particular war was the first time in the history of the planet when the entire world was at war. It was a war we could have lost. He told me Germany's propaganda people had made a movie about what a hero Hitler was in America. It even showed him in a ticker-tape parade in New York City. He said the folks in Washington gave it a lot of thought, the lingering racial tension in places around the country. You know what it's like, Aaron, even today. I won't pull any punches. I respect you too much for that. Doolittle told me without a blink that Roosevelt was fighting a world war he could have lost on two fronts and that he felt he didn't need to be giving Eisenhower in Europe or MacArthur in the Pacific a third front."

"Integration?"

"Yes," said Uncle Don.

"I never seen it that way, sure enough," said Aaron.

"No excuse for what they did, but there was a reason at the time," said Uncle Don.

"Hundred forty of our guys were court-martialed for speaking up and complaining about the way we were treated and seeing no action. Wasn't right, what they did to us, but I can see it the way you put it. Doesn't fit right, but it makes sense. Thanks."

"I don't like it any more than you do."

"So why'd they go and let the Red Tails—the colored guys—fly but not us? Makes no sense to me."

"Red Tails were in fighter planes—no crews. For you guys to pilot a bomber and lead a crew, or even to be bombardiers with the new equipment, they would have had to commission you to a grade higher than your crews. They were worried about some of the crew members not taking orders from a commissioned Negro."

"I hear that, man."

"Aaron, Jimmy Doolittle would have been honored to have had you with him over Tokyo. He would have been damned lucky to have had you."

Aaron looked up into Uncle Don's eyes to see if he was true. Seeing he was, he beamed. It was his first beam since the war—and it turned near into a silly grin as he sat there on the ottoman.

"Me dropping bombs on a factory in Tokyo. Can you just imagine it? Oh my, oh my, wouldn't that have been something now?"

Uncle Don looked at his watch, then at Aaron's grin.

"Aaron, is your sister in trouble? That's why we came. The Mission Methodist ladies are asking about her."

"If she's in trouble, I don't know it or where she is."

"Here's my address and phone number," said Uncle Don. "Can you let me know if you find where she is? People want to help."

"Uncle Don?" I asked.

Uncle Don looked over at me.

"Can I give him my address in Delphi Falls and my telephone number in case there's trouble and we can help?"

Don looked me in the eye. I imagined him thinking of his own eagerness to get in the war and to do something that mattered. He looked beyond me to the picture of the young sailor, William, who lost his life below decks on December 7, 1941. He looked over at Aaron.

"Okay with you, Aaron?"

"Fine by me," Aaron smiled. "You want my number? We'll trade numbers."

"That might come in handy," said Uncle Don. "I'd like talking planes with you sometime over a beer."

"First time I ever traded phone numbers with a white man," said Aaron.

"You'd like meeting a friend of mine, Hal Hoffman, over in Carlisle," said Uncle Don. "He flew B-17s—has a crop-dusting service now."

We all shook hands as Uncle Don and I left to drive back for Thanksgiving dessert. Aaron stood in his doorway watching us walk to the car.

Uncle Don stopped, turned, and walked back.

"Are you doing okay, Aaron? Any way I can help?"

"Oh, I'm doing fine. See that Chevy on the street?"

"I do. Nice car."

"It's mine, and it's all paid for. I'm making it a taxi. I'm doing just fine."

"Aaron, you might go visit the Mission Methodist people. Ask about your sister while you're there."

"Let me think on it," said Aaron.

"And, Aaron, it took us until nineteen twenty to give women a vote. We may be slow about things, but we'll make them right in the end."

Aaron smiled.

"If you ever need a taxi," said Aaron, "you got my number."

Uncle Don gave Aaron a cockpit thumbs-up, and we drove away.

I rolled my car window up.

"If I send a coded message today, when will it get to Mary Crane in the Crown?" I asked Uncle Don.

"The Crown? Where's the Crown?"

"Hard to explain. How long do you think it'll take to get to Delphi Falls?"

"There's no mail today, it bein' a holiday," said Uncle Don. "If it goes out tomorrow, it might get there by next Tuesday."

"We'll be back home on Sunday. Dang!"

"Write your message, Jerry. Not in code. Tonight you can call your dad collect and tell it to him, and he'll give it to whomever you'd like."

"Could I call Mary Crane and tell it to her straight out?"

Uncle Don looked over and smiled. He'd been a kid once. He remembered secrets and codes.

"Sure. It'll be my treat. That long-distance call is on me, my friend. Now let's go home and get some pie."

"Wait! I just remembered. Uncle Don, do you know where the Capital Hotel is?"

"We'll be driving right past it. Why?"

"Can you stop there, just for a minute? I have to run in and get something."

"What would you need at the Capital Hotel, Jerry?"

I lied the best I could without betraying trusts.

"Postcards, Uncle Don. I promised kids hotel postcards. Will you stop?"

"Sure, we'll stop."

I hated lying to Uncle Don, but I had to until I could figure everything out.

Next thing I remember was running into the hotel, through the lobby, and onto the elevator.

"Floor, please."

"Three."

I jumped off, turned toward room 305, and knocked.

Knock, knock, knock.

No answer.

Knock, knock, knock.

The door opened, and Ernest Hemingway was standing tall with his glasses on. That time he smiled.

"What's your news?" Hemingway asked.

I handed him the cipher wheel.

"Here, take this. It's a decoder thing so I can send you coded messages."

Hemingway grinned an approval at my intrigue. He took it from my hand and examined it closely. He knew exactly what it was.

"Jefferson made this for the State Department to use while they were in France. Jefferson and Adams used them regularly. It's my understanding that Franklin was jealous of it and thought it a trivial toy. He had no secrets that couldn't be discussed over a glass of wine."

"Wow, you know a lot," I said.

"I never held one. Clever device."

"My friends made it and sent it to me."

"Where did they see it to make a copy? This is an excellent reproduction."

"Somebody went to the Smithsonian and took a picture of it."

"I'm surprised it was there," said Hemingway. "Jefferson was self-indulgent and cheap. He only donated the books that created the Library of Congress because he was bankrupt and because we'd bailed him out."

Hemingway handed me an inch-high stack of preaddressed postcards.

"Here."

"Okay, Ernest, here's the deal," I said. "We found Aaron—you know, her brother. He lives in North Little Rock. As soon as we find where Anna Kristina is and the name of the man at the governor's office, I'll send you a code. I'll send you some codes anyway to make sure they work."

"Want a drink?" Hemingway asked.

I looked over at the bureau and saw the half-empty bottle of scotch on it and gave a grimace.

"Orange juice, son. Orange juice," Ernest said with a guffaw. He pointed to a pitcher of fresh-squeezed orange juice on the desk.

"I gotta go," I said. "Somebody's waiting. I'll find out everything I can."

Hemingway extended his hand.

"Papa Hemingway, can I ask you something?"

"Anything, my friend."

"Why do people treat people mean just because they're black or red or even yellow, like we called the Japanese in the war?"

Hemingway stroked his beard.

"Many don't open books, Jerry. They can't begin to imagine faraway lands and different cultures. They'll never see the brilliance of Spanish artists and warriors and bullfighters or the undying loyalty of the Asian people to their countries and families. They'll never know the gifts of art or design or the poetry of music and verse that came from Africa—from the gentle, soulful cultures that brought us jazz and the blues. People who don't know other cultures are frightened by them. Racism isn't about color, Jerry, it's about lazy intellect—about not wanting to know about or care about other cultures and the habits, traditions, and beliefs of other people."

"Books?" I said. "Books are hard sometimes."

"Reading is exercise for the brain, son. You have to think to read a book. Movies just program a brain. They don't exercise it."

"So if people learned about other cultures like you say, there wouldn't be any problems?"

"Maybe not quite that easy, Jerry. *Homo sapiens* is the only animal species that kills for pleasure. Up until now, mostly the males have killed, but that will change in time, I'm afraid."

"Can I ask you something?"

"Anything," said Hemingway.

"Promise you won't laugh?"

Hemingway lowered his eyelids in impatience.

"What does it mean, you know, the 'rape' word. What does it mean?"

Hemingway stood tall, stepped back, and gave me a gentle, curious smile.

"Your parents haven't had that talk with you, have they, Jerry?

"Talk?"

"The birds-and-bees talk."

"No," I said, fidgeting.

Hemingway smiled.

"Well make a note to ask them to, but if I were you, I'd wait until after New Year's. These things are best learned with a new start. New Year's would be good."

"Okay."

"But welcome aboard anyway," he said, smiling.

"Huh?" I said.

"Welcome aboard life, my friend. You've got everything it takes to make it one helluva ride."

He shook my hand like we were friends.

I stepped down the hall and waved over my shoulder, caught the elevator, and went back to the car with Uncle Don waiting in it.

He didn't say a word. He watched me stuff postcards into my back pocket as he drove away. I asked him about my visit.

"Why do they treat people the way they do down here, Uncle Don? When Dick and I took the bus downtown, we saw signs saying 'colored only' and that kind of thing. They wouldn't let us sit in the balcony at the movie—they said it was for colored only."

"That's a question for the ages," said Uncle Don. "I work in public health, trying to eradicate venereal diseases, with every color of skin. I see it daily. I don't think people want to be cruel. I think they're trained to be like that from over a hundred years of family traditions. And it's not only in the South. Don't let anyone kid you. There were slaves in New York and in places that would surprise you."

"Slavery? In New York?"

I understood slavery and how it ended. I didn't understand mean prejudice.

"Slavery is how it all started," said Uncle Don.

"I liked your story about World War Two," I said.

"I've wanted to say what I said today for a long time," said Uncle Don. "I never personally ran into a Negro pilot veteran before today. Quite a story…but what say we put this all behind us for now and go get some pie and take a look at that code wheel? I'll show you how easy it is. It's a great gadget. Where did it come from anyway?"

I didn't tell Uncle Don I'd just given my cipher wheel to Ernest Hemingway. I knew I could come up with a distraction if he brought it up again.

"Will you guys come up for Christmas?" I asked.

"Probably," said Uncle Don.

By the time I had eaten two pieces of pumpkin pie and one piece of apple pie, I barely had the stomach for the two scoops of ice cream Mom served up, which she never would have done had she known how much of the missing pie I was responsible for.

Between the Thanksgiving-turkey-and-stuffing feast, reliving in my mind the adventure I had had meeting the three angels and Ernest Hemingway and going with my uncle Don to southern and North Little Rock, and the three pieces of pie and two scoops of ice cream, my body was telling me I was going to require a late-afternoon sunset nap to let things settle in.

I stretched out on my cot, napped through supper's turkey-sandwich snacks, and didn't wake up until way after dark, when it was time to go to bed. When I woke in the vacant apartment, it was dark and quiet. There were no noises downstairs. A house with a new baby beds down early to prepare for those early-morning wake-ups.

Messages to Mary Crane would have to wait for another time. I'd personally deliver the list from the Mission Methodist Church to her when I got back. For the moment I was happy that my hero, Uncle Don, would be coming to Delphi Falls for Christmas. I couldn't have asked for a better present. I couldn't wait to show him off to my friends.

I sat up in the dark.

"Charlie, are you up here?"

"Charlie?"

"I did good today, Charlie. Thanks for your help."

Mom, Dick, and I were driving north by seven in the morning's early dark.

I leaned my head over, peering through the backseat side window and looking for the North Star.

CHAPTER FOURTEEN

BACK HOME ON THE RANGE

On Sunday at about dusk, I could see Dad in the distance stepping out on the porch and waving an outstretched arm at our gray '53 Chevy. The horses, Jack and Major, looked up from their grazing and trotted along behind us on the dirt drive. Dad grinned as our car pulled around behind the swings and came to a stop. He nodded when he saw Dick was driving, Mom was in the front seat, and I was in the back. He could see the sighs in our faces when Dick turned the engine off. We were finally home.

His grin was his greeting.

"How far did you drive today?" asked Dad.

"We stayed in a motel outside of Cleveland last night," said Mom. "It's good to be home."

"Did you drive all that way, Dick?"

"Today? No. Mom drove to Rochester, and I drove from there," said Dick. "We took turns all the way."

Dad shook his hand, congratulating him for a job well done. He made mention that he was proud. He walked over and gave Mom a welcome hug and a peck. He rubbed my head for good luck, welcoming me home.

"How come there's no snow?" I asked.

"Let's not rush it. It'll be here soon enough," said Dad.

I stepped over to say hello to the horses.

"Take the bags and boxes inside," said Dad.

"Leave the bags in the living room," said Mom, "I'll go through them and separate out what needs to be washed."

While we unloaded the car, Dad and Mom caught up on how Aunt Mary, Uncle Don, and the kids were and talked about how they'd confirmed that they were coming for their vacation all Christmas week through to New Years.

In light of my postcard and letter to the club, Dad decided to spare the story about the country club in Cortland and save it for another time.

"Anything to eat?" asked Dick. "I'm starving."

"Plenty of leftovers," said Dad. "Go wash up, and we'll call you when it's on the table."

I walked back to the car, opened the door, and reached onto the back window ledge, looking for my cipher wheel. All I found was my Baby Brownie camera.

"Mom, have you seen my cipher wheel?"

"Did you look under the seat?"

"It's not in the car."

"I don't have it, dear."

I closed the door behind me, catching Dick's eye.

"Don't look at me," said Dick. "You probably left it in Arkansas."

I turned and opened the car door again and searched the front and the back before I remembered. Ernest Hemingway. I slapped my forehead like I was such a lamebrain.

"Jerry, why don't you go see if Holbrook is still up at your camp, and then invite him down for supper if he is?" Dad said.

"Did he camp out?"

"I gave him a can of Spam and some eggs yesterday. My guess is he may still be up there or hiking one of the falls. Give him a shout."

I watched the cliff across the creek as I walked toward the waterfalls in the backyard. I was looking for the spot where the spring dripped water down the seventy-foot cliff. Our camp was on top, next to the mouth of that spring. I cupped my hands together and made my mourning-dove call.

"Whooo-weee-hooo-hooo-hooo!" I hooted.

I paused a few seconds.

"Whooo-weee-hooo-hooo-hooo!"

I paused.

By that time my horse Jack had trotted up to the call he knew so well from his old friend.

"Whooo-weee-hooo-hooo-hooo!"

I lowered my hands that time and looked up, and sure enough there was Holbrook, grinning on top of the cliff, hanging on to a tree, and waving back with big swipes. I motioned for him to come down and pointed at my mouth, indicating "supper." He grinned again and turned, disappearing into the woods. I walked back to where Dad and Mom were standing.

"He's coming. He probably has to put out the campfire and pack up, but he'll be down."

"Put your things away, and go wash up. We'll eat when he gets here," said Dad. "I'll drive him home after supper."

"I'm going to put some oats out for Jack and Major," I said. "I'll be there in a second."

I was remaking my acquaintances with the horses I hadn't seen for nearly two weeks when Holbrook appeared down at the front gate and slowly strolled up the drive.

"Did you ride any while I was gone?"

"I rode Jack bareback last week when I was waiting on the spaghetti dinner, but I only came here this time after work at Tully Bakery. I knew you'd be home today, so I asked my dad to drop me off. I still have some food your dad gave me."

"You had spaghetti here?"

"Yeah. We all did. The club met here to read your letter and see what you were all panicky about. Your dad made spaghetti."

"Shut up! I wasn't panicking."

"So how was it?"

"How was what?"

"The Mississippi River. Is it as big as they say?"

"Bigger. Muddy looking, though. It looks brown."

"Did you see any riverboats?"

"I saw two steamboats parked in Memphis, and I saw some barges on the river. Tugboats were pushing the barges. We saw one steamboat in Cincinnati, but that was on the Ohio River, not the Mississippi."

"That must have been so cool," said Holbrook.

"Did my dad see the letter I sent? It was secret."

"It was no big deal. We all worried about you is all."

I didn't answer Holbrook. I patted Jack on the neck a few times, and then Holbrook and I walked toward the house. I wanted to put it all behind me for a spell—the letter, Little Rock, and meeting Ole Charlie and Hemingway. I was still overwhelmed.

"Grab a chair, fellas. There're plenty of Thanksgiving leftovers," said Dad.

"Did you cook a turkey, Dad?" asked Dick.

"Mike came in from Lemoyne with his girlfriend, Son. He cooked the whole meal."

"Gourmet Mike cooked this?" I asked.

While he lived at home before going away to college, he was always putting his nose in the air about how our family ate like commoners and how he was above all that, proclaiming that he was a gourmet and that someday he'd be a world-famous doctor. Why, he even had a shoe box filled with little jars of spices and foods so bad that they didn't come in big jars. I'd seen a *National Geographic* in his room when he was in the eleventh grade, and I wouldn't have put it past him to eat ants, grasshoppers, frogs, or lizards, just like the people in the pictures in the magazine did. I convinced myself that my brother's gourmet habits were an addiction after I watched him order a raw egg in a malted milkshake one day at the malt shop in Manlius. As if all that weren't bad enough, Mike even cooked on a hot plate in his dorm room. The day I found out Gourmet Mike liked capers was the day I started including my older brother in my bedtime prayers. I had no idea what a caper was, but I just knew it couldn't be normal.

"Gourmet Mike cooked this stuff, Dad?" I asked again.

"Food, Jerry," said Mom. "Don't say 'stuff,' and don't call your brother 'Gourmet Mike.'"

"He did," said Dad. "Wouldn't let me do a thing all morning but read my paper."

My mind raced with the thoughts of frogs and capers and who knew what else they'd eat, those gourmet addicts.

Mom said grace, and Dick was the first to pick up a platter. He spooned some food off of it and passed it. Holbrook followed suit.

"How big was the baby again?" asked Dad.

"Eight pounds and four ounces," said Mom. "Momma and baby Terry are doing fine."

I looked across the table at Holbrook.

"Wait till you meet my uncle Don," I said. "He is so neat. He flew bombers in the war—big bombers."

Holbrook seemed preoccupied. "I know, you told me," he muttered. He looked at the morsel on his fork.

Now, Holbrook has always been an aficionado of Big Mike's spaghetti and sausage. He's often named my dad's Italian sausage as his favorite food of all time.

He lifted his fork, which had some bread stuffing on it, and looked over at Dad.

"Is this your sausage mixed in with the bread stuffing?"

I thought it strange, but after Holbrook said that, I could see Dad look the length of the table, peering at my mom for some help.

The woman was tired; she didn't pick up on his signals. Knowing he was on his own, Dad dealt with Holbrook's question.

"What do you mean?" asked Dad.

"These gray-black things in the bread stuffing—are they your sausage, the gray-black things?"

Dad looked at his watch.

"It's a gourmet stuffing," said Dad.

"Is it your Italian sausage or like a breakfast sausage?" asked Holbrook. "Just curious."

I wanted a little more detail about what Dad had meant by "gourmet" and decided to wait for answers. I set my fork down on my plate. I saw my dad hemming and hawing.

Dad offered him another cover-up.

"How about some gravy?" he asked.

Holbrook assumed Big Mike hadn't heard him.

"Is it your regular sausage in the bread stuffing?" Holbrook asked a bit louder.

"Will someone pass the sweet potatoes to Holbrook?" my dad asked, then completely changing the subject.

He looked around the table.

"There's plenty of butter, folks."

Holbrook was a relentless fan of Big Mike's sausage.

"Your sausage?" asked Holbrook.

I wasn't budging without answers. My food was growing cold.

Dad lowered his voice and mumbled "ahem."

"Escargot," he coughed.

"It's a what?" I asked.

Dad cleared his throat; he put his fist over his mouth.

"There's some celery in there too, and walnuts. Escargot," he coughed.

"Escargot?" asked Holbrook. "Did you say 'escargot'?"

"Yes."

"Is that anything like sausage?"

"It's more like a slug," said Dick.

"Dick!" Mom said, warning him with her eyes that it was time he keep his mouth shut. Brothers don't miss those looks.

Holbrook grinned with his eyes, knowing that Dick had to be kidding about the slug. He shoveled a forkful of the stuffing into his mouth, convinced it contained some kind of sausage, and started to reach for a roll.

"What is 'escargot,' anyway?" I asked.

"Snail," mumbled Dad.

With that, Holbrook froze, puckered his lips like he had sucked on a lemon, turned his eyes at Dad, leaned in, lifted his plate, and politely spit the mouthful onto its side rim.

"Dick, not one word!" Mom said.

"Escargot is a delicacy young Mike added to the stuffing," said Dad. "More cranberry, anybody?"

At that moment, if stuffing had been the only thing on the table and Holbrook and I hadn't eaten in four years, we would have sooner climbed the cliff to our camp for a lick of empty can lids of Spam than eaten a snail. Being as it was on our plates already, we chose to avoid the topic of it altogether so as not to draw attention to the fact that we were using our table knives to plow the stuffing to a corner of our plates. For the sake of sanitation, we wrapped our knives, which had touched the snail goop, in our napkins for possible burning or burial in the woods later.

I was hungry, but I wanted answers.

"In all the rest of this stuff—"

"Food, dear," said Mom. "Don't say 'stuff.'"

I kept my eye on Dad without so much as a blink.

"And don't lie to me."

"Don't be impudent, young man," said Mom.

"In all the rest of this stuff, are there any rutabagas?"

"Not one," said Dad.

"Are you just saying that?"

"No rutabagas, Son."

I trusted my dad—but I didn't trust Gourmet Mike.

"You promise?"

"I promise, Son."

From that point on, there wasn't a fork lifted by Holbrook or me that wasn't carefully examined and smell tested. It was a slow process getting to the pie after supper.

"I bet you boys will be happy to get back to school tomorrow," said Mom, changing the subject.

"The Christmas dance is coming up. Who you asking?" Holbrook asked.

I was inspecting every bite of food I lifted from my plate.

"I don't know. I'm thinking Donna Cerio if she hasn't been asked. Did you ask anybody?"

"Judy Finch," said Holbrook. "She said yes."

"She's a beauty too," said Dick.

"I think Randy or Mayor is going to ask Mary Margaret," I said.

"Ted Knapp asked Mary Crane already," said Holbrook.

Mom looked across the table at Dad.

A thought had come over her about teaching us that there's more to a person than just her beauty—that there are more meaningful values. But, of course, she wasn't a teen.

Dad had a notion of what she was thinking, but he quietly pointed at the stuffing on his plate as a hint to her that they'd already danced around an escargot debacle and that they might consider giving us a pass on the "pretty" issue this once.

Mom smirked and nodded her agreement.

"We're supposed to bring a tree ornament, even if we make it ourselves," said Holbrook.

"Where are they going to put the Christmas tree?" I asked.

"It'll be in the gym for the dance. Coach Driscoll cut one at his farm," said Holbrook. "Mary's on the decorating committee. She told me. That's when Ted Knapp asked her. He was helping Coach Driscoll and Mary bring the tree down off the hill."

"Well you can bet Minneapolis Moline Conway will be taking Judy Clancy," said Dick. "And Duba will probably ask Linda Sipfle. I'll ask somebody if anybody's left."

Dad and Mom were enjoying having the household back together at one table and listening to the chatter of their brood as Christmas neared. They both knew the culture shock Dick and I had experienced seeing the Jim Crow laws of parts of the South and decided then was not the time to bring it up. Things seemed to be getting back to the healthy, normal routine we'd become accustomed to living in front of the thundering waterfall. Fall and winters were quieter than springs and summers, as the doors remained closed, keeping out the cold and the noise.

The telephone rang, and I got up to go into Mom and Dad's bedroom to answer it.

"Hello?"

"Jerry?'

"Mary?"

"I was calling your dad to see when you guys would be getting home."

"We got here about two hours ago."

"Are you okay?"

"I'm okay. Just having supper."

"You didn't like Arkansas, huh?" said Mary.

"It was all right. Some of it was weird," I said. "I brought you a postcard, though."

"Can you and Holbrook get some guys to help us with the Christmas tree decorations?"

"Sure. When?"

"A night this week, after school. We want to get it up before the Christmas dance, and that's a week away," said Mary. "My dad will drive everybody home."

"You going with Ted Knapp?"

"Where did you hear that?"

"Are you?"

"Yes. He asked me."

As she was talking, I started to remember the full impact Little Rock had had on me.

Have you ever awakened from a dream and not been sure where you were or if you were in a nightmare or just a big adventure? Well that was how I felt at that moment, with Mary Crane on the other end of the telephone. There was far too much for me to think about before I could tell anyone about what had happened to me in Little Rock. I needed a chance to think it all through.

So I just blurted out the first thing that came to my mind.

"I got the address of that church you wanted for Aunt Lucy," I said. "We went there. They gave us a list of the kinds of things they need for their poor box. I'll give it to you tomorrow."

"What church?" asked Mary.

"On your postcard. You said to go to that church and to see what Aunt Lucy could send them for their poor box."

As soon as I mentioned Aunt Lucy, I slapped my head, remembering that Ole Charlie must have added all that to her postcard. I was stuck in a hard place, trying to think of how to get out of it without telling her about Ole Charlie.

"I lost the cipher wheel. Where did you buy that one you sent me?"

I couldn't very well tell anyone that I'd given mine to Ernest Hemingway. They would've locked me in a loony bin.

"We didn't buy it. Conway and Marty made them in woodshop."

"Can I get another one?"

"How did you lose yours?

"Uh…uh…I left it in a movie."

"You can have mine. I just used it to send you that postcard."

"Thanks."

"But my postcard never said what you said about Aunt Lucy."

I stalled to give myself time to think. I realized I had blabbed without thinking.

"Are you sure?"

"I'm so sure."

"Really?"

"Do you still have it? I mean the postcard. Look for yourself—it never said that."

"Hang on. I'll go look," I said.

I put the telephone receiver over my chest to muffle sound and stood there, stalling.

"I have it. You're right. It doesn't say that on it. My mistake."

I scratched my head.

"I'm such a numnuts," I mumbled to myself.

"Anyway, I got a list to give to Aunt Lucy."

"That'll be great," said Mary. "She wants to send things to the needy. She'll love it."

I scratched my head.

"It's like a miracle," said Mary. "I must have told you before you ever went down to Arkansas."

"Guess so," I said.

"Maybe we can get more kids to bring things that Aunt Lucy can send those folks," said Mary. "Anyway, see you in school."

"See ya."

Click.

I avoided having a heart attack after blabbing my big mouth and went back to the supper table, trying to figure out when, if ever, I'd be able to bring up Ole Charlie and the big mess in Little Rock.

I put the thought away when the lemon-meringue pie came out to distract me.

CHAPTER FIFTEEN

IT'S BEGINNING TO FEEL A LOT LIKE CHRISTMAS

By mid-December I had sent three postcards in code to Hemingway.

The first included a code name for me and read, "My code is 'bullfight.'" The coded message was "HMDGWVEDYRBIRVXPH."

The second was my telephone number: "New Woodstock 78." The coded message was "JSQCGAQYXVAPJR."

The third was the name of the village I lived in: "Delphi Falls, New York," or,

"QSBFUVAXBIYJSQKGJB."

They mostly were my way of saying "hello" and "how are you" and of letting him know that I was still waiting to find something out and that he shouldn't give up on me. The messages gave me practice with the code cipher wheel. Each day I would check the mailbox when I got off the school bus. I was hoping for some news from Arkansas—something from Ole Charlie or something from anybody, really.

No word yet.

I did get in trouble for saying that "science fiction is crap" at the supper table, and then I had to wash dishes for a week.

Mom asked me to explain myself and my bad language.

I was trying to announce that I wanted to be a writer like Hemingway or Mark Twain.

"If sentences are true, words are the passages to enlightenment of the soul," I said in my best Hemingway voice. "Science-fiction books are lies for people with no imaginations of their own. They're a bunch of crap from those who can't write."

"Where did you learn a word like enlightenment, Jerry?" asked Mom.

"I don't know. Mrs. Doxtator I think," I said.

I didn't want to tell her that Ernest Hemingway said it to me in his hotel room. She would have had me locked in a loony bin.

Dad put a dent in my thesis when he asked me to explain my favorite heroes, Superman and Captain America.

I was antsy, and it was making the few weeks before the Christmas school recess creep by. The Little Rock episode was fading in my memory. It was as if I was distancing myself from a bad dream.

The good news was that my uncle Don and aunt Mary had called to say they were on the road and would be driving into Delphi Falls any day.

Despite the heavy frost and snow flurries in the air, my friends and I were beginning to experience the fun of what being in high school with the older guys and gals was like, even if ninth graders were pretty low on the upper classmen's totem pole. Our first high school Christmas dance would come and go and would be a big success for us ninth graders in different ways and the source of many memories.

First, most of us brought something for Aunt Lucy to wrap and send to poorer families on her list. I had given up hope that she would get a note from the church in Little Rock with some important clues that I could send Hemingway.

Second, nearly everyone brought a Christmas ornament or decoration for the tree. Some had been bought at a discount at Mike Shea's store, and some, like holly sprigs tied with ribbons, had been made by hand. With decorating the gymnasium and the dance itself, everybody was getting into the Christmas spirit.

Third was simple—girls.

The night of the dance began with a freeze under a full moon as we crunched across the lawn and walked into the school.

We were greeted by Ted Knapp, Mary, Mayor, and Duba, who were standing on top of a table singing.

"Hark! The Herald Angels Sing," they chorused.

Dick was slapping strings on a washtub bass. Conway and Dwyer were shaking sleigh bells in rhythm.

Mrs. Cox had walked off and had given up on asking them to "get down from the table before someone falls and breaks a leg."

It was our first high school Christmas dance.

The gymnasium was decorated prettier than a Dey Brothers department-store holiday window up in Syracuse, with a model train puffing around all clickity-clackity. There was no square-dance calling like there usually was. After all, we were in ninth grade then, dressed to the nines like Andy Hardy and looking our Sunday best. It was Christmas, and that square-dance stuff was yesterday's mashed potatoes—well, at least it was for a high school Christmas dance. We still liked square dancing, mind you, but on this night, we were ready for more hugging with the fox-trots and less handshaking with all those "do-sa-dos" and "ala-man" lefts. This dance was all about radio-popular music like "How Much Is That Doggie in the Window?" or "That's Amore," which they played on a record machine Mary Crane had brought in. Her record machine had a close-down top and a carrying handle, if you can just imagine it. It was the latest thing in the early fifties. Its carrying case looked like a modern Smith-Corona portable typewriter.

At our first high school dance, the records were stacked up high on the record player, and we learned the term "record hop" for the first time.

And being as the dance was in the gymnasium, we all had to take our shoes off at the door and carry them so we wouldn't scuff the gym floor.

That's when we learned the new term "sock hop."

Oh my, but how I do remember the girls wearing their fanciest dresses, looking ever oh so nice, and we guys with our dad's ties and aftershave lotions, even if we still didn't shave. Some had on new sports coats, having grown out of their old Sunday ones or their hand-me-downs. We were grown-ups then (well, at least in our minds, we were), and it was long past the time when we used to sit around and wonder which girls wore brassieres. We didn't have to guess anymore. Now don't take that the wrong way—we meant no insensitivity, and we were always gentlemen. It was just that some teens thought fellows were adults when they had the start of a whisker stub or two and thought girls were adults when they wore brassieres. It was as simple and as innocent as that—nothing disrespectful was intended.

Ray Randall, our normal square-dance caller, had to dance to regular music for the first time. That made his girl from Homer happy, as she got to dance with him instead of just sitting there watching him sing, strum, and call squares. I danced the fox-trot, which my dad had taught me, as best I could. I'd sway back and forth like a tall sunflower stalk in a late summer breeze. Graceful as she was, Donna Cerio kept up, steering me around the floor when I went backward. She helped to make it look all that much easier. My mom had tried to teach me how to waltz, but I did the fox-trot to that too, I think.

Holbrook liked slow dancing with Judy Finch. He was particularly partial to it, avoiding jitterbugs at any cost. Jitterbugs weren't natural to him—and they might mess up his hair—so at the first strum or two on a new record he would know right off if it was fast or slow, and then he'd ask Judy if she'd like a cup of eggnog or punch and make his way off the floor during jitterbugs.

During a bathroom break, I found Holbrook, Mayor, and Randy and said, "Wow, wow, wee! This slow dancing is the best thing ever invented."

"You got that straight," said Mayor, pulling a paper towel from the dispenser. "I thought roller-skating was fun, but we can only hold their hands when we're roller-skating."

"Man, does Judy ever smell good," said Holbrook. "It must be some expensive French perfume she's using."

Holbrook took his comb out of his vest pocket, held it up to his head, decided his hair was perfect, and put it back in his pocket. That's when he went into song.

"I've got the world on a string, sittin' on a rainbow. Got the string around my finger."

"Did you ever believe in a million years that we'd be able to hold on to a girl for so long at one time?" I asked.

"And so close too," said Mayor.

"And get away with it. Almost like they like it," said Barber.

"I'll say," Randy said, grinning. "What are we doing in here, wasting time?"

"And they're holding on to us," said Holbrook. "Don't forget them apples."

"Never," said Mayor.

"Not in a million years. This is the best night of my whole life," I said. "Girl wise," I added.

"Did you guys see Teddy Knapp dancing with Mary?" asked Barber.

"He's a good dancer," said Mayor.

"Looking pretty chummy, those two," said Holbrook.

"What grade is he in?" asked Barber.

"I don't know, but he rides on our bus," said Holbrook. "He's our age."

"Get him in the club," said Barber.

"He's a really good basketball player," I said. "I scrimmage with him, Marty, Johnny Cook, and sometimes Gorman."

"They're gonna do a bunny hop next. Who's in for the bunny hop?" said Randy.

"Not me," Holbrook said, taking a last mirror peek at his hair.

Back in the gymnasium at the punch bowl, Judy Clancy ambled over to us.

"Hi, guys," she said.

"Hey, Judy. What's going on?" said Randy.

"You look nice," said Mayor.

"You're sweet. Thanks. I have an idea I'd like you boys to think about."

"Shoot," said Holbrook.

"You all did swell decorating the place," she said. "It's so festive and Christmasy."

"Mary was in charge," said Holbrook.

"She dreamed it all up," said Mayor.

"I just had an idea," said Judy. "It'd be a shame for this tall, beautiful tree and all the pretty Christmas decorations to sit alone here in the dark all through the two weeks of our Christmas vacation."

"I never thought beyond the dance," I said.

"You never thought beyond the girls," said Mayor.

"Well, that too," I said.

"Judy, what are you leading up to?" said Holbrook.

"What makes you think I'm leading up to something?" she asked.

"Look. I live with nearly a dozen girls. I know these things."

"Well, I was kind of thinking that the Delphi Falls Unity Church sure could use some decorating. This tree all decorated and lit up so pretty sure would make the midnight service on Christmas Eve special. Mary and I are singing with the choir."

Minneapolis Moline Conway walked up to us, looking for his best girl, Judy, with thoughts of dancing the bunny hop in his smile.

"How would we get a Christmas tree this tall and all decorated down to Delphi Falls without ruining it?" asked Barber.

"We'd stand it upright," Conway said.

"Huh?" said Barber.

"They don't call me Minneapolis Moline Conway for nothin'," he said. "We'll get it on my hay wagon standing up, and a bunch of you will get on with it and just hang on to it. I'll get her down there with the Minneapolis Moline. Don't worry about that."

"We can do that," Holbrook said, nodding his head.

Judy pinched Conway's cheek.

"Isn't he just adorable?" she said, grinning with squinty eyes.

"Just peachy," said Holbrook.

"Let's do it tonight," said Minneapolis Moline Conway. "I'll go get the tractor."

"Hold on! Just hold on!" said Holbrook. "I'm not ready to give up on a night of holding on to a girl and smelling her French perfume just yet. Who knows? Maybe even kissing might come up later, after the dance. Why would I ever leave her after the dance to move a pine tree down to Delphi Falls?"

"We can't do it until Monday, anyway," said Judy. "A bunch of us are going into Syracuse on Saturday, and we have choir practice most of Sunday."

Conway caught a glimpse of how a colorful Christmas light was making Judy's red lipstick sparkle just perfect. Those things tend to happen at the right time, and it brought him to his senses, in a manner of speaking.

"Holbrook does make a good point," he said, looking over at freckled-face, smiling Judy. "We'll do it Monday. School is out. We'll do it Monday morning."

"Monday—got it. Holbrook makes a real good point," I said, looking over at Donna Cerio, who was talking with Mary Margaret by the punch bowl.

That's about all it took for us growing boys to make a growing-boy decision. We were learning priorities and responsibilities. We voted to stay at the dance so we could hold on to girls on the dance floor, but we also voted to volunteer to help bring Conway's tractor over on Monday and to wake somebody up to unlock the school doors so we could get the tree and all the decorations.

"My dad can drive everybody after his milk-can run, and he even has a key to the school," said Randy. "He won't have to drive the school bus. No school."

"We'll decorate the Delphi Falls Unity Church all pretty-like," said Judy. "Maybe we can put the Christmas tree outside in front of the church."

Randy said his dad would get all the packages for the poor hauled over to Aunt Lucy's, too. She'd be home the next day, Saturday.

When all that was settled, we heard another record dropping on the record player and resumed holding girls, being held, and dancing. We were all prim and proper about our dance-floor etiquette, and dancing is all we did. But it did require holding, and we were getting good with that.

Uncle Don and Aunt Mary would be driving in as early as Monday, and I was excited, knowing I would be able to show off a real bomber pilot and my hero.

But at the moment, all I could hope for were a big, bright silver-dollar moon and a long good-night kiss that would start the Christmas season—and my first high school Christmas—off proper.

CHAPTER SIXTEEN

AUNT MARY'S EARLY CHRISTMAS PRESENT

By Monday morning winter had set in. Ten or more of us were standing about and rubbing the sleep from our eyes in the darkened gymnasium around the Christmas tree; some were yawning, a few were scratching their heads, and three had flashlights. Most were shivering from the winter's first deep-freeze cold.

"Oh, what a night," I said, looking at the dance decorations and thinking of the dance.

"I can still smell the perfume," said Holbrook.

"Whose idea was it to get such a tall tree, anyway?" said Mayor.

"I don't know," said Mary. "I just saw it and pointed at it up on Driscoll's hill."

"You sure you weren't pointing at Ted Knapp, and the tree got in the way?" said Mayor.

"Shut up!" said Mary.

"Jimmy, sweetie pie?" said Judy Clancy. "How are we ever going to move it in one piece?"

"Let me think," said Minneapolis Moline Conway.

"Well, while *sweetie pie* thinks about it, we'll have to lay it down just to get it through the doors," Holbrook said.

"We lay it down, and all the ornaments will fall off or break," said Mary.

"I'm thinking," said Conway.

As usual, Marty offered the brains behind a strategy. He walked to the tree and turned about facing everyone.

"We'll wrap her in burlap. Wrap her tight enough to hold the decorations and ornaments. Oh, they may come loose, but they won't break, and we won't lose them. We'll lay her down on the floor, heft her up, carry her out, set her on Conway's hay wagon, and haul her to Delphi Falls."

"That'll work," said Conway.

"Where can we get enough burlap?" Randy asked. "It's a big tree."

"It's too big to move," said Barber. "Wouldn't it be easier just to cut one in Delphi Falls and decorate it there?"

No one listened to Barber.

"If you want something big, you have to go to the biggest place," said Mr. Vaas. "The Knapp place is the biggest farm in the Crown. Our best chance for getting a lot of burlap is there."

"Can somebody drive me over...to the Knapps'? I'll ask them for some burlap bags for us to use," Mary said.

"You mean you'll be asking Teddy, don't ya?" said Mayor.

"Oh, grow up," Mary said. "He's out spreading this morning. He won't even be at the house."

That was when we knew why Teddy Knapp wasn't in the gym with Mary that morning. None of us had wanted to embarrass her by asking why he hadn't shown up, especially after the dance Friday night.

It was a little more than a half hour later when Mr. Vaas and Mary returned with the truck bed filled with enough empty feed sacks to wrap the tree. Mary was holding a pair of sheers to cut the stitching. They also had a roll of baling twine, which was more than enough to tie and bind everything.

It was early afternoon by the time the Christmas-tree cara-
van of Mr. Vaas's truck loaded with kids and Minneapolis Moline
Conway's tractor and hay wagon carrying the tree and some of the
gang was finally underway, heading toward Delphi Falls.

The first delay was minor. The wind caught Barber's hat just
right, and it flew off his head. The problem was that it wasn't
Barber's hat—it was his dad's favorite John Deere hat, and they
had to stop to retrieve it. Barber had taken it without asking and
didn't want to have to explain how he'd lost it—or worse, to have
to lie about grabbing it in the dark, thinking it was his. The only
other delay was when Holbrook was turning pale in the face and
had to pee. Minneapolis Moline Conway stopped the tractor and
told him to go behind the big maple on the side of the road.
Holbrook considered himself a gentleman but announced anyway,
to the entire crowd, that he couldn't pee in public. Judy Clancy
reminded him that it wouldn't have been a public matter had he
not announced it to the world. The girls separated from the boys
and moved into Mr. Vaas's truck, and they went on ahead. Conway
simply gave Holbrook the option of either taking care of his business behind the maple tree or being left to walk.

That worked.

The tall, robust Christmas tree survived the journey and was
soon standing graciously in front of the village church in Delphi
Falls. It had been carefully unwrapped and then had two ladders
standing on either side of it. Barber was balancing on one and
Randy was on the other. They were straightening the ornaments
and adjusting the lights, their hands numb and steam snorting
from their nostrils.

"Is this thing going to explode, it being outdoors like this, if we
plug her in?" asked Mayor.

"If the freeze stays, and it should, we'll be good," Marty said.
"But maybe if it warms up and rains, wet connecter plugs sure
might blow some fuses."

"This cold is here to stay, least till April," said Minneapolis Moline Conway.

While Judy Clancy and Mary were untangling a long extension cord the Barbers had loaned the church, the green four-door 1949 Oldsmobile pulled to a stop in front of the church and let out three quick, sharp honks of the horn.

"They're here!" I shouted. "It's my uncle Don and aunt Mary. They're here, everybody!"

I ran out to the curb. Aunt Mary was in the backseat with the baby in the portable crib. The next youngest was back there with her. Tommy and Timmy were in the front seat with Uncle Don. Travel weary as they all were, they managed grins and waves. The sight of the Christmas tree in front of the church brought them closer to Santa's visit.

Uncle Don left the engine running to keep the heater on but stepped out of the car.

"Hi, Uncle Don!" I said.

Uncle Don extended his hand to shake mine.

"Good to see you, Jerry," he said. "Merry Christmas, everybody."

I pointed and made the introductions. Each in turn waved a greeting.

"That's Barber on that ladder, and Randy is on the other. Mr. Vaas is inside checking the fuse box. This is Holbrook, Mayor, Bases, and Minneapolis Moline Conway. Over there are Mary Crane and Judy Clancy. There's more around here somewhere."

"Hello, everyone. We were about to drive by but saw you here and wanted to stop to say hi before we head down to the falls.

"I'll be home soon," I said.

"Jerry, your aunt Mary has something to tell you," said Uncle Don.

"Huh?" I said.

"She was going to wait until she saw you at home, but now is as good a time as any."

Don opened the driver's side door and asked me to get in. He closed the door behind me, turned, and made small talk with my friends.

When I got out of the car, I was beaming.

"Uncle Don, did you know what she wanted? Were you in on it?"

"I confess. Yes. We both know how disappointed you were with how busy I was when you came down to Little Rock. We agreed on this."

"What's going on?" asked Holbrook.

"My aunt Mary just gave me my Christmas present."

"Where is it?" asked Holbrook.

"Her present to me is twenty-four hours with Uncle Don here."

"You mean like he's your servant?" Mayor asked.

"This is my uncle Don. He flew a B-17 in the war. It's more like we can get him to tell us about what it was like flying B-17s and bombing Hitler and all that stuff," I said.

"That's a neat present," said Holbrook.

"Wow. When?" said Mayor. "Can we be there too?"

"Everybody can be there," I said.

"When?" Randy asked.

"Where?" Barber asked.

"She said twenty-four hours. I guess…well…Uncle Don, when can we do it?"

"It's your twenty-four hours, Jerry. Any time you say."

I looked at my friends and raised my voice.

"Who here wants to hear Uncle Don's B-17 war stories?"

Every hand went up.

"Where can we do it?" I asked. "Anybody got any ideas?"

"How about in the church?" Judy Clancy said.

"Our pond froze up," said Minneapolis Moline Conway. "We'll build a bonfire and hear stories and skate."

"You don't even have a pond," said Mary.

"It's the flat at the bottom edge of the cornfield. Rain soaks it every fall. The freeze makes it a good skating rink."

"What's the plan?" asked Uncle Don.

"Everybody, how about we get our skates and meet up at Conway's in two hours?" I said.

"I'll give rides to anybody who needs them," said Mr. Vaas.

"I can take a load of you in my car," said Uncle Don.

"Maybe after all that, they can come to our house and have hot chocolate to thaw out," I said.

Hearing me, Aunt Mary rolled down her back window just enough to speak out of it.

"We'll maybe even be able to get Big Mike to make some spaghetti for later. All your friends are invited."

I couldn't help but think that this was going to be my best Christmas ever.

Holbrook could imagine smelling the Italian sausage already.

"So what are the rules, Uncle Don?" I asked. "Can we ask you anything about the war, even if it's about a secret?" I asked.

"You can ask me anything, and if it's secret and I can't tell you, I'll let you know."

"Sounds very fair," said Mayor.

"There're two conditions," said Uncle Don.

"Conditions?" I said.

"First, for every story I tell you about my war experiences, one of you has to tell me a story of your own about the war—about something you remember."

"We can do that," said Randy. "What's the second?"

"If I don't want to talk about something, I just won't talk about it."

Wasn't a person standing there who didn't understand that. There were parts of that war we remembered and wanted to forget.

"Girls?" shouted Aunt Mary from the car's rear window.

Judy Clancy and Mary Crane stopped what they were doing with the extension cord and turned toward her.

"Try using wax wrapping paper, and tie it with string around all the electrical sockets. You'll have a better chance of their not shorting out."

"Gee, thanks," said Mary Crane.

Judy Clancy smiled and waved.

The time had been established, and the terms had been set.

Uncle Don and Aunt Mary drove off down to the falls while we finished decorating the tree.

I couldn't have asked for a better Christmas present. My hero, Uncle Don, a B-17 captain and pilot, for a full twenty-four hours starting that night.

"Wow" was all I could think.

CHAPTER SEVENTEEN

SKATING AND MEMORIES

We could catch a glow of Conway's bonfire over the horizon while driving up Cook's hill, and as we came over the top of it, we saw bursts of sparks billowing like butterflies up toward a wintery full moon. Instead of going the usual route down to the Reynolds's place and right, up the hill, to Conway's, I purposely had Uncle Don drive Holbrook, Mayor, Barber, and me the longer way around through town so I could show off Delphi Falls and point to where some of my friends lived. I also wanted to see if somebody had plugged in the Christmas tree at the church. No one had yet.

Conway and Judy Clancy had made the first true freezing winter night festive on short notice. Down past the milk barn on the flat of the cornfield, he and Dwyer had arranged unsplit fire logs on their ends side by side around the bonfire for sitting. They'd also laid long timber logs end to end so people could sit on them and lace up their skates. On an empty nail-keg barrel turned upside down, there was a large brown paper sack filled with marshmallows. Eight long roasting sticks, their ends whittled to a point, were leaning on the barrel like fishing poles for the taking.

There were maybe twenty-five kids milling about, laughing, joking, and talking about Friday night's dance. Everybody was having fun finding a place to sit or stand, warming their hands by the fire, or preparing to skate.

Uncle Don seemed to be enjoying being a Christmas present. He didn't usually like talking about the war, but he knew what a hero he was to me. He found a comfortable spot and stood near the log he would be sitting on. He looked up at the stars with a smile, watching the sparks take flight.

He looked over at me and offered me a friendly salute.

"At your service," he mouthed.

I looked over at Conway.

"Jimmy, does everyone know why we're doing this?" I asked.

"They all know," said Conway.

"Who wants to go first?" said Uncle Don.

I stood up and got people's attention.

"Everybody, this is my uncle Don. Uncle Don and his crew flew thirty-three missions with his B-17. We're so lucky he came back from the war safe in nineteen forty-five."

"He helped make it safe for us, you mean," said Mr. Vaas.

People around the bonfire smiled a genuine welcome to Uncle Don.

"Does everybody know the rules?" I said.

"Tell us," said Barber.

"We tell a war story for every story Uncle Don tells, or for every question he answers."

"I'll start," said Conway. "I remember in the early forties, maybe 1943, some soldier in his uniform came to school and told us how the army needed to make a lot of parachutes and life preservers so we could attack Hitler and keep our seamen safe. He told us they were starting a drive for the floss—you know, the pods from milkweed plants. Milkweed grows wild all around here. They paid ten cents for a big bag of milkweed floss pods that they could make into parachutes and life preservers. I collected a lot of sacks. Lots of kids did. My mom dropped 'em off in Apulia Station. "

"So did I," said Dwyer.

Jerry looked at Uncle Don.

"Your turn."

Uncle Don pointed the stick he had been roasting a marshmallow on over at Judy Clancy, offering her the charred, sweet delight so he could talk.

"I was a latecomer in the war. I was eighteen in forty-four when I got my draft notice. I joined the army air corps. After basic training and B-17 flight school, I was assigned to a B-17 and a crew, and we flew from our training base in South Dakota first to Long Island and then across the Atlantic to the base in England where we were stationed."

"Did you ever fly over the Crown in your bomber?" asked Mayor.

"As a matter of fact," said Uncle Don, "we did fly over Rochester so I could tip my wings for my mom and dad, and I remember we were ordered to fly below Syracuse and to follow Route twenty over to Schenectady and down the Hudson to Long Island. There were a lot of us in the air, so when we were spread out, some of us very well could have flown over here."

Mayor stood up.

"I remember hearing the rumbling of the bombers and being so scared that my brother and I would run and hide under the corn crib. I always cried until they passed over."

Bases stood up.

"I remember that. I would get down flat on the ground and not move in case they were Hitler's planes attacking like we saw them at the Saturday-morning picture show."

"I was in Cortland," I said. "That was before we moved here. I remember standing out in the backyard and crying and shaking in fear as the sky suddenly darkened with low-flying bombers. I had nightmares for a long time. I can still remember the ground rumbling with the noise."

"How many planes would fly together?" Mary Crane asked.

"Hundreds, usually," said Uncle Don. "I wasn't there on D-day, but they said there were ten thousand planes in the air on that day alone over the channel and Europe. My crew has taken off with as many as three thousand planes, bombers, and fighters."

"Why did you guys fly so low when you were going to Long Island?" asked Holbrook.

"Our movements were secret," said Uncle Don. "We flew low so we couldn't be counted easily. It's called 'bush hopping,' or 'flying under the radar.' Flying high could have given enemy spies time to count our forces."

"Amazing," said Mary Crane.

"How many bombing missions did you fly?" Duba asked.

"Thirty-three."

"That's what I thought Jerry said. I heard bomber crews could only fly twenty-five," said Duba.

"You could go home or ask for reassignment after twenty-five missions. My crew and I volunteered to stay on. We flew thirty-three missions."

"Did you ever bomb Berlin?" asked Holbrook.

"Our bombing missions were called 'precision bombing.' The first time we bombed Berlin, our lead plane got shot down. I became lead bomber during that mission."

"Did they all die?"

"Yes. Either in the crash or on the ground, shot by Germans."

"Could you see them when they went down?"

"We took pictures of the ship on fire for headquarters. Our mission took off at dawn so it was more dangerous. We were more visible to the enemy on the ground and in the air. It was a daylight hit by flak from ground cannons. I brought a scrapbook of pictures we took from our ship during missions. You can come by the house and take a look. I have the mission maps too. You might like to see those."

"Ship?" said Mary Crane. "You said you were on a ship."

"When they first dreamed up dropping bombs from airplanes back in the First World War, they started calling them 'airships.' I don't know. We called *Lady Helene* 'our ship'—most every pilot and crew called them that."

Randy raised his hand and stood up.

"I remember during the war, they had food and rubber shortages. My dad had to go to work at Carrier—they were making plane parts or something. The car tire treads on his thirty-seven Chrysler were gone, so he cut an old tire into tapered strips and stuffed them inside the tires and put the tube in. That let him get to work and back without blowing them out."

Randy looked over at his pop, who was sitting at the other end of the bonfire. He was wiping his eyes.

"Remember, Dad?"

Mr. Vaas nodded his head.

"They weren't happy times," said Uncle Don.

"They sure weren't," said Mr. Vaas. "But thanks to you boys and the women over there and in the Pacific, we got by. Randy there had to learn how to butcher a chicken and skin a rabbit at about four years of age. I still can't get that from my craw…having to teach him that. And then there were the women away at Red Cross working and volunteering and all."

He sat down and pursed his lips, remembering the nightmare of the war.

"I had to stay at my grandmother's during the war," said Mary Crane. "I remember when Daddy came home in uniform after it was over, I screamed and crawled under the bed sobbing, frightened because I didn't know who he was."

"My crew took pictures of the targets we bombed from the open bomb-bay doors in the belly of the plane," said Uncle Don.

"We took more when the bombs hit the target. That made it easier for headquarters to plan future missions."

Teddy Knapp stood up.

"Jamesville Penitentiary was one place where they held prisoners of war. Most of the farmhands had been drafted and were overseas, so they would bring POWs to various farms every day to help with the corn and the farm chores. My mother and grandmother fed them. One of them took a liking to me because I reminded him of his son who was my age and was back in Germany."

The formality of the back-and-forth storytelling soon broke into open conversations, marshmallow roasting, and ice-skating. When Uncle Don was telling Holbrook and me about the number of guns on a B-17, a car's headlights first flashed in the distance as it pulled into the Conway's barn driveway and came to a stop. Someone opened and got out of the passenger door and started walking quickly around the gate and down the fence line to where we were. I soon recognized her as one of the Gaines girls. It was Alda. She walked right over to Mary Crane, leaned down, and, cupping her hands, whispered into Mary's ear.

"She's there now?" Mary ask. "Doesn't she work in Syracuse today?"

"She's at our house," said Alda.

"Are you sure she wants me?"

"Honest. She's there now."

With that, Mary stood up.

"I've got to go," she said. "Jerry, maybe you should come too."

"What's up?" I asked.

Mary looked at Alda.

"Can we ride with you?"

"Sure," said Alda.

"What's going on?" I said.

"Are you coming or not?" said Mary.

"If Jerry's going, I'm going," said Holbrook.

"Us too," said Barber, Mayor, Randy, and Bases, all in unison.

Uncle Don could sense our urgency.

"I'll drive, fellas," he said. "Climb into the Olds."

Uncle Don waited for everyone to pile in and to pull the doors closed. By the time he backed out, Mr. Gaines was already driving Mary, Holbrook, Alda, and me back to his farm. Mr. Gaines stood waiting by his car for Uncle Don to pull in beside him and park. He extended his hand and introduced himself, and they shook hands.

"Welcome to our home," Mr. Gaines said.

"Merry Christmas," said Uncle Don. "It looks like a fine barn you have, Mr. Gaines. Cows and chickens?"

"A little bit of everything," said Mr. Gaines. "Call me Allen, son. I go best by Allen. Won't you come in and join the crowd?"

"Call me Don," said Uncle Don.

Inside the house the room was quiet. With the exception of the one light bulb hanging on the wire over the table, it was a kitchen of shadows. The waiting was suspenseful. Mrs. Gaines was standing in front of the sink beside a nervous Aunt Lucy. Mary Crane stepped in next to Aunt Lucy and held her hand.

"I thought you worked in the city on Mondays. Are you okay?" Mary asked.

Alda and Jackie were standing over where Barber, Holbrook, Randy, Bases, and I had gathered.

"They gave me off today. I'll go back in early tomorrow," said Aunt Lucy.

"Alda said you might be in trouble, Aunt Lucy," said Mary. "These are my friends. We all want to help."

Aunt Lucy put a palm over her mouth, sighed, and thanked us with her eyes for coming, tipping her head sideways.

"You're all so sweet for being here, Mary. Everybody, thank you."

"What kind of trouble?" Mary asked.

"Not me," said Aunt Lucy. "It's a girl in another state."

That jogged Uncle Don's memory, and he clearly remembered Aunt Lucy's name from his and my visit to the church in southern Little Rock. He looked over at me and mouthed "Aunt Lucy?" to see if I could remember hearing it.

I nodded yes.

"Listen to this letter," she said.

Aunt Lucy reached into her handbag and took several pages from an envelope in it. She stepped over to the kitchen table, held the pages under the hanging lamp bulb, and began reading the letter addressed to her.

Dear Sister Lucy,

We can't thank you enough for the carton boxes of joy your generous and warm-hearted friends have sent to us to share in our community among the less fortunate. Our souls are in God's hands, but many Christmases will be a little brighter because of your making these gifts. The purpose of this letter to you, my friend, isn't pleasant. One of our young parishioners is in dire trouble and in need of all the prayers we can send our Lord on her behalf. This Christmas will find this young lady about to give birth. I won't be mincing words, Lucy. She's a sister and sixteen, and the baby daddy is a white boy, and his father is an important man with the governor's office. He just sent a frightening message that they're taking this desperate little girl to Forrest City Hospital over near Memphis on Thursday the twenty-fourth. He's a very bad man, Sister Lucy. He's the muscle for the spineless governor who's keeping our children from getting new schoolbooks and from going to public schools. Early this week he had his own flesh-and-blood son, the baby daddy, leave two twenty-dollar bills with her to pay for a taxi to Forrest City. He told her that the state-highway patrol would know if she didn't go and that they would be following her all the way to keep her from trying any foolishness. The devil-man didn't say it, but we for sure are thinking that this baby won't survive this birthing. Lucy, we need your prayers. I don't have a telephone to call you, and I'm afraid to borrow one in case they listen. I don't want to bring trouble on anyone.

Signed,

Sarah Wilkins

"The twenty-fourth," I said. "That's Christmas Eve."

"Do you happen to know the young girl's name?" Uncle Don asked Aunt Lucy.

"I'm guessing it's Anna Kristina," she said. "That was one of the names on the list of people their church needed maternity and baby things for. Sarah wouldn't put her name in a letter like this in case—"

"I understand that," said Uncle Don.

"It only gives us four days," Uncle Don said, looking over at me.

"Are you going to help, Uncle Don?" I asked.

He nodded to indicate "maybe."

"Okay. I've got to do something right now," I said. "Nobody ask me any questions. Everybody has to stay quiet while I do it, and I'll tell you about it after. Okay?"

No one said a word. They watched Uncle Don nodding his approval of my taking the lead.

"Mr. Gaines, may I use your telephone, please?" I asked.

"Of course, son. Help yourself."

He pointed to the wall phone by the icebox.

I stepped over to the phone, reached up, and turned the crank twice.

"Operator, how can I help you?"

"Myrtie, this is Jerry."

"Why, hello, stranger. I haven't heard your voice in quite a while. How were your travels on Thanksgiving?"

"Myrtie, as much as I'd like to, I can't talk right now. There's an emergency, and I need some help."

If there were one person in the entire Crown who had her finger on the pulse of everything, knew most of the secrets, and could be relied on to help, it was Myrtie, our party-line telephone operator. Whether a home had a newer pick-up-to-connect phone or an original wall-hanging-crank-phone, Myrtie always answered either way. She and the party line had helped us solve many mysteries in the past.

"Anything, dear. Tell me."

"Myrtie, I need to make an emergency telephone call, but can you charge it to my dad?"

"Well, I don't know, Jerry. Will Big Mike go for—"

"Just make the call, son. I'll pay for it," Mr. Gaines said, interrupting.

I looked over at him and shook my head no. It wasn't necessary.

"Just do it, Myrtie. Please, it's an emergency."

There was a short pause on the line.

"Okay. Whatcha need?"

"I need you to get the Capital Hotel."

"Capital Hotel?" asked Myrtie.

"That's right, the Capital Hotel. It's in Little Rock, Arkansas. If you get them on the wire, ask for room number three hundred five."

"My goodness," said Myrtie. "Are you sure?"

"Myrtie, please?"

Myrtie went quiet, but I could hear her clicking things, humming to herself, and patching things.

I glanced over at Holbrook. He knew I was comfortable calling a hotel after working at the Hotel Syracuse all summer. This whole year had been a learning experience for us both.

We'd come a long way since Holbrook and I tried smoking the Meerschaum corncob pipes we'd talked Hastings out of in the cave late spring.

Long-distance telephone calls were expensive and rare in the early 1950s. Everyone standing around the kitchen was spellbound by the idea of one of their own even knowing how to make a long-distance telephone call, but they were also totally in the dark as to whom I was calling and why.

I heard a crackle in the earpiece and Myrtie's voice.

"Is this the Capital Hotel?" she said.

"Yes, ma'am, how may we be of service to you?"

"Long distance for room three hundred five, please?"

"Room three hundred five has left instructions that they are not to be disturbed."

"This is an emergency call."

"I'm sorry, Operator. Our guest is not to be disturbed."

"Myrtie…Myrtie," I stammered into the phone. "Tell them to ring room three hundred five and just say it's 'Bullfight' calling.

"Bullfight?" asked Myrtie.

"Bullfight!" I confirmed.

"Did you hear that, lady? Bullfight?" said Myrtie.

"I just don't know," said the hotel lady.

I was beside myself. I leaned into the mouthpiece and yelled, "Lady, he's going to be really mad if you don't!"

There were some delays, and finally Hemingway's voice came on the telephone.

"Jerry, is that you?"

"Yes, sir."

I said "sir" and not "Ernest" or "Papa" to avoid giving his identity away.

"It's hard to talk now, but I kinda found out what's going on down there."

"Speak slowly. Be deliberate, friend. Tell me."

"The man working with the governor's office, you know, he's the father of the guy who did you know what, sent her two twenty-dollar bills and told her she had to ride a taxicab on Thursday to a place called—"

I looked back over at Aunt Lucy for the name of the hospital.

"Forrest City Hospital," she whispered.

"Forrest City Hospital. It's near Memphis, I think."

"That vermin."

"I still don't know his name yet, the guy with the governor. All I know is he told her that the state-highway patrol will be following her so she doesn't try any funny business."

"Thursday?"

"Yes."

"That's Christmas Eve."

"I know."

"How appropriate…duplicitous cunning while the world is distracted by fantasy."

"I don't know what that means, but it doesn't matter. Are they going to kill her? Kill her baby?"

Faces in that kitchen grew tense just hearing the stark reality of the words, listening to me have to use them, and watching my face as I listened intently through the earpiece.

"This bastard is with the governor's office," said Hemingway, "and I don't think slime like him would risk a political career over a murder that could be found out. It's more likely that they'll sedate her and that the baby will be taken from the girl and given away, never to be seen in Little Rock, or in the state, ever again. They'll tell her it died during the birth."

"What can we do up here?" I asked. "Anything?"

"Where are you, Jerry?"

"I'm in Delphi Falls. My uncle Don is here visiting. He lives in Little Rock."

"This Uncle Don from Little Rock, does he know what's going on?"

"Kind of but not really," I said. "He's been telling us stories of his B-17 in the war."

"Oh? Where was he stationed?"

"In England someplace. He flew thirty-three missions. He even bombed Berlin."

"Thirty-three? Did you say thirty-three missions, Jerry?"

"Yes."

"What rank was he?"

"Uncle Don? Captain...He's a pilot."

"Jerry, this could be a very good piece of information. Listen to me carefully. I will wait for instructions. I want you to turn the entire matter over to your uncle, the captain. Let him come up with the strategy and a tactic for a plan. I'm here to serve in any capacity. Do we have an understanding?"

"Yes, sir."

"Are you certain you understand me?"

"I'm sure."

"Call me with a plan when you need me to do something."

"Okay."

"Make sure you tell the captain everything you know. He'll need good information to work from."

"Can I tell him your name?"

There was a pause.

"Let's not, son. There may be a time, but this isn't it. We need a hero right now, not a circus."

With that, Hemingway hung up the phone without saying good-bye, as did I.

I turned toward Uncle Don.

"Okay, here's the deal. Uncle Don, we're the Pompey Hollow Book Club. Mary over there is our president, but tonight we have to make you the boss. We have to help this girl in Little Rock and her baby, and you're a captain, so that's all there is to it. Will you help us?"

"Jerry, we need to talk."

"Will you help us?" I said.

"I don't know if—"

Mary Crane stepped up face to face with Uncle Don.

"Look, Uncle Don," she said. "We may be kids to some people, but we've caught burglars who've robbed twenty businesses. This year we caught Nazi POWs who escaped from Pine Camp. We caught a state-fair pickpocket ring from England. We did those things and even ran a farm for Farmer Parker because he hurt his back. We learned to do all this from the examples set by heroes like you who sacrificed your lives for our freedom."

"That's admirable," said Uncle Don. "I'm very proud of you... but I have responsibilities, a job, and children."

Mary leaned into Uncle Don's face.

"Uncle Don, in all of the times we've tried to do good, in all of the times we've caught or trapped bad people, never once was a person's life at stake. Never once. But now one is. It sounds like it could be two lives at stake. We need you to help us. Help Aunt Lucy—and that girl in Little Rock. I'm begging you. Are you going to help or not?"

Uncle Don stared into Mary's eyes as she made our case and her plea. He broke his stare and looked over at me and then into the eyes of about everyone in the kitchen. I can only assume now that his mind back then was thinking of the bigger picture—the inhumanity of it all. He looked over at me again as if he understood the discomfort I'd felt in Little Rock, seeing the ambivalence to Jim Crow at its worst.

"I need to talk with Jerry alone for a minute," Uncle Don said.

With that, he took me by the arm, led me out the side door into the cold, and closed the door behind us.

"You lied to me! I want to know why. Make it good," he snapped.

I was crushed. Uncle Don was my hero. His thinking I would ever betray him wrenched my gut.

"Huh?"

"You lied to me."

"I promise I didn't lie. Uncle Don, I would never lie to you."

"So you just had to stop at that hotel to pick up some postcards, right?"

His eyes locked on mine with a "gotcha," and he searched for the truth.

"Oh, that," I said.

"No time for games, Jerry. Who did you call in Little Rock?"

"I can't say. I mean, I promised."

"I can't help. There can't be secrets with something this important."

My head was spinning. I didn't want to lose my hero's confidence in me, and I didn't want to break my confidence with Hemingway. Looking through the side-door window, I could see a bible resting on a side table.

"Uncle Don, do you believe in God?"

I knew he did, but I had to make a point.

Uncle Don started and then straightened his back.

"Well of course."

"Do you believe in guardian angels? Do you believe in real guardian angels?"

Uncle Don relaxed his posture and smiled. He pursed his lips, nodding his head as he smiled. He went into a trance as he looked at the door to the outdoor privy.

"We had German fighter planes attacking us from every direction. The Nazis even had special training on how to attack the B-17 with all our guns and shoot us down. There was always flak exploding all around us. We were even in the real danger of bumping into one another—there were that many planes in the air. Missions were a few hours of hell in and a few hours of hell back to the base. Jerry, you bet I believe in guardian angels. Wasn't one of my thirty-three missions when I didn't speak with my guardian angels all the way out and all the way home. They kept me alert and awake and my crew alive. Of course I believe in guardian angels."

"Well you're just going to have to trust me now," I said. "Will you help? If you do, I have somebody in Little Rock who will help you and will do anything you tell him to do, but I can't tell you his name. At least right now I can't."

Uncle Don trusted me. I could tell he didn't give it another thought. He backed up the step and into the kitchen, tweaked his chin, and circled the table twice. He paused. He looked down at the seated Mr. Gaines.

"What do you think, Allen?" he asked Mr. Gaines.

"The girl is in all kinds of worry. She surely is, my friend."

"Pretty helpless, too, it looks," said Uncle Don. "Alone."

"Birthing with a man around is hard enough, but alone at her age? Oh my Lordy, the fear and desperation that must be in that chile's heart."

"Shall we?" Uncle Don asked, raising his brows in anticipation of a response.

"I'm too old to say no. It's the least we can do," said Mr. Gaines. "'Sides…we haven't had this much excitement in this kitchen in nigh on—well, for years now."

With that, Uncle Don spun about and barked at us.

"Clear the room!"

"Huh?" said Mary.

"Everybody leaves!" said Uncle Don.

"Can't we be here?" I asked. "It's not fair."

"You put me in charge. Now I'm setting the rules. You will all have to leave. Jerry, walk your friends over to the house, and get some hot chocolate—maybe some spaghetti. Mr. Gaines, the ladies, and I have some thinking to do. We're going to come up with a plan—a strategy."

"For real?" I asked.

"For real," said Uncle Don. "We'll let you all in on it just as soon as we know what it is."

Mae spoke up.

"Alda, Jackie, put your coats on, and go with your friends. We'll come fetch you when the men are ready."

Alda looked at Mary and then over at me.

"Can we?" she asked.

"Sure you can. You two are in the club same as anybody else who wants to join," said Mary. "Come on."

"Walk straight home," said Uncle Don. "You should be there in ten, maybe fifteen minutes. Don't lallygag in case we call and need you."

"After you get a plan, we can help?" I asked.

"Yes," said Uncle Don.

"Are you mad at me?" I whispered to Uncle Don.

"I could never be upset with someone for keeping his word," said Uncle Don.

I remember grinning nervously.

"By the way, Jerry. Do you remember that Aaron fellow we went to see on Thanksgiving—the girl's brother?"

"Sure I do."

"I got him a job with my crop-duster friend, Hal Hoffman, in Carlisle."

"What doing? Fixing planes?"

"He's flying a crop duster. He dusts the rice fields."

"I thought he had a taxi."

"He does both. Now he has a smile on his face."

"Does he know about the trouble his sister is in?"

"I don't know, but he's about to. Take off with your friends, and let Allen and me plan. Tell your aunt Mary I'll be late."

"I have you for twenty-four hours," I said. "Does this count?"

Don smiled and held the door open for us to leave.

With that, Mary Crane; Holbrook; Randy; Bases; Mayor; the two Gaines girls, Alda and Jackie; and I all pulled our coats on, stepped from the house, and started walking the half mile to the falls. Last thing we heard before the door closed behind us was Allen's voice.

"Mae, Aunt Lucy, how about let's have some food on the table? Our guest can't be thinking proper on an empty stomach. Let's eat first and socialize, and we'll come up with somethin' to get this young girl out of her mess over a good hot pot of chicory coffee and cinnamon."

CHAPTER EIGHTEEN

HEAVENLY INTERMISSION

As we stepped on the road and started walking the hill from the Gaineses' place down to Maxwell's corner, Holbrook was the first to ask me the big question. At the time I was thinking how the kitchen meeting we'd just had had made me feel older somehow and more grown-up.

"Who did you call in there, Jerry?" he asked. "Who was that you were talking to?"

"A man I met in Little Rock. No big deal. He's a good guy and said he'd help us if we need him to. He told me he didn't like what was going on down there either."

"So how did you get in the middle of all this mess, anyway?" Mayor asked.

I realized Jackie and Alda were walking with us, and I didn't want to make them uncomfortable, so I tried to dodge the question of what I'd seen in Arkansas.

"It's a long story," I said. "Not now, though. I already told you all what it was like down there in my letter. I wasn't kidding."

Barber looked over at Alda and Jackie, who were walking beside Mary.

"You two are so lucky you're here and not living in Little Rock," he said.

"Why?" asked Jackie. "Is it awful down there?"

I remember her innocence reminding us that we were all embarrassed about the way it was in Little Rock. We chose not to elaborate on the mess for Jackie and Alda, who were seventh graders. Mary Crane took the lead.

"Oh, it's nothing. Just that some people can be real jerks," said Mary.

We soon were stepping through the gate of our long dirt drive to the house. It was then that I imagined seeing some kind of light flash or sparkle on the barn-garage roof in the distance.

"Did anybody see that?" I asked.

"See what?" said Holbrook.

"That light," I said.

"What light?" said Holbrook. "I can see lights inside the house. Is that what you mean?"

That's the first time in weeks that it all came back to me. I remembered the angel congress they'd had in my upstairs sleeping room in Little Rock and how Ole Charlie had told me all about the angel congresses they'd had on Dad's, Big Mike's, barn-garage roof. I knew that if I saw a light again, especially on the barn-garage roof, it might be a signal for me.

And I did.

"Why don't you guys go on inside and get some hot chocolate or whatever," I said. "I want to check on Jack and Major and see if they have enough hay."

"I'll help you," said Holbrook.

"Naw. You go inside too. Get some Italian sausage. I'll be in shortly."

I got no more argument from Holbrook. I stood and watched everyone walk up to the front door, knock, and be welcomed in by my mom.

After they closed the door behind them, I walked over to the side of the barn-garage where the horse-stable shed was.

I used the loudest whisper-voice I could manage.

"Charlie? Was that you flashing the light? Are you here, Charlie?"

Almost as soon as I finished the sentence, Ole Charlie appeared just above the transom on the roof. Sure enough, he was standing up on top of the barn-garage in his bib overalls.

"Jerry, bless you, young man," said Ole Charlie.

"Where did you disappear to, Charlie? I've been asking for you and hunting for you everywhere I go and looking a fool sometimes."

"Jerry, Angel Arnold and I need to talk with you. Can you come up here with us? It won't take long. He's around on the backside looking at the white rock reflecting the moon's glow."

I knew that Ole Charlie said they always held their angel congresses on the barn-garage roof.

I remember peering over to the house to see if anyone was looking out a window. I looked up at Ole Charlie.

"Charlie, can you, like, do something or, like, say something so I can just float up there, like that?"

"What?"

"Can't you, like, snap your finger, and then I'll just appear up on the roof with you guys?"

"I'm an angel, son. I'm not a magician. Get a ladder, and take it around back so no one sees."

"I thought you said no one but me could see you, Charlie. That's what you said."

"They can't see me, son. They can see you. Now go around back."

"Okay," I said.

"And please hurry. Time's a-wasting," said Ole Charlie.

When I tried to balance the twelve-foot-tall ladder, it swirled around in a circle or two and about fell backward into the creek;

but I was finally able to steer it back around and to settle it on the edge of the barn-garage roof. I climbed up, and, hanging onto it, I backed onto the roof and sat on the shingles, waiting for Ole Charlie and Angel Arnold to come to me.

Angel Arnold wasn't smiling. He had more of a prayerful look in his eyes.

"Young man," he said. "Good and decent people are about to begin their journey on a venture of great peril and deep personal sacrifice. They're about to try to help someone in need—to save one of God's children from harm's way."

"I telephoned Ernest Hemingway, Angel Arnold, long distance," I said. "I really did. He promised to help, just like you said he would."

"Jerry, this is most important, what I want to say. You need to see to it that your father also knows about this. Just take him aside, and tell him everything. Do it tonight, as soon as you climb down the ladder and go up to the house. If he's the man Angel Charlie says he is, he'll know what to do."

"He is," said Ole Charlie. "Big Mike is a special man."

"Anything else?" I asked.

"Jerry, you're a good lad," said Angel Arnold. "It's been a pleasure meeting you. Heaven thanks you for your important bedtime prayers. It's only fair I tell you that you won't be seeing us again after you climb down and step off the ladder," said Angel Arnold.

"Never?"

"You won't have any memory of seeing us, either," said Ole Charlie.

"That's not fair."

"One day you'll understand, Jerry," said Angel Arnold.

"Will I remember Ernest Hemingway?"

"You will, and he will help because of your courage, not because of anything we've done. He admires you."

"I still don't think it's fair."

"You'll know this is best, son, one day," said Ole Charlie.

"So I'll remember it someday?"

"One day when you're closer to God you'll be better able to understand it all, perhaps."

"Closer? I say my bedtime prayers every night. That's pretty close."

"Perhaps 'nearer' might be a better word, son. In the meantime, you have much growing and living to do. Your life needs no more distractions from us. Your friends need the Jerry they grew up with."

I remember hanging onto the ladder rung, trying to get a good last look at Ole Charlie as an angel so I would never forget him.

"Now go tell your dad, Big Mike," said Ole Charlie. "Tell him right away. He can help."

I turned and put my foot down on the third rung on the ladder.

"I promise," I said.

Holding the sides, I began stepping down carefully.

"And Jerry?" said Ole Charlie.

"Yes?"

"Merry Christmas, my friend."

I remember now how I waved at Ole Charlie and Angel Arnold as I climbed down each rung and finally stepped to the ground.

"Merry Christmas, Charlie. Bye."

After that moment all I could remember was running into the house to tell my dad about the girl in Little Rock and about Uncle Don and Mr. Gaines meeting up at the Gaines farm to work on coming up with a plan.

CHAPTER NINETEEN

THE WAR ROOM

This meeting has become so legendary over sixty years,
I've learned every detail of it.

"Do you go by 'Don' or 'Uncle Don,' young man?" Allen asked. "And do you like cotton-fried puffballs?"

"Either one is fine," said Uncle Don. "Most up here call me Uncle Don because of Jerry. And yes, I do like puffballs. How do you season them?"

Mae carried her black iron skillet over and rested two puffball slices on Uncle Don's plate. He leaned in and sniffed the air about the plate.

"Ah. Bacon drippings and garlic. Maybe a touch of fennel," said Uncle Don.

Mae was sporting a curious look and wondering if Uncle Don was being truthful or just polite about liking her puffballs at all. But it looked as though he'd guessed right on all counts, including the fennel.

"It was the year I got my Eagle Scout badge," said Uncle Don. "One of us discovered puffballs while hiking and setting up camp out in a wood near Rochester. I lived there growing up. When we found some puffballs on a trail, one of the guys in the troop told us how his mom prepared them. He showed me how to clean them using my jackknife. I practiced on two or three and got pretty good at it. I'd slice them thin with chunks of diced Spam and then cook them in a campfire iron skillet. They're great with eggs, too."

"I could have used you on the Pullman," smiled Allen. "You have a real flair."

"Is that what you did before farming, Allen—work the railroad?"

"Not just the railroad, son. I was always a Pullman man. Chicago to New Orleans and back for twenty-two years. Pullman is more than just a railroad, Uncle Don."

"Oh, you bet it is. I've seen a few Pullman cars," said Uncle Don. "They sure do know how to go first class, all right."

"I started as porter but I really wanted to be a chef and to cook every meal."

"Did they promote you?" Uncle Don asked.

"Pullman was slow on pay for blacks. Gave us about seventy-eight dollars a month. As a porter, a brother would get tips too, but I wanted to cook. I gave up the tips, slept on a board in the baggage car between meals, and never got out of the kitchen when I worked, but I sure was the chef back in the day. Cooked a meal for my boss man, is what started it. He liked my cooking and made me a chef."

Uncle Don looked over at Allen as he told the story. He had a sense that when Allen told the story to his children, he was most likely a Pullman chef who hadn't experienced any of the added "complications" of the hard times blacks had gone through. He would keep Allen's confidence. He could see the smile in the old man's eyes bubbling up from his memories of many happy years on the rails.

"I bet you saw a lot of things and met a lot of folks over those twenty years," said Uncle Don.

"Twenty-two years, son. Oh, I did," said Allen. "I 'spect I saw it all. One passenger I knowed more than eleven years gave me this here farm on cash payout. He surely did."

"God bless that man," said Mae.

"I always told him my dream of someday being a farmer and raising chickens and hogs and corn. Don't you know he waited for me to step off the train in Chicago one time and told me he owned a place up this neck of the woods and did me right by offering to carry the paper way he has? I pay him every December and will until it's paid for. Never miss."

"With your travels down to New Orleans all those years, no doubt you've seen what it's been like in the South—for the black, I mean," said Uncle Don.

Allen chose not to address that open sore. He broke his gaze and turned his head to Uncle Don.

"Do you favor corned-beef hash, son?" he asked. "I make a good hash."

"How do you serve it, you being a chef?" asked Uncle Don. "Do you rest a poached egg on top?"

"I do. How about you?" said Allen. "We can do two eggs if you'd like. We have plenty of eggs."

"I met a chef at a hotel on Long Island one time. Chef Josh, as I recall," said Uncle Don. "He told me the best way to eat really good corned-beef hash is with an egg over easy draped on top like a blanket. He said it'd spread more egg goodness into the hash than one poached would. It really works."

"Woman," said Allen. "How about corned-beef hash for our friend and ole Allen here? You ladies too. Join us if you're of a mind."

"Coming right up," smiled Mae. "I'm thinking it'll be with eggs over easy?"

Uncle Don smiled.

"Aunt Lucy," said Uncle Don. "You do some good work sending out those care packages. I know the ladies in that church in southern Little Rock are appreciative."

"I do what I can," said Aunt Lucy. "My boss lady pays my postage for those big boxes. Bless her heart. She let me off today to come here. I pray we can help that little girl. I surely do. I've never sent packages out of state before. Just don't know what got in me to do it this time, but the Lord has spoken, and He's given us a young girl to help."

"Praise the Lord," said Mae.

"Allen," said Uncle Don. "Now don't take me wrong, but I would like to ask you to teach me all you can about the black experience, especially what you know about it in the South from your traveling through it so much. I'm searching for hints of clues as to what we might be able to do. Something I can grab on to."

"You want me to tell you what it's like to be a black man?"

"Allen, I could write ten books about what it's like to be black in the South, and I wouldn't come close to it. But if I'm to help this girl, I sort of have to know the black experience the way it is to see my options."

"I never spoke of this in this house, and I trust you'll take it on out of here with you when you go," said Allen.

"What we share goes nowhere," said Uncle Don. "You have my word."

"In nineteen twenty-seven a brother was hung and shot, and his body was dragged through the streets of Little Rock. They dropped his corpse at Ninth and Broadway, in the black part of town. Thousands of vigilantes showed up and burned him, broke into stores and homes, and threw neighborhood store fixtures and house furniture on the flames for kindling."

"Twenty-seven was some time ago, Allen," said Uncle Don. "It's not that intense anymore, don't you think?"

"Being black, especially in the South, a soul doesn't have all that many options," said Allen.

"I'm serious," said Uncle Don.

Allen reflected on it for a moment.

"One thing was certain, son," said Allen. "The blacks and rail-roads have gone together for a hundred years. We built them as slaves, and now they hire us cheaper than whites to ride as porters. Ya see, white folks in the South don't mind us riding through their towns on a rail or carrying their luggage. They just don't want us living too close to them."

"Sounds like you're saying it's an out-of-sight, out-of-mind kind of thing, as they say?"

Mae cracked an egg in the skillet and stepped over to the table as it spattered. She pointed the spatula.

"What are you thinking, young man?" she asked.

"Oh, I'm just thinking."

She stepped back over to her skillet.

The food was served, and silence filled the room with thoughts. As he was cleaning his plate, sopping up what was left with a folded piece of buttered toast, Uncle Don looked up.

"If maybe there was some way we could hide her out until after the baby was born," said Uncle Don.

"I know one thing, son," said Allen. "If Jim Crow don't want that baby around, that baby won't be around long."

Uncle Don looked over at Allen. He could feel the angst in the man's voice. It was a voice that had to be guarded and held back in a white man's world for years. Maybe then Uncle Don thought of the bombing missions he'd flown to rid the world of an inflamed bigotry.

"It won't be easy," he said. "But maybe we have to come up with some way to get the girl out of Arkansas altogether."

"It's been some time now, but if I remember it right," said Allen, "looking out the Pullman window across the Mississippi from Memphis, that highway to Little Rock is straight as an arrow. They could have highway-patrol cars lined up there like fence posts, watching every move she makes. It's hard enough to hide a black pregnant girl in the daylight, especially if they're following her. I don't see how you'll get her past all that."

"That's true," said Uncle Don. "And if that man in the governor's office is connected to any of the hate groups, that could make things worse...and more dangerous for everyone."

"Well we know he is, or we wouldn't be having this talk," said Allen.

"We have to save that child," said Aunt Lucy.

"And her baby," said Mae.

"Allen, teach me black," said Uncle Don.

"What on earth!" said Aunt Lucy.

"Simmer down," said Allen. "I know just what the man means."

"In the South," Uncle Don added. "Yes, teach me black in the South."

Uncle Don leaned in to listen.

Allen rested his forearms on the table and clasped his hands. He gazed down to the tabletop, gathering his thoughts as though he were transporting himself into his memory of the South.

"Ain't no jobs less we take little or no pay, so brothers have to learn how to get by on their own. Some take the good road and work several jobs to support their families or start businesses in their vicinity."

"What's a 'vicinity'?" said Uncle Don.

"White man calls it a neighborhood. Southern blacks live in the vicinity—could be the vicinity of the church, vicinity of the warehouse, or maybe the vicinity of a store."

"Interesting," said Uncle Don.

"Some cut hair or have a ladies' salon. Some have pushcarts selling home-grown vegetables or delivering eggs or skinned rabbits. I'm up in Syracuse every Saturday selling my eggs and chickens at the university and to restaurants. This way, by having their own businesses in cities, they dealin' with their own kind, and nobody outside is minding their business like some do, especially in the South."

"So in their neighborhoods, or 'vicinities,' they have networks and ways of doing things—ways of bartering and getting things done?" said Uncle Don.

"Well, yes, but for their own kind," said Allen. "A white man wouldn't get into their circle."

"I wonder why that is," said Uncle Don. "Not even if a white man could help them?"

"It's more than color, son. If a black man is twenty cents an hour and a white man is a dollar fifty for the same hour, better the white not come around. It's a prideful reminder we ain't equal—a hurt. At least black man to black man, we know we're equal, and we can understand one another."

"What could help a black man feel successful? What would it take?"

Allen thought and pointed to a side table.

"See that table yonder?"

"I do. The one with the books stacked up on it?"

"That's how a black man knows he's rich. Books in the house—books that will get read—mean success. Books make us rich. They're our ticket up."

"Okay, that's good," said Uncle Don.

"It's more than that," said Mae.

"Woman, what could be better than books?" asked Allen.

"A father at home and the books too," said Mae. "Now that's something."

Allen smiled. In all his life, it had never dawned on him to not "be there" for his family.

"Thank you, Jesus," said Mae.

"I can see what you call vicinity stores and services serving their own circle. But take the Pullman workers. You all got outside of neighborhoods—outside of towns, even—and mixed with whites. Who else would do that? What other businesses would rely on whites from time to time?"

"Taxicabs," said Allen.

"Taxis?" said Uncle Don.

"You'll sometimes have two, three men chip in to pay for buying a car and chip in to drive, and they'll go all about chauffeuring near every neighborhood when they're called."

Uncle Don reflected on that and took his wallet out of his back pocket. He pulled a slip of paper from it.

"Allen, you've given me an idea. Might I use your telephone to make a long-distance call?"

"On the wall," said Allen, pointing to the telephone.

"I'll keep track of expenses," said Uncle Don.

"You'll do no such thing!" said Allen. "Make all the calls you need."

Uncle Don stood up and walked to the wall.

"Ladies, maybe this would be a proper time for coffee," said Allen. "You might consider using the large church urn, Mae—and plenty of chicory and cinnamon. It could be a late night."

Uncle Don picked up the earpiece, leaned in to the mouthpiece, and cranked the handle around twice.

"Operator."

"Operator, I'm making a long-distance call. I need to connect to North Little Rock, Arkansas. The number is Pulaski four hundred seven, please."

"Pulaski four hundred seven in North Little Rock, Arkansas?" said Myrtie.

"That's right," said Uncle Don.

"I'll connect you if they answer," said Myrtie.

"Little Rock, how may I help you?" said a voice through the earpiece.

"Long distance calling for Pulaski four hundred seven. Can you ring it, please?"

"Are you paid, operator?"

"We're paid," said Myrtie.

"One moment, please," said the Little Rock operator. "I'll connect you."

Allen stood up and stepped over to Uncle Don. He held his palm over his mouth and whispered to him.

"You might be careful what you say. Somebody could be listening."

Uncle Don winked at him, understanding his point.

"Hello?"

"There's your party," said Myrtie.

"Aaron?"

"Who's calling?"

"Aaron, this is Don."

"Hey, my man. How are you?"

"We're visiting relatives for Christmas."

"Oh, that's nice. Whereabouts are you?"

Uncle Don didn't want to be overheard by someone in Arkansas.

"Small farm. We'll catch up when I get back."

"Well, you have a good Christmas, my friend. I'll tell Hal Hoffman you called."

"How's the crop dusting coming, Aaron?"

"It's slowed for the winter, but I'm getting good at it. It's a light plane but loaded with power. I can get it to the end of the field and pull her straight up and twist and roll her down again."

"That takes some speed. Not quite like your old B-25 days, I'm guessing."

"Oh, Don, now that you bring it up, you'll never believe it. Hal Hoffman was trying the best he could to get hold of a B-17 from the army salvage, but most had wrecked, and it was slim pickings."

"I haven't seen the numbers, Aaron, but I'd think most of the B-17s they made either crashed or were shot down. We had heavy losses in flight-school training, crashing into each other."

"Well he did find a B-25. Funny you should mention it."

"You're joking me, right?"

"A B-25!"

"A Jimmy Doolittle B-25? A 'bombs-over-Tokyo' B-25? Well, I'll be."

"Sure as I'm sitting here, he found three at a war surplus lot in Savannah. He took me there with him to look them over. I told him which one was in the best shape. I told him what parts he may be needing down the road."

"Well, you would know."

"I got it running like a champ. He let me fly it to the dirt field behind the diner, the field we have for the dusters. Took some getting used to the feel of the big old lady again, getting it back here and all, but Hal Hoffman was patient and let me take my time."

"Congratulations, Aaron."

"This winter, when I'm not driving my cab, I'm our mechanic on the planes. He has two dusters and the old B-25 now. We built a tin hangar. I take good care of them."

"Aaron, I need to ask you a question."

"Ask, my friend."

"Don't take it wrong, but I need to ask if you've been in contact with Anna Kristina."

"No, man. Ah…well…no, man. I wouldn't know what to say."

"Aaron, I need to tell you that she may be in some kind of trouble, and she could use some help. Can't talk about it now, but can I count on you?"

"You can count on me. Anything—just tell me. Can I ask for something, my brother?"

"Anything."

"Can you not tell her my name or anything like that, and let me do it if the time is ever right?"

"You have my word, good buddy."

"Thank you, my brother."

"Aaron, I'll call you at this number or at Hal Hoffman's hangar if I come up with something."

"I'll be at one or the other unless I'm out in my cab."

The two said their good-byes and hung up.

Uncle Don could see Allen smiling over at him over his coffee cup. It was as if Allen could sense Uncle Don was speaking with a black man in Arkansas and was treating him with respect.

Without hesitation, Uncle Don turned the phone crank two more times.

"Operator."

"Operator, can you please ring New Woodstock seventy-eight?"

"Big Mike's place. I sure will."

"Thank you."

"Do I know you?" asked Myrtie.

"I don't think so; I'm Jerry's uncle Don."

"Well congratulations on having your baby boy. It's nice to make your acquaintance. I'm Myrtie."

"Hello, Myrtie."

"Connecting you."

"Hello?"

"Hello, who's this?"

"Dick."

"Hi, Dick, this is your uncle Don. Is Jerry there? I need to talk with him."

"Dad took him and went over there to meet you. Are you at the Gaineses'? They left half an hour ago. They should have been there by now."

"I think I hear them. Thanks, Dick. Bye."

Just as Dick spoke, there was a knock on the side door of the Gaineses' kitchen. Allen walked over and opened it. In stepped Big Mike, Mike Shea, Doc Webb, and I.

We stood around the kitchen table with our coats on as Mae handed coffee cups out to Dad, Mike Shea, and Doc.

CHAPTER TWENTY

STEADY AS SHE GOES

"We're not here to kibitz, Uncle Don," said Dad. Jerry filled me in on what's going on, and we're only here to help if we can."

"Mighty thoughtful, gentlemen, but I still don't have what I'd call a good plan yet. Trying to put the puzzle pieces together with what little I know."

"Everybody? Uncle Don? Allen? Ladies? Say hello to my friends here, Doc Webb and Mike Shea."

"Oh, we know Dr. Webb and Mr. Shea," said Allen. "Welcome to our home, gentlemen. Help yourself to the coffee. It's a fresh pot, and there's plenty of it."

Everyone made their pleasantries. Dad, Mike Shea, and Doc took their coats off—I did too—and we joined Allen and sat around the table, watching Uncle Don pace back and forth in the shadows of the kitchen.

"Mae," said Dad. "Happen to have a sheet of paper and a crayon I can use?"

"Certainly."

She stepped from a side table and handed paper and a crayon to him. He stood up.

"Uncle Don," he said. "You're best at putting things in order in your head. Mind if I help you get it kick-started? Maybe we can help."

"I need all the help I can get," said Uncle Don.

Dad took the crayon and smudged a small dot in the center of the large sheet of paper. He held it up for everyone to see.

"Everyone," he said. "What do you see on this sheet of paper?"

"A dot," I said.

"It's a dot," said Uncle Don.

"Yep, looks like a dot to me," said Allen.

"It must be a trick question," said Doc. "What's on the sheet of paper, Big Mike?"

"You all see the dot. Well it's there, all right. But see all the white space around the dot. It's a full sheet of blank paper with a small dot in the middle."

"I get your point," said Uncle Don. "I've been thinking inside the box, and you want me to think outside the box?"

"Exactly, son."

"Want to give me a hint as to how I can think out of the box on this?" asked Uncle Don.

"If you dream it, you can achieve it."

"I'm not getting your point."

"What've you done so far?"

"Well, I called the girl's brother to tell him I might need his help."

"Anything else?"

"Allen here has been helping me learn the black culture in the South to maybe give me some windows of opportunity for possible approaches."

"Anything else?'

"Not that I can think of. No, wait—Jerry called someone he knows in Little Rock who said he would help."

"It's time to dream it up," said Big Mike.

"I'm still not getting it," said Uncle Don. "I can't just dream up a plan."

"Uncle Don, elbow grease comes in 'cans,' not 'cant's.' Pretend that you're a magician and that you could make anything happen with just the mere snap of your finger. What would you do right now?"

"Anything?"

"You're a magician. Absolutely anything. Just dream it up, and snap your finger."

"Well first thing is I would go down there, but it's a three-day drive, and we don't have three days."

"I forgot to tell you the magician rules," said Dad.

"What!" said Uncle Don. "Magician rules?"

"Magician rule number one, son. You can't say 'but' as a magician. No 'buts' allowed. So that puts you down in Little Rock. What next?"

"That's right," said Doc. "You're down in Little Rock. Now what's next?"

"Well, I'd figure a way to get the girl and to take her to safety. Then I'd hide her out until after the baby was born."

Uncle Don circled the table two times, prancing faster each time, first around the front and then sliding past the sitting gentlemen around the back. Ideas were stirring in him.

"Uncle Don," said Mike Shea. "How many troops would you need to have with you to help her to safety? How big of a team d'you suppose?"

"I'd need a woman to look after the girl. She's pretty well along. Maybe two more to be lookouts, maybe, to carry things, or to be backup. Three in all would do it. The two already in Little Rock... that'd make five."

Dad looked across the table at Mike Shea.

"You thinking what I'm thinking?"

"I am," said Mike Shea. "You game?"

"I am," said Dad.

"You game, Doc?" said Mike Shea.

"I'm in," said Doc. "Not sure what you're talking about, but count me in."

"Put your team together," said Dad. "We're putting up the money for airline tickets to fly into Little Rock and for whatever expenses you may have down there. Money you may need for you and your team."

"You mean it?"

"Pick your team."

"Flying into Memphis would probably be safer," said Uncle Don. "We'll get a rental car and drive to Little Rock. Highway patrol for Arkansas won't be in Memphis on the lookout, whereas they might be at the Little Rock airport."

"They won't be looking for folks coming into the state—just for folks leaving," said Allen. "But best they not see you either way."

"Pick your team, Son," said Dad.

Uncle Don looked over at me.

"Jerry?"

I stood up and said, "Holbrook and Mary Crane and I are the team—you know, to help save the girl!"

"Not yet. But can you call your contact again and ask him something for me?"

"Sure, I'll call. But Holbrook, Mary Crane, and I are going with you. We're your team for Little Rock. Now, what do you want me to tell him?"

"I'll write it down so you can get it straight. Go get him on the phone."

"Mr. Gaines?" I said, pointing over to the telephone on the wall.

"Be our guest," said Allen.

I turned the crank around twice.

"Operator?"

"Myrtie, this is Jerry. Will you get me the Capital Hotel in Little Rock, Arkansas, long distance, and ask for room three hundred five?"

"I have my notes here, Jerry. Do I say 'bullfight' this time?"

"If you have to, yes."

Uncle Don handed me a sheet of paper with instructions written on it.

"Jerry, is that you?" asked Hemingway.

"Yes. We sort of have a plan. Want to hear it?"

"Shoot!"

"Hold on, I have to read it."

"Take your time."

I read it to him:

"We'll need somebody with a car that can't be traced to Little Rock and a driver pretending to be a cabby. He has to be a white guy, the driver, and he'll pick the girl up at the Mission Methodist Church like he's the taxi she called. Then we'll need him to take her to a place that we haven't picked yet, but we'll figure it out tonight or tomorrow and tell you."

"Done! I fit the bill. I already have the car. It's parked in the side lot of the hotel. It's a Hertz renter from the Memphis airport. They'll never trace it back to Little Rock."

"Can't they trace it to you?"

"How? In case you forgot, I'm Manolin Santiago, my friend."

"That's right! I remember now. Perfect. Is that name with the car too?"

"With the car too. I'll wear my best disguise."

"You're great," I said.

"No, you are, my good man. Call me with further instructions."

"I'll be sure to call, but plan for it to be this Wednesday at five o'clock. That's when you'll pick her up at the mission like you're her taxi driver taking her to the hospital in Forrest City."

"So is that where I'm to take her?"

"No, but we don't know where you'll take her yet. She'll think that's where you're taking her."

We both hung up.

Uncle Don took the earphone from my hand and gave her two full cranks.

"Operator."

"Myrtie, can you get Pulaski four hundred seven in North Little Rock, Arkansas, on the wire for me, please?"

While Myrtie went through her machinations, Uncle Don turned to the group.

"I think the pieces are starting to fit together," he said.

Big Mike, Mike Shea, the Doc, Allen, and the rest looked on in awe, almost as if they were in the middle of the Humphrey Bogart movie *Casablanca*. At about that time Mae stepped over to Uncle Don and leaned in to his ear.

"You bring that girl here, young man," she said firmly. "We're that little lady's family now. We'll be all she's got, but we'll sure enough be all she'll ever need. You bring that girl here."

"Praise Jesus," said Aunt Lucy.

"Hello?" a voice said over the earpiece.

"Aaron? Don here."

"Whatcha got for me, Captain?"

"I need you to write down this name."

"Hold on."

"I'll wait."

"Okay, give it to me."

"Sarah Wilkins. Write that down."

"Sarah Wilkins—got it."

"She's the lady I need you to find at the Methodist church mission in southern Little Rock."

"I know that mission. I said grace there a time or two. Even went to a funeral at the church back in the forties."

"When you find her, give her this message. Ready?"

"Ready."

"Tell her Aunt Lucy has arranged a taxi to come for Anna Kristina to take her to Forrest City on Wednesday at five o'clock. Tell her Aunt Lucy said it's important she be ready to go to keep the fare down."

"So am I picking her up in my cab?"

"No, that's all taken care of. I don't want there to be a chance for you to get caught."

"You want a white guy to do it."

"Right. They won't suspect a white guy would help her."

"What do I do?"

"Nothing yet. Just go about your normal activities, but not too far from a telephone. I'll get back to you, I promise."

"Okay."

"Can you go tonight and give Sarah Wilkins the message?"

"As soon as we hang up, I'll head down there. I'll be back in an hour, maybe an hour and a half."

"Be careful not to make a big deal out of it in case there's someone watching her. If you see any highway patrol, don't pay attention to them. Just tell her Aunt Lucy has a taxi coming for Anna Kristina to take her to Forrest City on Wednesday at five o'clock. Be sure to tell her Aunt Lucy said it's important she be ready to go so the fare doesn't run up."

"Got it."

"She'll know its code," said Uncle Don. "She'll know 'Aunt Lucy' is code that everything will be handled. Just tell her those words I told you and leave. Don't hang around."

"I'm on my way."

Uncle Don let the earpiece hang down, clacking into the wall as it swung, while he stepped to the table and opened his wallet. He picked paper notes and business cards from it. Leaving it on the table, he took one of the cards back to the telephone and picked up the earpiece again. He cranked it twice.

"Operator?"

"Myrtie, I need Conway seven hundred ninety-one in Carlisle, Arkansas, on the wire, please."

"Busy night," said Myrtie.

While Myrtie was connecting the call, Uncle Don turned and looked at me.

"Jerry, where are your friends right now?"

"Some are at the house and a bunch are probably still ice-skating at Conway's. Why?"

"No, not those friends. Where're Holbrook and Mary Crane?"

"At the house. They're having spaghetti."

"You need to run back and pack a small bag and tell them to pack and be ready too. Pack warm—a heavy coat and maybe your long johns. And what if their parents won't let them go?"

"Oh, they can go."

"Why don't I drive Jerry to the falls," said Doc Webb. "I can take Holbrook and Mary Crane to their houses to pack."

"Perfect," said Uncle Don. "If we have to, can we meet up back here, Mae?"

"Of course you can," said Mae. "You do whatever you have to and then bring that girl here, where she'll be loved and nurtured."

Myrtie rang the number.

"Hoffman Dusters, Hal speaking," said Hal Hoffman.

"Connected," said Myrtie.

"Hold on, Hal," said Uncle Don.

He looked over and caught me starting toward the door.

"Wait up a sec, Jerry...Don't leave until after this call."

He turned to the mouthpiece on the wall.

"Hal? It's Don."

"Why, hello, stranger, you new poppa, you. How's the latest addition to that growing litter of yours? I'm lighting up a cigar on New Year's."

"Mary and the kids send their love to you and Janet, and happy Christmas. We're upstate in New York with Big Mike and Missus."

"Snow there?"

"No snow yet, but it's freezing," said Uncle Don.

"We got the Christmas card. Why do I have honor of this long-distance call, my friend?"

"Hal, you're going to have to bear with me. I'm going to take you back a ways. It's important, Hal."

"Okay, I'll play your game."

"Do you remember Rheine?"

"Oh, hell yes, I do. How could I forget it? It was our first mission out. It was a predawn scramble. Sirens going off everywhere and all hell breaking loose with everybody running about."

"They needed a precision-bomb attack on all the bridges on the Dortmund-Ems-Kanal to get ahead of two German tank divisions retreating and on their way to cross them," said Uncle Don.

"I remember we leveled them."

"We got 'em all," said Uncle Don.

"I think it was a thousand of us going out," said Hal Hoffman. "Maybe more took off on that raid."

"That's it," said Uncle Don. "That's the morning. It was for the ground troops and tanks wrapping up the Battle of the Bulge."

"What brought all this up, Don? You getting nostalgic on me in your old age, buddy?"

"Aaron told me about your B-25 acquisition, Hal. He tells me it's some special bird—a real lady in the sky."

"I can't wait for you to get back here and to try her out with me. She's a beauty."

"So how's he working out for you?"

"Aaron?"

"Yes."

"He's quite the mechanic. Great pilot, too. We're going to sell rides in her in the summer."

"Hal, what would you say if I told you I needed the loan of a B-25 for twenty-four, maybe forty-eight hours this coming Wednesday? I'd have it back sometime after Christmas."

"You need a B-25?"

"Yes…a B-25."

"You need the loan of a B-25?"

"Yes, sir."

"You having some Christmas eggnog, are you, Don? Into the early bubbly, are we?"

"I'm not drinking, Hal. Not a drop. I'm as serious as a heart attack. I need the B-25. Aaron told me all about it."

"So it's a conspiracy between you two, eh," said Hal Hoffman. "Dare I ask why you need it?"

"Something's come up. I was going to use a car, but I heard about your B-25. Let's leave it at that. But we might save a life with it."

"It's yours, my friend. It'll be fueled and ready. If you need me, I'll be there too."

"I wouldn't be around the airfield if you don't have to be. The less you know for now, the better."

"It ain't much of an airfield, Don. It's a strip of mud in the rain. Dusters don't take much runway. This old turtle with wings takes its own sweet time thinking about lifting off."

"How's it look now—the runway?"

"It's dry. You can get her up to speed."

"Like I say, if you don't need to be around Wednesday, it might be smart to not be."

"Roger that," said Hal. "Wednesday I'll be home with the family. Don, it has almost the same cockpit configuration as our old B-17s. Do you think you can fly her?"

"Not sure, but I think I already got that flying part and getting her up and all handled," said Uncle Don.

"I'm not even going to ask, but I can guess," said Hal Hoffman. "He's good—real good."

Uncle Don looked over at Allen, had an idea, and spoke up into the phone for Allen's benefit.

"Hal, none of my business, but can I ask how much Aaron costs—his flying and mechanical work? Is he a bargain?"

Allen looked up and waited to hear the answer. Hal was brief.

"For dusting, I gave him a choice of either being the mechanic and keeping seventy percent of dusting fees after fuel when he flies or—"

Uncle Don repeated that so Allen could hear it.

"So for flying the duster, you gave him a choice of either being the mechanic and keeping seventy percent of dusting fees after fuel when he flies or—"

"Or a straight dollar fifty an hour for everything," said Hal Hoffman.

"Or a straight dollar fifty an hour for everything? That's a good wage," said Uncle Don.

"He's a good talent," said Hal Hoffman.

"Merry Christmas, my friend," said Uncle Don.

"Oh, and Don?" said Hal. "I'll leave my old sheepskin flight jumpsuit in the plane in case one of you needs it."

Uncle Don smiled and hung up the earpiece.

"Did you catch all that, Allen?"

Allen was wearing a most contented smile because a brother was being treated fairly in the South.

Uncle Don pointed his finger over at me.

"Jerry, it's your turn. Come and get your friend back on the telephone."

He picked up the earpiece again and held it out for me to take from him. I cranked the phone twice.

"Operator?"

Myrtie, I need the Capital—

"I know, the Capital Hotel in Little Rock, room three hundred five."

"Yes."

"It sure sounds like you're all up to another something or another," mumbled Myrtie.

The connections became easier with each call to the hotel.

"Jerry?" Hemingway said.

"Yes, hi. Well, we have more to the plan, I think."

"Let me have it."

I held my hand over the mouthpiece and asked Aunt Lucy if she had the address of the Mission Methodist Church in southern Little Rock. She pulled the envelope from her purse. It was in the upper left corner.

"Okay, write this address down."

I read the address to Hemingway and asked him to read it back. He had it perfect.

Uncle Don interrupted me.

"Let me speak to him, Jerry."

"Huh?" I stuttered.

"Let me talk to him. Don't worry, I won't ask him any questions."

I told Hemingway to hold on for instructions and handed the earpiece to Uncle Don. Without even saying "hello," Uncle Don started talking.

"Your passenger's name is Anna Kristina. She's expecting her cab at the Methodist on Wednesday at five o'clock sharp. She'll be under the impression that you'll be taking her to the Forrest City Hospital, which would be about an hour-and-a-half drive."

"Anna Kristina, Methodist, Wednesday at five o'clock. Going to Forrest City Hospital—understood," said Hemingway.

"Make sure she's in the backseat."

"Good thinking," said Hemingway. "Gives less of an appearance of familiarity."

"Do you know Carlisle, Arkansas?" asked Uncle Don. "It's on the way to Forrest City and not far from Little Rock."

"I've passed through it before driving in from Memphis, I think," said Hemingway.

"There's a highway truck diner in the town—Red's Diner."

"Red's Diner. Got it. I remember seeing their flashing neon sign."

"Pull in to that diner like you have to go in and take a leak."

"And the girl?" asked Hemingway.

"No coloreds allowed in the diner—that's what the sign on their door says," said Uncle Don. "So we'll oblige them. She'll have to stay in the car. Park as far on the left as you can, close to the dirt driveway next to the diner's west side."

"And I go inside?"

"Yes. We need to stall for time."

"There's a chill in the air tonight. The clouds hint it may be colder on Wednesday. Do I leave the car running?"

"Why not? It'll keep the heater warm."

"I just get out and go inside?"

"Yes, go inside, go to the men's room, and then stall. Have a cup of coffee and a piece of pie."

"And here's where I'm not supposed to ask you any questions, right?"

"Don't lock the car doors," said Uncle Don.

"Are you the captain, by any chance?" asked Hemingway.

"Actually, I was a lieutenant in the service. I'm a captain in the reserves now."

"Good job, Captain. Will there be reason for me to stay around Little Rock?"

"No reason."

"So if I think what's going to happen does happen, I could drive right to Memphis and catch a flight out?"

"Yes. If we're able to pull it off, it'll happen fast."

"It's going to be my pleasure to serve under you, Captain."

"Thanks, Mister. I don't know who you are, but thanks."

"When it's all over, Captain, ask my friend Jerry. He will speak the truth."

Uncle Don handed me the phone receiver.

"Merry Christmas," I said.

"Merry Christmas, my friend," said Hemingway. "Don't forget about that New Year's research assignment."

"Remind me again."

"The birds and the bees, my friend. The birds-and-bees talk."

"Oh, that. Yeah."

We both hung up.

"Jerry," said Uncle Don. "How soon can you get your club together for a meeting? We're going to need help on this end."

"This should be an SOS," I said.

"What does that mean? I mean, I know what 'SOS' means, but—"

"More kids and the older guys too. The older guys have the cars and trucks."

"How soon can they meet?"

"In maybe an hour. You want them at the house or the cemetery? They won't all fit in this kitchen."

"At the house," said Dad. "Better tell everybody to put a move on."

"I'll set it up when Doc takes me. Barber is there. He calls all the meetings."

"Good. Off you go."

Just as I was ready to go out the kitchen door, I remembered an important fact. I turned around to look at Uncle Don.

"No! Wait! Most everybody is over at Conway's ice-skating. Nobody will be home to get Barber's phone call."

"We could go there, but I'll need to be near a telephone," said Uncle Don.

"How about if we set it for in the morning? Nine or ten?"

"When are you going to want to fly down there, Uncle Don?" asked Dad.

"Wednesday," said Uncle Don. "If the highway patrol is out like everyone's saying, we don't want them to see any unnatural movement too early and have the chance to react."

"The element of surprise," said Mike Shea.

"Bully!" said Doc.

"Ten, at the house," said Dad. "I'll have donuts."

"Ten will work, I'll be better prepared," said Uncle Don.

"Are you going to tell Aaron?" I asked.

"He's headed to the Methodist mission now," said Uncle Don. "I'll call him later or in the morning before we meet."

I ran outside with Doc and jumped in his jeep. We headed off to the falls.

"Doc, think you can drive Holbrook and Mary Crane to their houses to pack a bag and then get them back here? Maybe they should sleep on the floor at our house so none of us miss the meeting."

"Bully, young man. Bully! You can count on me."

Big Mike, Mike Shea, and Allen were sitting at the table, watching in amazement. They were seeing the clear-headed thinking required to form battle strategies and tactics coming back to an experienced war veteran who was grappling with duty after duty without missing a single small detail. They sipped their coffee with a certain pride only a father could know.

Uncle Don turned the crank again and got the airline on the wire. He made reservations for the four of us to fly from Syracuse to Memphis on Wednesday morning. We had one whole day to plan our trip.

He scribbled some notes on a piece of paper and pulled on his coat. He turned and thanked the ladies for their patience and the puffballs. He tipped his hat.

"Gentlemen?" he said to my dad and Mike Shea as he prepared to leave.

He turned and shook Allen's hand.

"Best corned-beef hash I've ever had, Allen. See you in a couple days."

"You like pickled tongue?" asked Allen, standing up to say good-bye.

"I do indeed, with a good beer," said Uncle Don. "Can't wait to try yours. Horseradish too."

"Allen, morning comes early for you here on the farm," said Big Mike. "Thanks for the coffee."

Allen smiled, happy he was involved in something that could change a life and maybe even save one.

"Ladies?" said Mike Shea. "We'll be off."

"What can Aunt Lucy and I do to help?" asked Mae.

"Just go about planning a good Christmas for your families, ladies," said Mike Shea. "Folks will be looking forward to a glorious midnight service, as always. That big tree out front of the church is quite a nice surprise this year."

"Mae, we'll drop the girls, Jackie and Alda, back here," said Dad.

Mae had a tear in her eye.

"We are so blessed to have our girls grow up here in the Crown. We are so blessed."

Everyone said his or her thanks for the hospitality, gave proper hugs, and left the Gaines place, heading to the falls.

CHAPTER TWENTY-ONE

THE MORNING SOS MEETING

It's much easier to describe the mood that morning now that it's been more than sixty years. I do remember thinking that life would never be the same again for me. Up until the experience of going to Little Rock and seeing things I couldn't even imagine Jim Crow times, like how people were being treated. The Pompey Hollow Book Club members had taken on many assignments in the past—we'd caught burglars, thwarted thieves, and grabbed pickpockets—but we'd never known murderers. Crooks were bullies, and we weren't afraid of bullies. Murderers were different. It didn't matter if it was only a threat of murder. To us, someone who would threaten to murder someone was sick—and still a murderer. This experience was about to change our lives forever.

Dad, Mike Shea, Allen, and the doc were standing in the kitchen with Mom and Mae, drinking coffee. Aunt Lucy had to be at work in the city.

Must have been twenty people who came early for the meeting. Cars dropped them off and then drove back to farms to continue chores. As the kids walked in, they each got a donut and a paper cup of hot chocolate and then sat down in a circle on the living room floor without talking, waiting for some direction. We knew the seriousness of an SOS and that it'd be Duba, Dick, Conway, or Dwyer who would take the lead and start the official meeting.

Uncle Don came out of a bedroom, rolling up his sleeves to just above his wrists. He walked into the kitchen and poured himself a cup of coffee and stood by Dad and Aunt Mary in the kitchen. Mike Shea, Allen, and Doc had moved out toward the dining room to take it all in. The little kids were in Mom and Dad's room playing with my mom.

"Listen up," Duba said.

Dick stepped up and stood next to the upright piano.

"Let's not waste any time. How many of you know what's going on and what we're trying to do? I know you've been gabbin' amongst yourselves."

Every hand went up.

"Good, so we all know why we're here. We're here to listen to the plan Uncle Don and Mr. Gaines have come up with. After that we'll see what we all can do to help."

Dick looked over at Uncle Don, nodding for him to take the lead. Uncle Don took a last sip of his coffee, set it down on the counter, and stepped over by the upright. He wasted no time.

"Tomorrow's the big day," he said.

Looking around, he decided to test the room.

"Who's in?"

Every right arm in the room went up like a rocket.

"I grew up in Rochester," he began.

"Now I live in Little Rock, Arkansas. That's a long way away. Let me ask you all a question. How many of you think I could have some old friends in Rochester and some new friends in Little Rock at the same time?"

We agreed it was very likely.

"Well, to be safe on this mission, we have to assume that anybody we deal with down in Arkansas might have connections up here or anywhere else, for that matter."

"We don't tell secrets," said Dick. "What's your point?"

Marty Bays, the smart one, spoke up.

"His point is simple. Loose lips sink ships. Whatever we learn today we have to keep to ourselves, or we could jeopardize the whole plan."

"He's right," said Uncle Don. "If the wrong ears hear it up here, they may just tell people who know people in Little Rock."

Dick stood up.

"Raise your right arms, everybody. Now repeat after me."

Arms went up.

"I pledge to keep everything I hear in this meeting secret, and I pledge I won't talk with anyone who's not in this room now about it."

He looked around the room at all the raised arms.

"If you pledge to do that, say, 'I pledge,'" said Dick.

It was unanimous.

Uncle Don took over again.

"We're going in to Little Rock," said Uncle Don. "We're going to fly to Memphis. Then we'll sneak into Arkansas tomorrow. After we get there, we're going to try to get the girl without anyone knowing and bring her to Delphi Falls, back here to the Gaineses' place."

"Who's going?" asked Marty.

"Jerry, Mary Crane, and Holbrook are going with me. They decided."

"So how do you get her out? You going to fly back from Memphis?" asked Dick.

Uncle Don didn't answer him.

"They can't fly," said Duba. "People at the airports will be watching the planes if the governor is involved in this."

"No airports," said Uncle Don. "But let me keep that part of it secret. It'll be better that way."

I could feel the tension building in the room.

"But we'll need fuel once we're up here," he added. "Lots of fuel. By then we'll be on reserves."

You could have heard a pin drop. It was then that everyone in the room knew that Uncle Don was going to fly a plane himself and that nobody would be on a regular passenger airline coming back.

"Regular gas or, like, airplane fuel?" asked Marty.

"Airplane fuel, full mix," said Uncle Don.

"There's Binghamton airport—that's on Route eleven— or there's the Syracuse airport, Hancock Field," said Big Mike. "They'll both have fuel."

"If you land at one of those airports, tell us," said Dick. "We'll pick you up and bring you here."

"Oh, we can't land at those," said Uncle Don. "We could be seen or get caught, at least on the way in."

"How will you get word to us if there's an emergency?" asked Dick.

"Good question," said Uncle Don. "Does anybody around here have a shortwave radio?"

"Myrtie does. Just call the New Woodstock operator, Myrtie," said Duba. "She'll pick up."

"For certain?"

"She'll pick up," said Dick. "She did it for civil defense in the war, and she does it now for the sheriff in case of emergencies."

Don made notes in his spiral notebook.

"What's your plan, then?" asked Duba.

"We'll have enough fuel to get here, land, and then takeoff to go to one of those airfields for fuel."

"I don't get it," said Mayor. "Can't you get caught just as easy if you go to an airport after you come here?"

"I get it!" said Marty. "It won't matter by then if they don't have any passengers."

"And not if we don't take off for a few days after we land here," said Uncle Don.

"Let the trail cool—get them off the scent," said Holbrook.

"That means you're going to have to land it around here some-where, doesn't it?" said Marty. "Around Delphi Falls somewhere."

"Dang," I said.

I can remember the chills that ran up my spine at just the anticipation of thinking about actually being in that airplane with Uncle Don flying it.

"How much runway are you going to need?" asked Conway.

"For takeoff we'll need an even eight hundred feet loaded," said Uncle Don. "I'm thinking maybe five hundred feet with a lighter load."

"Holy Cobako!" Dwyer said. "A body might think you're going to fly a bomber."

Uncle Don didn't flinch.

"The highway is out if it's a bomber," said Conway. "The wings would be too wide and would catch fence posts or telephone poles."

"Is that true?" asked Holbrook. "Are you going to fly a B-17?"

Uncle Don looked over at Allen and didn't answer.

"We'll need five or six hundred feet of runway," he said. "No roads."

"What direction will you be coming in from?" asked Conway. "I mean, once you got here. Will you be circling around?"

"Why would you need to know?" said Uncle Don.

"If we know that, we can tell you where you can land the fastest."

Uncle Don picked up his spiral note pad and looked at his notes.

"We'll be avoiding airports the best we can for as long as we can, so we'll be flying from visual references to Chattanooga. From there, if the sky is clear, we'll follow the old US Eleven all the way up here to Route Twenty."

"That's Cherry Valley," shouted Barber.

"If I remember my jigsaw-puzzle map of the United States of America," said Marty, "that means flying east then north. Won't it burn more fuel, flying out of your way like that? That's a long trip."

"It's a precaution," said Uncle Don. "First off, if we play our cards right, no one will even suspect we're using a plane. But if we are seen, the more sure they are that we're headed east, the better. They'll think Nashville or Charleston. They'll be thinking east, not north."

"Well then," said Conway. "Do you know where Oran Delphi Road is and where it crosses Route Twenty? We'll take you there and show you if you don't know."

"I know exactly where it is," said Uncle Don. "I went to Syracuse University after the war and drove it many times. It's at the foot— the lowest point—of the big hills between Pompey Center and Cazenovia," said Uncle Don.

"Hang south on it there, on Oran Delphi, and turn right at that corner. We'll have six cars lined up with our headlights on, marking the field on the left of Oran Delphi where you can land. It's Barber's field."

"Where will you be lined up with the cars?"

"How about on the side of the field every twenty feet so you can see more of the runway with our headlight beams?"

"Front end of the field would be better. Park a few feet apart at the front end of the runway with your headlights beaming down the runway. If we can see the line of lights facing away down the field, we'll know to drop in from behind them and land in front of them. If it's too dark or fog is up, we'll know to come in from the north over them and trust there's enough runway to bring her to a full stop."

"Oh, you'll have enough runway," said Barber.

"What kind of field is it?" asked Uncle Don.

"It's a field," said Barber. "What do you mean, what kind?"

"What's it used for—corn, beans, or hay? It all makes a difference."

"Hay," said Barber.

"Why would that make a difference?" asked Randy.

"If the ground's been plowed and is rough, it could break off our front wheel. We'd be able to land, but we'd keep the nose up until the last minute."

"It's hay. It's cut too," said Barber.

"But we ain't promising no woodchuck holes," said Duba.

"That's about it," said Uncle Don. "Takeoff will be at five o'clock—that's six Eastern Time. Little Rock is an hour earlier. We should be touching down here sometime between ten and eleven, depending on the winds."

"We'll be there to pick you up and give you rides," said Dick.

"There'll be a few tarps in the plane," said Uncle Don. "We could use some help covering the props and engines."

That's the time when my mom stepped into the living room. She was as nervous as any momma would have been, but she buckled up and had her say.

"Everybody?" she said. "Can we all just bow our heads and say a prayer to ourselves that everyone is safe throughout this whole wonderful thing you're doing? I know there're several different religions in this room, so just bow your head and say it any way you want or believe. God will hear us all equally well."

The room had been silent for what seemed like a minute or two when Minneapolis Moline Conway spoke up.

"Those with cars or tractors who can do the runway duty tomorrow, meet up at my place after milking today. We'll go see what the field looks like in the dark and mark our posts."

Uncle Don blessed himself, raised his head, and stepped back into the kitchen to get a cup of coffee.

The meeting pretty much broke up with my dad opening a few flat boxes of doughnuts and kids waiting for rides.

CHAPTER TWENTY-TWO

WE WERE OFF!

The next morning was almost a blur. Mary Crane and Holbrook had slept over, but none of us had gotten a good night's sleep; instead we were thinking about the trouble we might be getting into going to Little Rock. Mom had Wheaties in three bowls waiting for us on the table along with milk and sugar and three spoons.

"There's no Christmas tree here, Jerry. Don't you guys put up a tree?" asked Mary Crane.

"Santa brings our tree," I said. "With the kids here, it's more fun that way when they wake up."

"That's so nice," said Mary. "Was it like that for you, too?"

"It's always been like that."

We were just filling time. None of us had any idea as to what to expect next. We stood at the counter and munched our Wheaties, and I was thinking about whether we would be back for Christmas the next day or in trouble in Little Rock. We were waiting for Uncle Don to appear and to tell us what to do. Dad came in the side door and in through the laundry room. He was dressed up in his suit, tie, and overcoat. He had already been to the bakery in Homer and back.

"Uncle Don's outside. Finish your breakfast, and we'll go."

"Are you going with us, Dad?"

"Only wish I could. I'm taking you to the airport."

Holbrook and I grabbed our coats from a chair and began stuffing things in my knapsack. Mary had a small suitcase already packed resting on the piano bench in the living room. When Dad saw the bags, he reminded us that we would be coming home that night and wouldn't need all those things. We hung on to our winter coats and walked out to the car.

"If you have gloves or mittens, I'd go get them," said Uncle Don.

Inside Mom went through a box in the front hall closet and found gloves and winter hats that fit each of us.

Mary, Holbrook, and I sat in the backseat. We could see snow flurries starting to dance in the swirling wind. It didn't appear to be a wet snow. Dad drove the car, and Uncle Don sat in the passenger seat turning pages in his small spiral notepad. To this day, I can remember sitting in the backseat and thinking that we were actually going on the thirty-fourth mission along with Uncle Don and feeling we'd be safe as long as he was with us. Holbrook had never flown, and Dad suggested we get him a barf bag from behind the seat in the plane just in case he needed it. Mary had been up with Flying Eddie in his biplane back in November, so she was fine with flying. I was too. When I was nine, my dad thought it would be a great adventure for me to ride on an American Airlines Flagship DC-3 all alone to Watertown. I remembered how fun it had been, and although I was scared about the trouble we could get into in Arkansas later that day, I couldn't wait to feel the takeoff again. I like the part when the thrust of the plane building speed during takeoff pushes you back into your seat until the wheels leave the ground, and then how you feel weightless a time or two as the plane climbs altitude.

Dad pulled up to the airport terminal and put the car in "park."

"On the radio this morning, they predicted that this snow is going to build," said Dad. "Will it be a problem?"

Uncle Don didn't respond.

He later told me that in all of his thirty-three missions, there had never been a weather option. If the Allies had become weather dependent, Hitler would have known when to attack and when to dig in just by watching the weather reports. Bombers and fighters had to take off in any weather.

He turned sideward in his seat and looked each of us in the eye, one at a time.

"If any of you want to change your mind about going, now's the time to speak up. I won't mind at all if any of you choose to stay here."

None of us so much as blinked. We were ready to go.

"So," said Uncle Don. "Listen carefully."

He turned full round and kneeled in the front seat with his back leaning on the dashboard.

"Do you remember what I told your friends about my growing up in Rochester and now living in Little Rock and how easy it would be for me to know people in both areas?"

"Sure, we remember," said Mary.

"Good. Now I want you to know that everybody on the airplane today will be just like that. They're all coming from here, Syracuse, and flying to Memphis with us. Think they'll know people in both cities?"

"Probably," I said.

"Isn't Memphis in another state, though?" asked Mary. "We're going to Arkansas."

"It's right on the border of Arkansas and not all that far from Little Rock."

"Oh," said Mary.

"Best way to not spill a secret is to not talk," said Uncle Don. "Best way to not talk is to sleep."

"Really?" said Mary. She stuck out her lip and puffed a curl from her eye.

"Can't I just look out the window?" asked Holbrook.

"Yes, sure. Look all you want. Just don't get into conversations with anyone and risk spilling the beans. The few hours we'll be there will be critical, and we don't want to be sending out advance signals to anyone."

"What if somebody asks me why I'm flying to Memphis?" asked Mary.

"Here's a trick," said Uncle Don. "Just say the word 'Christmas' if anybody asks you anything. Just say one word: 'Christmas.'"

"Okay," I said. "Christmas. I can do that."

"Most people know that kids are taught not to talk with strangers. If you just say 'Christmas,' they'll be good with that. Just say it, and go on your way."

"Anything else we should know?" asked Mary.

"Mary, I didn't want to tell you too far in advance so you wouldn't worry."

"Tell me what?"

"The girl we're going to get is pretty far along."

"Oh, I know she's pregnant. Aunt Lucy told me all about it."

"Well, there's more to it, Mary. We think she's due this month sometime. I need you to stay close to her and to try to keep her as calm as possible. She's very young and should listen to you. Keep reminding her that you're Aunt Lucy's close friend."

"I can do that. Don't worry."

"Anything else?" I asked.

"Try not to talk with one another on the plane or in the airports, just in case someone could overhear you."

"Is that like flying on radio silence, Uncle Don?" Holbrook asked. "Like in *Thirty Seconds Over Tokyo* with Spencer Tracy?"

"Exactly," said Uncle Don.

"Wow. This is so good!" I said.

"But try to sleep. We have a lot to do when we get down there and not much time to do it," said Uncle Don. "After we land just stick close to me, try to keep up, and listen for my instructions."

"Uncle Don," said Mary. "I promise we won't disappoint you."

"So let's go," he said.

Dad gave us a thumbs-up as we climbed out of the car. Then, forming a single-file line, we followed Uncle Don to the airline counter, where a lady handed him our tickets. We then walked down a sidewalk and onto the airplane, where a stewardess in a pretty blue suit and a hat smiled and welcomed us on board. We found a row that had two seats on either side of the aisle. Uncle Don pointed to one and let Mary sit next to a window, and he sat beside her. Holbrook was next to the window on the other side, and I sat in the aisle seat next to him.

"Everybody, buckle up," said Uncle Don.

I remember seeing the two engines and propellers out our window first belching smoke and then beginning to spin, and it reminded me that Uncle Don's B-17 had had four engines, just like the DC-6 we were about to fly in. I remember the airplane taxiing down the runway, and I remember hearing the noise and whir of the racing engines as we started to take off. I remember being pushed back into my seat by the force as we leaped forward and raced down the runway, and I can remember the look in Holbrook's eyes after takeoff as we bounced, weightless, a couple of times.

The next thing I remember is waking up in Memphis with the airplane stopped and the engines turned off.

We followed Uncle Don like goslings. He walked at a normal pace so as to not attract attention. From time to time he would look around to see if we were all with him. We walked past a big bale of cotton by the side door and through the airline terminal. There was a Christmas tree in the middle of the terminal and some decorations on the walls. We didn't stop for anything. Uncle Don walked right through the building and out the front door. Without skipping a pause, we found our way to the second row of cars in the parking lot and passed in front of a Buick with a Tennessee plate on it, an Oldsmobile with a Mississippi plate, two Chevrolets with Tennessee plates, and an old Plymouth with a plate so muddy I couldn't read it. That's when Uncle Don pointed to a Chevrolet to the left of the Plymouth. Through the window I could see Aaron, Anna Kristina's brother, the man Uncle Don and I had met in North Little Rock on Thanksgiving. He was sitting behind the wheel in the driver's seat.

Uncle Don turned about, searching for people who might have been watching us. He saw no one.

"Holbrook!" he said in a loud whisper. "Get in the front. Crouch down on the floor, and stay down."

He then stepped to the back door and opened it.

"Mary Crane, you jump in the back and slide over, but sit on the seat. Jerry, get in and crouch on the floor in front of her, and stay down."

We moved like we were well-trained robots. We trusted Uncle Don implicitly, and we assumed he and the driver of the car had it all planned out. None of us said a word simply because Uncle Don's last order to us on the subject had been not to talk.

I heard the car start and felt it pulling away. I could tell when we were stopped at a stoplight and which way we were turning when we turned. I remember it wasn't too long before I looked up from the floor and out through the rear window and saw the tall steel girders of a bridge we were driving over. Just before we drove off the end of the bridge on the other side, Don started to talk.

"Okay, stay down until we get there," said Uncle Don. "Everybody, don't get up, but this here is Aaron driving the car. Aaron is my friend and is helping us today."

"Hello, everybody," said Aaron. "God bless you."

I tapped Uncle Don on the leg to get his attention, and then I pointed at my mouth to see if we could talk.

"You can talk. Just stay down until we get there," said Uncle Don.

"Hi, Aaron, remember me?"

"I remember you, young man. God bless you for coming."

"Was that the Mississippi Bridge we just went over?" I asked.

"The mighty Mississippi, it surely was," said Aaron. "Welcome to Arkansas, everybody."

"Why are we on the floor?" asked Holbrook.

"A car full of people is always looked at if there's suspicion of foul play – they are suspicious of what may look like a gang. A man and his daughter with a driver in a taxi wouldn't draw any attention."

"Especially if the car is coming into Arkansas and aren't trying to skip out," Aaron added with a grin.

"When will we be there?" asked Mary.

"Carlisle, Arkansas, is one hundred and six miles from Memphis," said Uncle Don. "We should be there by three o'clock. That'll give us a couple of hours to walk through everything and to get ready."

There was silence most of the way. Holbrook broke the silence by telling us how much he'd enjoyed flying and the flight down. He said that if he'd had better eyes, he would have liked to join the Air Force and fly like Uncle Don.

"It's a good memory for you," said Uncle Don.

"Yeah, and I took the barf bag to remind me of it," said Holbrook.

Even with the tension in the air, we couldn't help but laugh.

In time the car slowed and pulled off the highway. It never came to a stop. Almost in a crawl, it turned right on what felt and sounded like our gravel-and-dirt driveway in Delphi Falls.

"Don, if you'll jump out and get the hangar door, I'll pull in, and then we can unload inside the hangar," said Aaron. "It takes a good yank, but it'll lift."

"Everybody," said Uncle Don. "Stay put until we're inside with the door closed."

He got out of the car, and we could hear an overhead door rolling up. It was still climbing as the car made its way into the dark hangar and stopped right beside an enormous B-25 bomber in army green with a star on its tail.

By that time Aaron was out of the car. He stepped over to the doorway and looked outside to see if anyone was watching. With a heave on its chain, the entrance door started to come back down, putting us in darkness. I heard the sharp clunk of a breaker switch, and then four bulbs inside the hangar were lit.

"You can get out now," said Uncle Don.

I remember standing under the wing of the bomber in awe, staring up at the enormous plane (at least it was enormous to me) that undoubtedly had a history we'd listened to on the radio news throughout the war.

"I thought it would be bigger," said Holbrook. "Look at how big the engines are, though."

"It's a medium bomber, son," said Aaron. "Designed with speed in mind for quick drops and fast turnarounds and used more for air cover than for strategic bombing like the big boys, the B-17s, or the B-29s."

"Aaron, can you open the bomb-bay doors for loading?" asked Uncle Don.

"Will do," said Aaron.

"Jerry and Holbrook," said Uncle Don. "There's a mattress rolled up and tied with some rope somewhere. Find it and lift it up into the cargo hole of the plane. Then find the four tarps somewhere on the floor—"

"They's over by the office," said Aaron.

"Over by the office," said Uncle Don. "Get them loaded up."

"Keep the tarps rolled," said Aaron. "They's all the seats we'll have back there. Y'all 'ill need them to sit on."

"What can I do?" asked Mary Crane.

Uncle Don pulled a pamphlet book from his coat pocket. It was a pamphlet that Dad had gotten from Dr. Brudney in Fabius. He handed it to her.

"Read this, Mary. It's about all the signs to look for when someone is close to having a baby."

Mary looked up in a blank stare.

"Just read it," said Uncle Don.

Then he turned about.

"Let's go, everybody. Put a move on. Get it done, and then we'll tell you what's next."

With that, Uncle Don waited for Aaron to drop the bomb-bay doors and to climb down from the plane. He and Aaron stepped around in front of the B-25.

"What's the plan, Aaron? She's your bird."

"Huh?" Aaron said. "You're flying her, Captain. Ain't that the plan?"

"Now why would I want to be flying your plane?" said Uncle Don. "Besides, it's a ship I'm not checked out on. No way am I flying it, especially with a talent as good as you standing right here in the same hangar."

With that, Uncle Don stood at attention and snapped a salute to Aaron.

"Awaiting your orders, Captain!" he said.

"You mean—" Aaron said.

Uncle Don held his salute without as much as a smirk. He was dead serious. Aaron bolted up and stood tall, returning the salute. It was a salute he'd been waiting to return since 1942. It was a salute of respect from Captain Uncle Don, a seasoned veteran with thirty-three missions into Hitler's hellhole behind him. That meant something to the man—it truly did. That was so important to Aaron that he didn't waste a moment on tears.

"Anna Kristina is being picked up at five sharp," Aaron said. "That means that between five fifteen and five thirty, the car should be pulling into the diner's parking lot."

Aaron looked down at his wristwatch.

"Let's set our watches to three twenty-two," said Aaron. "In about an hour, at four thirty, I want to do the full walk-through preflight check of this lady while she's here in the hangar. She'll be ready to fly before we pull her out."

He handed Uncle Don the routine-checklist sheet every B-25 had to go through before takeoff.

"After preflight checkout we'll open the doors, rev her high, and taxi down next to a clump of pine trees by the rice silos behind the diner. That'll hide the plane from view. If anyone should see us while we're taxiing, they'll think we're off and already long gone before anything happens. It'll also be chocked close enough so getting the girl from the car in the parking lot on board won't be too far a walk for her. She'll be scared enough without adding a hike way down to the other end of the runway."

"Sounds like a plan," said Uncle Don. "You'll have the ship revved and ready to bust loose and take off. I'll bring the girl from the car and get her on board."

"No disrespect, Captain, but that's a negative," said Aaron. "I'll go get the girl. She's my sister. She may not know my face, but for sure the last thing the girl will be trusting tonight is a white man. I'll be getting her on board. I'll pull the chocks and throw them in, too. You be in that left seat and ready to take off when we're boarded, and we won't look back."

"Yes, sir," said Uncle Don with a salute. "Where's the wind likely to be coming from this time of day?"

"Well, that's the bad news, now ain't it," said Aaron. "It'll most likely be a tail wind coming from that end of the runway. The wind will be with you and harder to take off in, but I figured it'll be safer if no one's able to see the plane startin' up or takin' off. To do that, we're going to have to take off from the wrong end of the runway."

"You give me a good cockpit tour, and I'll get her up," said Uncle Don. "We're not carrying any guns, bombs, or ammo. We

should be light enough to do a Doolittle." (Uncle Don was refer-
ring to Jimmy Doolittle's B-25s taking off from the short aircraft
carrier to bomb Tokyo in 1942.)

"Get her up, do a hard bank starboard around, and point her
to Chattanooga," said Aaron.

"Count on it," said Uncle Don. "Then you'll take over from
there, Captain. The left seat will be yours on this mission."

Aaron pursed his lips; gave a shy, proud twist of his head;
looked up at the B-25 cockpit's front window with a twinkle in his
eye; and then twinkled another look over to the clock on the wall
in the back of the hangar. He was savoring the moment for himself, feeling every second of it, and locking into memory how it felt
and what it was like to be looked at and treated as an equal.

"Where's the coffee urn?" said Uncle Don. "Let's get some
joe, and then you can give me a walk-through of this great lady,
Captain."

"Over in the office," said Aaron. "Follow me, but we're out of
sugar."

CHAPTER TWENTY-THREE

MAESTRO, IF YOU PLEASE!

Aaron climbed into the pilot's seat, preparing to taxi the plane partway down the dirt runway into hiding. Uncle Don was waiting below to close the hangar door behind us after we pulled out. Holbrook, Mary Crane, and I were on board, sitting in the dark. The shaking screech of the engines cranking up one at a time inside the tin hangar was deafening. Each engine and prop turned slowly and then seemed to gasp for air, suddenly bursting into a spin. We held our ears but kept our eyes open, looking for signals or instruction. Aaron was waiting for Uncle Don's signal that the coast was clear for the taxi out of the hangar. He turned his head about and shouted back to us.

"I'd put your coats on if I were you. It's gonna get cold back there when we finally take off."

Holbrook gave him a thumbs-up as the engine's RPM increased, revving up into high decibels. Uncle Don waved an all-clear signal with his handkerchief, and the B-25's front wheel hopped up as the brakes were released, and she started to roll out of the hangar. Outside Aaron pushed on the brakes, and we came to a rocking stop while Uncle Don pulled the hangar overhead closed. Holbrook and I moved about and lowered the boarding ladder from the belly of the plane. Uncle Don padlocked the hangar door, walked underneath it, and climbed up and in. Aaron waited for us to pull the ladder up and lock it. He released the brakes again while still at a high rev, and the plane jolted forward, that time picking up a convincing takeoff speed. We rolled down the runway to the clump of pine trees and the rice silos behind the diner. Just past the trees and out of sight, he stepped on the right brake, causing the plane to swing about sharply as he lowered the revs, turning it almost in a three-sixty turn. He brought it to a full stop and quickly shut down the two engines. The silence with the engines off caused a vacuum in the back. It was like our ears had popped. These were all new sounds and silences to Holbrook, Mary Crane, and me. With every sight or sound in that plane, one of the same planes that had helped us win the war, the steadfast appreciation we'd already had as kids for the bravery of guys like Uncle Don and Aaron deepened.

Uncle Don pointed a finger at me until he had my attention.

"You're the only one here who knows what your friend looks like. Think you can get to the other side of those pine trees over there without being seen and watch for him?"

All I remember thinking was that Holbrook and I had played this game a million times in the woods over our falls back home in Delphi Falls. We were so good at stealth that we could stalk a crow without being seen. We once watched a beaver build a dam for two days without ever being noticed.

"I can do it," I said.

"The second you see him drive in, run back here fast and tell us."

With that, Uncle Don looked at his watch. He looked up to the front of the B-25 and caught Aaron's eye.

"Ready in seventeen!" barked Uncle Don.

Aaron looked down at his watch and computed what time it would be seventeen minutes from that very second. He climbed out from the pilot's seat, crawled back with us, sat on a tarp next to Holbrook. Then he took his leather-and-sheepskin flight suit from a bag and rolled it out on the floor.

Uncle Don lowered the bomb-bay doors, all the time keeping his eyes on his wristwatch. At the proper moment he pointed to me to get ready. He clicked his finger.

"Now!" he said.

I didn't wait. I rolled onto my stomach and hung my legs down the bomb-bay opening, ready to drop myself to the ground. Uncle Don had intended for me to climb down the boarding ladder, but he grabbed my wrist, and we locked together as he leaned out from the plane and lowered me down far enough that I could drop down without getting hurt.

"Go! Run!" said Uncle Don.

The second I took off running, he started lowering a ladder to the ground carefully, not letting it fall. Entering through the bomb-bay doors would be easier for the pregnant girl than entering on the boarding ladder. Seeing me leave, Aaron crawled over and sat in the bomb-bay door opening with his feet hanging over it, holding the ladder post. He was waiting for the signal from me that the car with his sister had pulled in. Mary lowered her head down through the opening, watching for my signal. Uncle Don crawled up front and climbed into the pilot's seat, examining his takeoff-checklist sheet, and then began flipping switches in antici-pation. He tightened a comfort grip on the wheel and looked all about the pilot's cabin. He turned his head.

"Holbrook and Mary," he shouted. "When the bomb-bay door is closed and locked, open the mattress out flat. There should be two blankets inside. After the girl is on board, try to make her comfortable. You may have to hang on to her and roll the mattress in half over her to keep her from bouncing around during takeoff. We'll be lifting off right away, so watch your footing."

"That'll help keep her warm too," said Aaron.

That's when everything started up like a train car full of fireworks busting loose. I sure enough saw Ernest Hemingway driving in with a girl in the backseat. I about peed my pants. I turned and bolted back to the B-25, waving my arms to signal to them.

"They're here!" I shouted.

"They're here!" Mary yelled, relaying my signal.

I was panting by the time I reached the plane and looked up through the bomb-bay doors.

"They just pulled in," I shouted up.

"Stay where you are," said Aaron. "I'm coming down."

Aaron stepped onto the ladder and lowered himself to the ground. As he stepped away from the plane, he looked at me and said, "Jerry, you have to stand still now. Hold the ladder, and do not move a muscle. Stand still while he starts the engines. It's very dangerous, with the props and all. You cannot move one inch from this ladder. Do you understand me?"

"Yes, sir," I said. "I understand."

"Good. Now, when your friend comes down the ladder, you tell him the same thing."

"Holbrook?"

"Yes, Holbrook."

"Will do," I said.

With that, Aaron looked up and shouted, "Don! Can you hear me?"

"Loud and clear," shouted Uncle Don."

"We're all clear!" shouted Aaron.

"Roger that," said Uncle Don.

Aaron turned like an infantryman and walked at a good pace through the trees, disappearing around the side of the rice silos. Almost the second he was out of sight, Uncle Don turned a switch to start the left engine. It whined a shrill and whined again until it belched a billow of black smoke, and then the engine caught spark and whirred the propeller at a high rev. He turned his head and shouted for Holbrook.

"Holbrook, time for you to climb down and get ready to help the girl get on board! Mary Crane, can you hear me?"

"I can hear you!" shouted Mary Crane.

"Once she's onboard, you get her settled because we'll be rolling and taking off just as soon as we get the doors locked!"

"I will! I'll take care of her!" shouted Mary.

With that, the right engine started turning. It busted and popped, coughed, and stalled out. It stirred again, that time sounding a familiar whine, turning, and turning until it puffed a black smoke, and the propeller chomped and instantly spun free, ready to fly.

I remember hanging onto the ladder, waiting for what seemed like forever, and then seeing Aaron and the girl coming around the rice silos and circling behind the trees. Aaron had his arm around her and was helping her keep from tripping in the turf. He was holding her coat and a pillowcase with all her belongings in it. I can remember how Anna Kristina was carrying her baby low in her belly, how her clothes didn't fit well, and how her eyes were as big as quarters and filled with trepidation and fear. The only thing she trusted, perhaps, was her brother, Aaron, but we later learned that her first thought was that she wasn't certain he hadn't sold us out to get on somebody's good side.

As they walked, not a word was spoken between them. Anna Kristina didn't show any fear of climbing the ladder or any sign that she needed help. Mary Crane was at the top with a smile of her own and one for Aunt Lucy, and she helped the girl over to the mattress. Aaron sent Holbrook and me up the ladder next. He was last to climb. He paused just as his head was at the top rung and looked back to see if we had been seen. The Christmas Eve, it seemed, was in our favor. Not a creature was stirring.

He lifted the ladder in and raised the bomb-bay doors and locked them.

"All aboard and secure, Captain," he shouted.

The engines had been at the highest rev for the past minute or two in ready anticipation of our takeoff. Uncle Don lifted both his feet from the brakes and pressed on one, and the B-25 lunged forward, turning about and heading to the base of the runway. Without pause, Uncle Don stomped the alternate brake pedal to turn the plane again, and it pulled around in a half circle, the engines revving at the highest RPMs. And then like a frog, it leaped forward.

Just as he had done on thirty-three missions, Don counted to himself: "Five seconds, ten seconds." He could feel it in his fingers.

The hangar in the background was coming closer—closer. "Fifteen seconds." And then, "It's time, sweetheart," he mumbled through clenched teeth.

Uncle Don arm-wrestled the wheel back, showing no weakness. And in twenty-three seconds, we lifted off the ground.

"Grab something and hang on!" yelled Aaron.

The B-25 had lifted to maybe two thousand feet when, without warning, it rolled nearly on its side into a starboard bank to turn right and right again until we were heading due east. Uncle Don later told us that while looking down during takeoff, he could see three cars in the diner's parking lot: two regular cars and one state-highway patrol car with the trooper 'bubble' light on its roof.

Aaron grabbed the sheepskin flight suit and began to pull it on. He turned a flashlight on and crawled on his hands and knees over to the mattress. He paused and stared into Anna Kristina's eyes. She was beyond fright. She had no more despair to give. She had been through a lot for a sixteen-year-old girl. All she had then was the comfort of Mary Crane's warm hand and a promise that Aunt Lucy, who she'd never met, was at the other end of this nightmare. She looked at Aaron. She wanted to believe his eyes. She so wanted him not to be a stranger. He took her other hand.

"Don't be afraid, Anna Kristina," he said. "No need to be afraid ever again."

"I'm not afraid," she said, asserting the independence he'd years ago abandoned her with. "I'm scared, but I'm not afraid."

It seemed in her reserve she showed he would have to earn her trust. He had abandoned her all these years. She was happy to see her brother for the first time she could ever recall. It seemed she wasn't put off by not having been family with him for all that time. Anna Kristina had grown up in a culture of people who could still remember slavery as their heritage, a culture of people who'd had members of their families sold off and separated from them— who'd had no rights to do anything about it other than pray to God or sing to the soul or to all their own kin, no matter where they were. But he wasn't taken from her, he left her life on his own. He would have to earn her trust. This night was a good start.

Aaron crawled into the front cockpit. Uncle Don turned and saluted him, unbuckled his seat belt and shoulder-harness straps, and gave him the left seat and with it, full command of the B-25. Uncle Don took the right seat.

Uncle Don after saluting Captain Aaron.

"Jerry!" he shouted back.

I made my way up to the cockpit's opening.

"Yes?" I said.

"There're two footlocker boxes back there," said Uncle Don. "One has a bucket and two relief tubes in it. The other has some sandwiches and soda pop."

"Okay," I answered without putting a mind to it.

"If anyone has to go, tell them to use the bucket or the relief tubes," said Uncle Don.

"Huh?" I said.

"You'll figure it out. Open and show the two lockers to Mary Crane."

The plane seemed to be settling down, rolling less, and flying more smoothly than it had during our takeoff on the dirt field. We were then plowing along through the clouds in a darkening sky at what I think was ten thousand feet.

With Aaron in control, Uncle Don opened a map out, examining it and folding it down to the area he was interested in studying.

"I'm reckoning an hour and a half to Chattanooga," he said.

"That feels about right," said Aaron.

"Then set a heading one fifty degrees north to Binghamton, and then set a heading zero one zero degrees to our destination. We'll use visual references to bring her in."

"What's the field look like?" said Aaron.

"That's just it," said Uncle Don. "It's a field on a farm near our Delphi Falls. I figured it safer that way, out of sight. It should be frozen, though, and not muddy. If the winds are with us, we'll still have a three- or four-hundred-mile reserve on fuel to get us back to Binghamton to fuel up for return."

"This lady sure loves to fly," said Aaron. "She's looking forward to stretching her wings. With a little luck, we'll bring her in jus' fine."

"Well, we're lucky you're the captain," said Uncle Don.

Aaron beamed a toothy, childlike grin.

"Me? How's that?" Aaron asked.

"We couldn't be any luckier than this," said Uncle Don. "We have a top-rate medium-bomber pilot who trained in the freezing-cold Michigan winters like flying us into what I think may just be some weather when we get there."

"Full moon tonight," said Aaron. "Good nighttime visuals in the snow under a full moon."

Aaron returns salute and takes command

CHAPTER TWENTY-FOUR

BETTER WATCH OUT, BETTER NOT CRY!

The very second Uncle Don looked down and had a visual reckoning of Chattanooga, Tennessee, below, two things happened.

Aaron banked the B-25 onto a one fifty degrees bearing north to Binghamton, putting the setting sun on his portside window, and the Barbers's telephone rang back in Delphi Falls.

"Hello?"

"Mrs. Barber, this is Jimmy Conway. Is Barber around?"

"He's just come in from shoveling snow away from the front of the barn doors. Hang on, dear."

"Hello?"

"Barber," said Minneapolis Moline Conway. "On the radio today, Deacon Doubleday said this is going to be a record snowfall. No letup in sight until after dark. Worst since forty-nine."

"My dad says with the winds, it could drift six or eight feet," said Barber.

"We only have a couple hours before they'll be here. We have to move fast. Can you set up a meeting? Your place would be fastest."

"Set up a meeting with who, Jimmy? Jerry, Holbrook, and Mary Crane aren't even here."

"Get anybody who can come. It's Christmas Eve, I know. It'll be tough finding everybody. For sure, Randy and his pap; try Bases; Mayor; Marty, for sure; Dwyer, Duba; Dick; and Sheriff John Price, if you can find him."

"I'll try."

"Any others who can get rides to your place through the snow and winds?"

"Do you want Judy Clancy or maybe Alda and Jackie?"

"They're all in choir practice for tonight's Christmas service— if they're still having one."

"The hayfield they're supposed to be landing on is a mess. There must be two feet of snow on it already. We never did get the snow fence up. It's blowing all across Oran Delphi and piling up in the field. No way can they land there."

"Make your calls!" said Minneapolis Moline Conway. "Set it up right away. I'm heading out the door and down to your place with the Moline and the plow. We'll get her cleared."

"I'll make the calls," said Barber.

Just as he was about to hang up, Conway had a thought.

"Oh, wait," he said. "How about trying Mike Shea, Big Mike, and the Doc?"

"Then how about Mr. Gaines, too?" said Barber.

"Give it a shot. Nothing to lose asking. I'll see ya when I see ya." *Click.*

Mrs. Barber was a short, portly woman with a ready smile but a stern demeanor. She had to be strong since she had to feed a room filled with farmhands breakfast at five in the morning and dinner at twelve o'clock. She was Mrs. Clause that night, with her hand-sewn, Christmasy red apron about her. There was a sprig of holly safety-pinned to it. She had the fireplace crackling ablaze and had stacked a five-foot-high pile of firewood at its side. The huge, round dining room table had been cleared of salt and pepper shakers for a meeting. She was in the kitchen warming cider in a soup caldron and had a passel of mugs and a stack of cinnamon sticks on the dining room table, ready to go with the cider for the young ones. There was a jug of rum for the older folks in case they favored a nip or two in their cider to cut the bone chill.

Thanks to Doc's jeep and Mr. Vaas's milk-can-hauler rig, the dining-room gathering around the table was ample. The adults there were Mike Shea, Doc Webb, my dad, Allen Gaines, Mr. Barber, and Mr. Vaas. Our group included Minneapolis Moline Conway, Duba, Dick, Jimmy Dwyer, Mayor, Randy Vaas, Bases, Barber, and Marty Bays. Most everyone else Barber had tried to call had been either at their grandparents' homes for Christmas or outside shoveling snow and unable to hear the telephone ring. Just as the meeting was about to start, Sheriff John Price opened the side door. He stomped his feet on the mat and shook snow from his hat before he walked in.

"How'd you get here, Sheriff John?" asked Mike Shea.

"Tire chains on all four tires," said Sheriff John. "A bag of sand in the trunk just in case."

Without interrupting the meeting, Mrs. Barber came in and set her big caldron down on the edge of the table with a gentle clunk. She ladled cider from it and carefully slid one tall mug at a time for the nearest to grab and slide to the next, who would pass it on until everyone had a mug warming his hands.

Conway started.

"I've already called Farmer Parker," said Conway. "He said we can use his horses tonight if we need them."

"Sarge and Sallie," said Marty Bays. "I've worked with them. Good idea."

"Marty, you know horses better than most," said Mr. Barber. "How long would it take to get a team here from Farmer Parker's farm?"

"Hard to say, in this weather," said Marty. "On dry ground with a load, a team can travel at eight point eight feet per second, bout five miles per hour. We'll harness 'em up, and I'll be riding on the back of old Sarge and steering them both this way. May get more speed without a haul. Given we still have some daylight left, maybe a half hour over here, it'll be dark. Once I get them through Delphi Falls, even if it's dark, I'll get an eyeball on your house lights here and follow them. Trick is, how you going to get me over to Farmer Parker's?"

Marty was real smart—or did I tell you that already?

"Well we three had to come in my jeep," said Doc. "Big Mike got his Olds stuck in a bank at our place. My jeep is all that would make it up the Reynolds' hill to Fabius to get Mike Shea. In a couple hours, the roads won't be passable."

"It's not letting up, folks," said Sheriff John.

"I think I can speak for the elders here," said Dad. "They've already been in the air an hour or so. Tell us what you need from us, and we'll try to help you make it happen."

"Hear, hear!" said Doc.

"Well first things first," said Conway. "We need to clear an airstrip on that hayfield."

"Did you bring your plow?" asked Barber.

"She's out front," said Conway.

"Well that handles the snowplowing," said Mayor.

"But we promised your uncle Don headlight beams at the bottom end of the runway," said Conway. "There ain't no way we're going to get eight or ten cars down there on the field in this snow."

"No cars and no headlight beams. There's no sense even plowing if they can't see the field to land," said Mayor.

That's when Doc Webb stood up and stepped around the table and out into the kitchen.

Conway felt he was losing control of the meeting.

"I guess besides Doc's Jeep, maybe Sheriff John's car and our Minneapolis Moline tractor are the only things that can get through. And if there are no lights on the landing strip, what good would a plowed field be?"

"I just said that," said Mayor.

It was during some back and forth on the topic of headlights on the landing strip that Doc came back into the room with a smile on his face. He stepped to the side of Mrs. Barber, picked up the rum keg, and flavored his cider. He passed the keg to Mike Shea. Then, while still standing, he spoke.

"Barber?" said Doc. "Do you happen to have a wagon around here that'll hitch to Conway's Moline tractor?"

Mr. Barber answered for Barber.

"We have two," he said. "One flat-bedded hay wagon, and one just a buckboard rigged for pulling with a tractor."

"Well, let's get them hitched up. I just called ole man Moore… You all know him from the apple farm up on Cherry Valley at Pompey Hollow Road."

"Judy and I've been there for the apple festival," said Conway. "I know where it is."

"We know the Moores," said Mr. Barber.

"Well," said Doc. "Mr. Moore just happens to have some spares and is lending you eight smudge pots to use for light on the air-strip. They'll burn all night in a blizzard if they need to…but you'll have to go get them."

"An airplane would be able to see smudge pots from the air for miles," said Marty.

"I'll see if Myrtie can keep her shortwave tuned in," said Sheriff John. "Just in case they call in from the plane."

"What will the roads be like when they get close, say, two or three hours from now?" asked Marty.

"Unpassable, most likely," said Sheriff John Price.

The room had broken into warm cider–inspired mutterings, speculations, "what ifs," and a number of other dysfunctional, go-nowhere utterances when Mrs. Barber walked in to the dining room with a refilled kettle of warm cider and began rapping on the table with her tin cider ladle.

Crack, crack, crack, crack.

The room came to a respectful silence.

"Here you are!" she said. "Blabbing away like old hens at a tea-party social while a frightened little sixteen-year-old pregnant girl is flying in the freezing cold somewhere between us and God."

She paused and waited for any signs of intelligent life among those at the table. Other than Conway, who was speechless but sitting there with his mouth open like he was about to say something, she found none. Mrs. Barber and her ladle officially took charge.

"So the roads will be impassable, will they? Just where is the girl supposed to be going when she gets here?"

"Our place," said Allen Gaines.

"Could your tractor get through, Jimmy?" asked Mrs. Barber. "Get through from the airstrip down Oran Delphi to the Gaineses' place?"

"Not after maybe three hours of snow buildup and winds—not without plowing," said Jimmy Conway.

Mrs. Barber raised her fist, grasping the ladle, rested it to her chin in thought, and looked over at Marty Bays.

"Could horses get through?"

"If they could see, but in the dark and blinded by snow, probably not," said Marty.

"Wagon wheels wouldn't make it either," said Mayor.

Those in the room began to mutter again. Once again Mrs. Barber cracked the ladle on the table.

Crack, crack, crack, crack.

"Marty!" she yelled. "You ride in Doc's jeep with Big Mike and Mike Shea. Doc, drop him at Farmer Parker's."

"Can do," said Doc.

"Marty, harness up Farmer Parker's horses and get back here while the roads are passable and while you can still see."

"Why here, Mom?" asked Barber.

"Straw loft of the old feed barn, Son."

"Huh?" said Barber.

"There's a horse-drawn bobsled up there. It'll carry four or five. A couple of you help get it down. Get her rigged up for a team of horses. You might grease the runners, Dale. If wheels won't make it through the snow, that bobsled sleigh surely will."

Why, you've never seen anything like it in your life. The entire crowd set their cider down carefully and began to applaud. They'd been sitting around sipping it and all the time thinking the worst, and they'd hardly imagined something so simple answering their prayers.

And then Marty threw a wet dishtowel on the moment.

"Horses can pull the sled—that's for sure. The sled can ride the snow—that's for sure," said Marty.

"Marty!" said Mrs. Barber. "Don't be mealymouthed, and don't beat around no bushes, lad. You want to say something, stop dancing, and say it."

"This here is dairy-farm country, he said. "And there ain't any streetlamps, and I don't care how good a team of horses is. It'd never make its way that far in the dark."

"They'll be a full moon tonight," said Randy Vaas.

"Won't be enough if it's still coming down," said Marty.

Crack, crack, crack, crack.

"Dale!" yelled Mrs. Barber. "You, Mayor, and Randy Vaas go pull the bobsled down like I told you, and tidy her up in the lower bay. Do it quick, and then hook a wagon up to our tractor. Then you're going to string lights from the plane strip all the way to the

Gaineses' place so the horses can make their way. And that'll be that!"

"No offense, Gertrude," said Mike Shea. "It may be the rum talking, dear, but that's more than two miles, and I haven't yet seen a cord stretch that far, and I surely don't have that many lights in the store. Oh, you'd be welcome to them if I did, but they just don't exist. Not that many."

At that, Mrs. Barber felt she had to clear her name.

"Mike Shea, don't you be suggesting I'm on the rum. Firstly, everyone knows I do not imbibe, and secondly, apparently, despite what the Lord gave you in height and business know-how, he missed giving you common sense."

"Well, I wasn't meaning—" said Mike Shea.

"Just in case everyone in this room can't remember, even though you've all been here on this very farm near every year since I can remember for the harvest hayride and dance—"

"We love it," said Mayor. "The whole Crown comes."

"Well, it just so happens we have in the hayloft of the feed barn the near eighty kerosene lanterns we use to decorate the hayride and barn dance? They'll burn a half ounce per hour. Dale, after you boys get the bobsled down and rigged, pull all the lanterns down and put three ounces of kerosene in each."

"Yes, Ma."

"And take Randy Vass and Mayor with you, and go string them on fence posts from the airstrip through Delphi Falls and then all down the road to the Gaineses' farm."

"Should we—" Barber said.

"And light them before you hang them," Mrs. Barber said, anticipating his question. "Stay with them until you know the burn is good."

"Better hang them on fence posts all the way to Big Mike's place so Marty can drop off Uncle Don, Mary Crane, Holbrook, and Jerry there," said Duba.

"Drop Aaron by at our place," said Allen Gaines.

"Who's Aaron?" asked Marty.

"Aaron is the girl's brother. He may be flying the plane," said Allen.

Dad told me later about the moment when it was announced that Anna Kristina's brother, Aaron, was flying the plane. He told me there wasn't a person around that table who even thought twice about what Allen had said. Made him so proud that race, color, creed, or any other such man-made contrivances had no place in the Crown. We were all too busy helping save a girl and her baby, and that was all anyone cared about. Only made sense for her brother to come too.

"Take plenty of stick matches," said Mr. Barber. "One of you drive the tractor. One of you set in the wagon and light the lanterns and hand them out to the one hanging them. Should go smooth. Stretch them out. Remember that they need to guide the horses, not light up the whole village."

The room was silent, and a sense of awe seemed to flow through it. Such a difficult evening was made possible to overcome by a mug of cider and a moment shared between friends.

Crack, crack, crack, crack.

"So let's get going," said Mrs. Barber. "Conway, you and your team take Dick, Duba, and Jimmy Dwyer and head up to Moore's place and get the smudge pots. Don't forget to light them. Ask him how. Dale, you and your team get the bobsled down and all the lanterns and go hang them all. Take a roll of hay-bale string case you need it. Marty, you go with Doc. Harness up Farmer Parker's horses, and bring them over here. Put them in the cow barn until we need them."

Mr. Barber smiled and then lifted and lowered his mug of flavored cider in a toast to the love of his life.

"A toast, gentlemen!" Mr. Barber said.

Every mug in the room went up.

"To my bride," he said.

Mrs. Barber's face turned beet red.

"Why, woman," said Mr. Barber. "You sure cut up that turkey in short order. My goodness, we're all so proud of you."

Mrs. Barber smiled and set her ladle down.

"Whoever said a woman couldn't run the show ain't never been to a farm," she said. "Now go on, everybody, and git. Lots to do before they get here."

The room started to clear as people unfolded into groups.

"And Merry Christmas!" Mrs. Barber said.

CHAPTER TWENTY-FIVE

OUT ON THE LAWN AROSE SUCH A CLATTER

Passing over the heart of West Virginia, the B-25 took us up to ten thousand feet.

"Looks like we'll be following the Blue Ridge Mountains," said Uncle Don. "Then over the Pennsylvania mountains on up to Binghamton."

Aaron had both his hands gripping the wheel. He was comfortable with the smoothness of the ride. He felt good inside with his friend Uncle Don sharing the cockpit.

"We'll be fine," said Aaron. "The snowcaps on the mountaintops make me think there'll be some weather ahead. We can handle it."

"Reminds me of the Eighth," said Uncle Don.

"The Eighth?" asked Aaron. "You mean the Eighth Army Air Corps?"

"Some of the pilots who flew deep into Germany to drop their loads and then turned back in daylight would take the long way back. They'd fly around and go over the Alps," said Uncle Don. "Little or no flak over the Alps."

"Must have been somethin'," said Aaron. "That sure must have been somethin'."

"You're as good as the best I've flown with, Aaron. You're right up there with the best."

Aaron pursed his lips and looked ahead into the horizon with a sparkle in his eyes. Then he smiled. He was ready to set the heading on zero-one-zero degree bearing north.

"Might as well keep her up here at ten thousand," said Uncle Don. "We'll give those babies down there plenty of room to clear under us."

In the back Mary was trying to get Anna Kristina to rest. Holbrook and I had bundled them best we could with the mattress, folding it around them. Then we'd wrapped a tarp around that. We figured their combined body heat would keep them warm. Mary held Anna Kristina's hand and told her stories about the Pompey Hollow Book Club. She told them about how we'd saved bunnies when we were ten. She told them about the bad guys we'd caught—the store burglars, the escaped POW guys, and the pickpocket.

Anna Kristina had no idea of where we were taking her or of what was in store for her future, but it wasn't important at the moment, it seemed. She knew her baby would be safe. Anna Kristina never took her eyes off Mary Crane's face. She listened intently to her every word, almost as if she were her momma and telling her a bedtime story. Anna Kristina was older than Mary by three years on the calendar, but she was still a child—a wonderful, eager-to-learn child. She was building trust in her new friend. At one point during a pause in a story, she looked over at Mary, catching her eye.

"I s'pose this book club is…well…like a body would have to be a real somethin' to get in a club like that."

"What do you mean?" asked Mary Crane.

"Well…I don't know. Never mind. Just me bein' silly."

"Why, Anna Kristina, are you asking me if you could join the Pompey Hollow Book Club?"

"I didn't mean no dis—"

"Didn't anybody tell you?" Mary asked, interrupting her.

"Tell me?" whispered Anna Kristina.

"Why, young lady, we are the Pompey Hollow Book Club, and we came all the way down to Little Rock to protect you. And you know what that means, don't ya?"

"No?"

"Tell Anna Kristina what that means, Holbrook."

"That means you're automatically in the club," said Holbrook.

Anna Kristina's eyes widened.

"Really?"

"Really!" I said.

"It's official!" Mary said. "Show her, guys."

Holbrook and I gave her a thumbs-up.

"Welcome to the club," I said.

"You mean people like me can—"

"Listen to you," said Mary. "Carrying on and all. Why, yes, we need people just like us in the club. The more the merrier. You're just like us. We could tell that right off. You're one of us!"

Her big, beautiful eyes glistened with tears of wonderment.

Mary looked away and puffed a curl from over her eye.

"Well, are you in?" asked Mary.

"Huh?" said Anna Kristina.

"Are you in or not," said Mary.

She turned her head and looked Anna Kristina in the eye.

Anna Kristina smiled, squeezed Mary's hand, and closed her eyes to dream.

She fell asleep somewhere over the foothills of the Pennsylvania mountains.

Up in Delphi Falls, the smudge pots had been brought down
from the Moores' house. They were set in place and burning,
throwing off tongues of flames lapping at the winds. The snow had
stopped falling, and the glow of a full moon then blanketed the
valley with a silent carpet of calm. Myrtie, the telephone operator,
had been alerted of the situation and was listening for the shortwave, just in case. Each kerosene lantern sparkled its own character, and they dotted the land all the way from the airstrip down on
Oran Delphi Road up to the village, over past the Gaineses' place,
and then down to our falls.

Those who weren't standing around the smudge pots keeping
warm or riding with Minneapolis Moline Conway and matting
down the airstrip were either in the Barber house, sitting by the
fire, or up at the church, rehearsing for the services that evening.
Everyone at the Barbers' or by the smudge pots was waiting in the
silence, listening for sounds. They were listening for the sound of
a B-25 bomber.

Mrs. Barber held young Bobby on her lap on the rocker and
read aloud.

"The moon on the breast of the new-fallen snow gave a luster of
midday to objects below," Mrs. Barber read. Her voice was soft and
as warm as the wonderful tale.

That's when it came.

Rumbling sounds came from the distance first—we couldn't
tell from where. They grew louder until the ground vibrated as

they came closer. The old farmhouse shivered, causing a shake that tinkled the china cups hanging on the hooks on the wall by the buffet table. The plane was fifteen hundred feet in the air and flying directly over the Barbers' house.

Varoom!

"That's them. They're coming north up from DeRuyter Lake. They're supposed to be coming across Route Twenty, the Cherry Valley," Marty yelled.

"They're in trouble then!" yelled Barber.

With that, everyone in the house except Bobby grabbed a coat and ran outside. Mrs. Barber scurried out behind them in her housedress and Christmas apron. They ran into the middle of Oran Delphi Road to watch for the plane, which had disappeared by then. Trained by every war movie since the forties, a few were waiting to hear the crash.

None came.

"Let's wait," said Marty. "We'll see what they're up to up there."

"Dale!" said Mrs. Barber. "Run in to the house and get my coat and some galoshes! Tell Bobby to stay put. Marty, you go get the horses and pull the bobsled rig out here."

"Shouldn't we wait here on the road?" said Marty.

"Wait for what?" said Mrs. Barber. "They're here. They'll be landing, and a little girl needs our help—and fast. Git!"

With that, Marty skipped off, running to the old hay barn to pull the team of horses out. They were already hitched up and waiting.

"Randy, you, Dale, and Mayor run down to the airstrip on foot case they need you," said Mrs. Barber. "We'll pick you up if we catch up. Go on, now."

"Are you going too, Ma?" Barber asked.

"The girl's in girl trouble, Son. She needs a woman. Go on with them—git!"

As Marty pulled the horse team and bobsled onto Oran Delphi Road and then stopped, he saw the B-25 coming back up over the center of the road at about one thousand feet.

"They're circling around," yelled Marty. "That's what they're doing, by golly. They're checking out the runway."

Mrs. Barber climbed in and sat on the bobsled's bench.

With that, Marty—one of the best horsemen in the Crown—took the reins into firm handgrips, and in one motion, he brought the straps down on the rumps of Sarge and Sallie with a gentle clap.

"Giddayup! Ktch, Ktch. Let's go, you hosses!" he said, growling.

The horses worked up from a light step through the snow to a good cadence with the bobsled gliding effortlessly behind them. Marty calculated the center of the road and the fence line and followed the glow of the lanterns, hurrying down toward the base of the landing strip.

Marty would shout "gee!" for the team to guide left and "haw" for the team to guide right.

FLUMP...FLUMP...FLUMP, The muffled hooves marched in the unplowed snow, their steps making a sound like "*flump*" each time one landed.

Steam snorting from their velvet nostrils, the horses seemed to have full confidence in Marty's hand, and they welcomed the warming run on such a cold night.

Varoom!

That time the B-25 banked and circled to the west of Oran Delphi Road and began its approach to land. In the plane we had to circle twice for Aaron and Uncle Don to get good visuals so they could study our approach.

Outside on the ground, Mrs. Barber and Marty reached the base of the airstrip and turned onto the snow-covered airfield just as the B-25 roared down to about twenty-feet above the smudge pots.

As soon as our plane cleared the burning barrels, Marty yelled, "Haw! Haw! Haw! Giddayup now, Hosses!"

The bobsled swerved right and slid around and sped up to reach our moving plane, which had finally touched down and was quickly whining its engines to a full stop.

Inside, Uncle Don was making suggestions.

"Aaron, you might shut her down to save fuel. She'll still have to make it back to Binghamton to fuel up."

"Roger that," said Aaron.

Uncle Don looked out the cockpit window and saw the Minneapolis Moline tractor and the plow at the edge of the field.

"Looks like that tractor over there has all we'll need to turn this lady around when the time comes for takeoff," said Uncle Don.

With that, they both went through their disciplines and switched off switches and checked all the gauges. Aaron unstrapped his harness, turned in his seat, and stepped into the back cargo first. Don went back next.

"How's everybody making it back here?" asked Aaron with a smile. "Everybody doin' okay?"

"That landing was so cool!" I said.

"Well, we're here!" Mary Crane said. "We're finally here! Yay!"

I helped Holbrook unwrap the girls from the tarp and the mattress.

Uncle Don told us to stand back, and then he pulled the lever that lowered the bomb-bay doors. Aaron knelt down and, leaning on his side, stuck his head down and out. He watched Marty pull the team of horses and the bobsled up just outside the reach of the starboard wing. Since he'd been based in Detroit during the war, Aaron was no stranger to snowstorms. He gathered the chocks and dropped them through the opening. They fell to the ground. He was certain, on the snowy hayfield, that the plane wouldn't roll, but procedure was procedure, and he was among the best.

"Holbrook. Jerry," he said. "Drop the tarps down. Let's get a team to cover the engines. Tie them on with a good seal. We don't need moisture in the engine or the sparks."

Then he lowered the ladder.

"Miss Mary, will you help Anna Kristina down this ladder? I think your chariot awaits," said Aaron.

Mary and Anna Kristina made their way down the ladder and over to the bobsled.

"Hello, honey," said Mrs. Barber. "You climb in here with me, where it's warm."

"Are you Aunt Lucy?" asked Anna Kristina.

"No, honey, I'm Mrs. Barber. Aunt Lucy is up at the church. It'll be Christmas tomorrow, ya know, dear."

"I know," said Anna Kristina as she stepped over the side rail and sat down next to Mrs. Barber. "Santa already gave me a present."

Mrs. Barber saw the whole day and evening as a blessing—almost as a miracle. She looked at the "Santa moment" through her own eyes – the safe landing was the gift from Santa.

"Oh, I just know he did," Mrs. Barber said as she wrapped a blanket around the girl and pulled her close. "I just know he did, honey."

Mary Crane sat in front of them, turned, and faced them.

Anna Kristina looked over at Mary Crane and whispered, "He really did."

Mary smiled.

Inside the plane, after all the tarps had been dropped to the ground, Aaron looked about for last-minute details.

"Holbrook and Jerry," said Aaron. "You climb down first."

We climbed out, purposely taking our time stepping down the rungs of the ladder, inhaling in the sights and the smells of this once-in-a-lifetime memory.

"You next, Don," said Aaron.

Uncle Don saluted Aaron.

"After you, Captain!" he said.

Aaron looked up at Uncle Don and smiled. He nodded his head as though to thank Uncle Don for the respect, returned the salute, and stepped down the ladder. With that, Uncle Don cranked up the bomb-bay doors. He then let himself down the boarding passage and closed that up once he was out.

Uncle Don looked about.

"Folks? Everyone? Thanks for your help. The strip was perfect. I'd like everybody to meet Aaron, our pilot-captain tonight. And over there is his sister, Anna Kristina."

By that time Dick, Duba, Minneapolis Moline Conway, and Dwyer were hovering around the B-25, staring up at it and soaking it in like they were in a dream.

Aaron started to ask for help with the chocks and tarps. Dick saw him and anticipated his thought.

"You guys go on," said Dick. "We'll take care of the plane."

"But, it's important—" Aaron said.

"You all go on, now," said Minneapolis Moline Conway. "We'll cover the engines and chock her."

"Can you snuff the smudge pots out so they don't draw too much attention?" asked Uncle Don.

"We plan to," said Duba. "We're going to load them up and take them back to Moore's, where they belong, tonight. We have the lids to snuff them out."

With that, Uncle Don and Aaron stepped through the snow and climbed onto the bobsled. They sat behind Mrs. Barber and Anna Kristina. Holbrook and I sat backward behind them with our legs stuck up over the back. Randy, Mayor, and Barber stayed at the smudge pots to help.

"Well let's just get this little lady home by a warm fire, where she belongs," said Mrs. Barber.

Marty raised the straps and lowered them firmly onto the rumps of the horses.

"Giddayup!" he said. "Let's go, you hosses."

The bobsled lurched forward.

"Gee!" Marty said. "Gee!"

The team of horses bore left and circled around the entire B-25. I remember looking up at it—the bulging engines, the cockpit, and the stout, able wings. That plane had so many stories to tell. It could have seen Tokyo. It was a sight we would never forget. It was a memory of a war we had all lived through but had only seen through the Saturday-morning picture-show newsreels.

Wasn't long before Marty yelled back, "Hang on!"

The bobsled made it over the side-road gulley and up onto Oran Delphi Road, and we headed to Delphi Falls. Marty could see all eight kerosene lanterns on the fence posts at the edge of the village. The full moon was bright.

We could hear "*flump, flump, flump*" as the hooves marched in the unplowed snow.

Marty cocked his head around and spoke out of the side of his mouth.

"I thought the plan was that you guys were going to fly in over Cherry Valley, come in on Route Twenty, and turn in from the north. What happened to that?"

"Fog," said Aaron. "That whole hilltop was covered in fog. Couldn't get a visual."

"We couldn't see where Eleven and Twenty come together," said Uncle Don. "Thick fog."

"So what'd you do?" asked Marty.

"I knew Cazenovia Lake," said Uncle Don. "And I knew DeRuyter Lake. We took her up to five thousand feet and looked around. Once we found DeRuyter Lake, I told Aaron to follow Oran Delphi all the way up from the south. Jerry had told me that Barber's place is the first farm on the right outside the village, so once we got a visual on that, everything made sense."

"Then we saw the fire barrels," said Aaron. "The rest was easy, after a couple of flyovers. Just a few buzzovers for visuals."

Mary Crane, Holbrook, and I looked back at the scene we were leaving. The smudge pots were still blazing, burning the day into our memories. Mary leaned forward and held Anna Kristina's right hand. Anna Kristina shook in the cold as she held Mrs. Barber's left hand. She watched the barns and then the homes we passed as we entered the village of Delphi Falls, her trip near half over.

CHAPTER TWENTY-SIX

HE IS BORN TONIGHT!

Gaily they ring
while people sing
songs of good cheer,
Christmas is here.
Merry, merry, merry, merry Christmas.
Merry, merry, merry, merry Christmas.

The village was dark. There were Christmas lights strung on some porches as we slid by the homes one by one. There were lit candles on some windowsills and wreaths on front doors. Three snowmen on that many front yards proudly stood guard for the happy childhood memories they would one day become. The full moon rose above the church like the star the three wise men had followed the night Jesus was born. The tree in front of it was bright with cheery Christmas lights. The limbs had been brushed with a broom to remove the heavy snow they had collected in the storm. Every window was aglow with a warm yellow-gold light. The bobsled pulled on past it all.

Marty turned his head around.

"Here?" said Marty.

"Let's g'wan and take her home to the Gaineses' place," said Mrs. Barber. "No sense stopping here and risking getting caught in another snowstorm."

"Ktch, ktch," said Marty. He slapped the reins gently down on the rumps of Sarge and Sallie.

Just as they turned on Delphi Road to head down to the Gaineses' farm, Anna Kristina shouted, "Oh no!"

"What, dear?" Mrs. Barber asked. "Nothing to be afraid of. We're here with you."

"Oh no!" Anna Kristina said in a shrill voice.

"What is it?" asked Mary. "Are you okay?"

Mrs. Barber opened the front of the blanket that was folded around Anna Kristina. She gently reached her hand under it.

"Her water's broke," Mrs. Barber said as calmly as she could.

"What's happening?" Anna Kristina asked in a fearful voice that matched the fear in her eyes.

"Marty, back us up. Back us up now. Take us to the church."

"Whoa!" said Marty.

The team of horses stopped instantly.

"Back!" Marty said. "Back! Back! Back!"

Again in the middle of Oran Delphi Road, Marty barked new orders to the horses.

"Haw, team, haw. Giddayup!"

The team guided the bobsled left and sprung into a trot back through town. In front of the church, Marty pulled hard on the reins.

"Whoa!"

Uncle Don and Aaron jumped from the bobsled. They each put an arm around Anna Kristina's back and clasped their hands together, cradling her. They lifted and carried her to the steps of the church. Holbrook pulled the church door open; Mrs. Barber stepped in quickly and called for calm with folks inside wondering what was happening while crying for help from the choir, who had an otherwise empty church because of the weather.

"We're having a baby!" she yelled.

In 1953 a farm woman wouldn't have needed to hear another word or an ounce of direction. Having babies was just as natural to them as dying on the farm.

"Keep singing, ladies," said Judy Clancy. "A baby is born tonight. Sing!"

"Hallelujah!" the choir said in unison.

The Davenport girl sat at the piano and led the choir into blessed Christmas songs. Mrs. Barber signaled for Jackie and Alda to come meet Anna Kristina. As they approached her, they looked down and smiled at her.

"Can we get her a cushion to lie on, Mrs. Barber?" said Alda.

"That's a nice idea, dear," said Mrs. Barber. "Boys, help the girls take two of the church-bench cushions, and let's get them under this girl."

They comforted the girl. Alda and Jackie each held one of her hands. Mary walked over to them, holding Aunt Lucy's hand.

"Anna Kristina," said Mary. "This is Aunt Lucy."

Anna Kristina looked up and smiled. She looked into Alda's eyes. She looked over into Jackie's eyes. She looked back at Aunt Lucy's smile. Aaron leaned over her and set her pillowcase with her belongings in it next to her for comfort.

In the background the choir sang "Silent Night."

Anna Kristina looked up into Mary Crane's eyes. She reached for her hand.

"Where am I?" she whispered.

"You're almost home," said Mary Crane.

"Am I going to die?"

"No, no, dear," said Aunt Lucy. "You're going to live. That baby inside you is going to live. Why, child, you have blessed our Christmas just being here."

"You're home and free," said Aaron.

"And later, after we go to sleep," said Alda, "is when Santa will come."

Anna Kristina lifted her hand over to her pillowcase. She reached inside it and felt around under the cotton cloth.

"I already seen Santa," she said. "He had a white beard and everything, just like in the store window."

"Was he in the store?" asked Mary Crane.

"No," said Anna Kristina. "He was the man who drove me to the hospital but we didn't get there. Honest."

Anna Kristina pulled two packages from her pillow sack. She looked at me and made memory certain I was Jerry and then handed me one of the packages.

"This is for you," she said. "He said he was Saint Nicholas. That's what Santa's real name is. He told me."

Anna Kristina cramped up with a whimpered moan. The ladies asked the men to step away as they went about their business. The breathing and moaning sounded painful, but it was necessary. Just as the choir was rejoicing at the birth of Jesus, the baby spat out a cry, letting us know that he was there and cold. Mrs. Barber handed him to Aunt Lucy, who swaddled the infant and laid him on Anna Kristina's breast.

"Whatcha going to name this beautiful little baby boy?" asked Aunt Lucy.

"Such a handsome baby," said Mary Crane. "He got a name yet, Anna Kristina?"

"Nicholas," Anna Kristina whispered as she lifted the baby to her face. She kissed him ever so gently.

"Hello, Nicholas," she whispered.

A white Christmas in Delphi Falls

EPILOGUE

MERRY CHRISTMAS!

My gift from the Saint Nick who drove Anna Kristina to the diner was the book *The Old Man and the Sea*, by Ernest Hemingway himself. He had autographed it and written, "To my friend Jerry. Signed, 'Papa' (Manolin Santiago)."

Uncle Don saw it, looked up at me, and smiled.

Uncle Don is gone now, but he was always so proud of the Thanksgiving and Christmas we spent together. He would say, "It's almost as if your guardian angel orchestrated that whole time."

Hemingway's gift to Anna Kristina was the same book. He autographed hers too.

"It's good to have an end to a journey but it is the journey that matters in the end. Signed, Ernest Hemingway."

Both Anna Kristina and Nicholas finished school as members of the Gaines family. They both went to college and became teachers.

They are a happy part of the Gaines family to this day, living happily ever after.

This story is my Christmas gift to you. I hope it makes a difference in your life. I hope it helps you make a difference in other people's lives. It's not too late to start.

Merry Christmas.

A citizen of the world, Hemingway fought for freedom and
equality

Jackie and Alda's grade in school in the Crown (1950s)

THE VOICES

I'm a vernacular storyteller. I point out, with an unvarnished candor, that nearly every boy I grew up with carried an owned or borrowed copy of one of two books—*The Adventures of Huckleberry Finn* or *Tom Sawyer.*

Many of us became fixated on the boyhood independence those books promised. I would disguise their covers with borrowed dust jackets from other more literary and noble books. It was all a lie; I would read *Moby Dick*'s dust cover just so that I might feign familiarity with the book, and then I'd join Tom and Huckleberry Finn; or I'd use the *Red Badge of Courage*'s dust cover—that worked too—and I'd jump inside and on a river raft with the slave, Jim. The dialects Mr. Twain had etched on those pages overshadowed any grammatical whimsy found in Ms. Doxtator's ninth grade English class. Mark Twain wrote *Huckleberry Finn* while living in Elmira, which is a mere frog's jump from Delphi Falls, so we were comfortable in our conviction that his grammar was proper, since he was the one published in books. Our kindly Miss Doxtator's heart was in the right place, and she meant well—she surely did—but she hadn't gotten the latest news on advancements in proper grammar.

—JMA

Uncle Don and His Crew

1944–1945
The Crew of B17 "Lady Helene"

Donald G. Lederman, Pilot
John F. Pakola, Copilot
William T. Martin, Tail Gunner
August D. Cervetti, Waist Gunner
Frank A. Serene, Radio Operator
Willard E. Dingley, Engineer
Leonard Carmell, Navigator
Paul Redkovich, Turret/Togglier (Bombardier)
Erwin Chojnacki, Waist Gunner

Thirty-Three Missions in 1945

January 20, Rheine; January 21, Mannheim; February 3, Berlin; February 6, Chemnitz; February 14, Chemnitz; February 15, Cottbus; February 20, Nuremberg; February 21, Nuremberg; February 22, Ansbach; February 23, Kitzingen; February 25, Munich; February 27, Leipzig; February 28, Kassel; March 1, Ulm; March 5, Chemnitz; March 10, Soest; March 12, Siegen; March 15, Oranienburg; March 18, Berlin (became lead bomber); March 19, Jena; March 24, Varel; March 28, Hanover; March 30, Hamburg; April 3, Kiel; April 4, Kiel; April 5, Nuremburg; April 8, Grafenwoehr; April 9, Schleissheim; April 10, Neuruppin; April 14, Royan; April 15, Royan; April 16, Soulac-sur-Mer; and April 20, Nauen.

My sister Mary and her husband, Donald, are real.
They are presented as Aunt Mary and Uncle Don, respec-
tively, in this story.

My sister Mary and her husband, Donald, are real.
They are presented as Aunt Mary and Uncle Don, respec-
tively, in this story.

Thirty-Three Missions in 1945

January 20, Rheine; January 21, Mannheim; February 3, Berlin; February 6, Chemnitz; February 14, Chemnitz; February 15, Cottbus; February 20, Nuremberg; February 21, Nuremberg; February 22, Ansbach; February 23, Kitzingen; February 25, Munich; February 27, Leipzig; February 28, Kassel; March 1, Ulm; March 5, Chemnitz; March 10, Soest; March 12, Siegen; March 15, Oranienburg; March 18, Berlin (became lead bomber); March 19, Jena; March 24, Varel; March 28, Hanover; March 30, Hamburg; April 3, Kiel; April 4, Kiel; April 5, Nuremburg; April 8, Grafenwoehr; April 9, Schleissheim; April 10, Neuruppin; April 14, Royan; April 15, Royan; April 16, Soulac-sur-Mer; and April 20, Nauen.

Also by Jerome Mark Antil

The Pompey Hollow Book Club
(Set circa 1949)
Little York Books (ISBN: 978-0-9847187-4-0 (TPB))

The Book of Charlie, book two of The Pompey Hollow Book Club
Series
(Set circa Halloween 1953)
Little York Books (ISBN: 978-0-9893044-3-6 (TPB))

Mary Crane and Séance with Sherlock!, book three of The Pompey
Hollow Book Club Series
(Set circa 1953, two weeks after Halloween)
Little York Books (ISBN: 978-0-9893044-5-0)

The Long Stem in the Lobby
Little York Books (ISBN: 978-0-9847187-6-4 (HC))

Aventuras de Pascua del Club de Lectura Pompey Hollow
(Set circa 1949)
Little York Books (ISBN: 978-0-9847187-7-1). Available on Kindle.

Handbook for Weekend Dads...and anytime grandparents
Little York Books (ISBN: 978-0-9893044-0-5 (TPB))

Cup of joe before takeoff

In 1945 every B-17 captain was given a .410 shotgun for
crash survival (to hunt food)

Lightning Source UK Ltd.
Milton Keynes UK .
UKHW041858130920
369800UK00001B/15

9 780997 180213